ONLY THIS SUMMER

Acclaim for Radclyffe's Fiction

"Medical drama, gossipy lesbian romance, and angsty backstory all get equal time in [*Unrivaled*,] Radclyffe's fifth PMC Hospital Romance…[F]ans of small community dynamics and workplace romance without ethical complications will find this hits the spot."—*Publishers Weekly*

"*Dangerous Waters* is a bumpy ride through a devastating time with powerful events and resolute characters. Radclyffe gives us the strong, dedicated women we love to read in a story that keeps us turning pages until the end."—*Lambda Literary Review*

"Radclyffe's *Dangerous Waters* has the feel of a tense television drama, as the narrative interchanges between hurricane trackers and first responders. Sawyer and Dara butt heads in the beginning as each moves for some level of control during the storm's approach, and the interference of a lovely television reporter adds an engaging love triangle threat to the sexual tension brewing between them."—*RT Book Reviews*

"*Love After Hours*, the fourth in Radclyffe's Rivers Community series, evokes the sense of a continuing drama as Gina and Carrie's slow-burning romance intertwines with details of other Rivers residents. They become part of a greater picture where friends and family support each other in personal and recreational endeavors. Vivid settings and characters draw in the reader…" —*RT Book Reviews*

Secret Hearts "delivers exactly what it says on the tin: poignant story, sweet romance, great characters, chemistry and hot sex scenes. Radclyffe knows how to pen a good lesbian romance." —*LezReviewBooks Blog*

Wild Shores "will hook you early. Radclyffe weaves a chance encounter into all-out steamy romance. These strong, dynamic women have great conversations, and fantastic chemistry." —*The Romantic Reader Blog*

In **2016 RWA/OCC Book Buyers Best award winner for suspense and mystery with romantic elements** *Price of Honor* "Radclyffe is master of the action-thriller series...The old familiar characters are there, but enough new blood is introduced to give it a fresh feel and open new avenues for intrigue."—*Curve Magazine*

In *Prescription for Love* "Radclyffe populates her small town with colorful characters, among the most memorable being Flann's little sister, Margie, and Abby's 15-year-old trans son, Blake...This romantic drama has plenty of heart and soul." —*Publishers Weekly*

2013 RWA/New England Bean Pot award winner for contemporary romance *Crossroads* "will draw the reader in and make her heart ache, willing the two main characters to find love and a life together. It's a story that lingers long after coming to 'the end.'"—*Lambda Literary*

In **2012 RWA/FTHRW Lories and RWA HODRW Aspen Gold award winner** *Firestorm* "Radclyffe brings another hot lesbian romance for her readers."—*The Lesbrary*

Foreword Review Book of the Year finalist and IPPY silver medalist *Trauma Alert* "is hard to put down and it will sizzle in the reader's hands. The characters are hot, the sex scenes explicit and explosive, and the book is moved along by an interesting plot with well drawn secondary characters. The real star of this show is the attraction between the two characters, both of whom resist and then fall head over heels."—*Lambda Literary Reviews*

Lambda Literary Award Finalist *Best Lesbian Romance 2010* features "stories [that] are diverse in tone, style, and subject, making for more variety than in many, similar anthologies... well written, each containing a satisfying, surprising twist. Best Lesbian Romance series editor Radclyffe has assembled a respectable crop of 17 authors for this year's offering."—*Curve Magazine*

Applause for L.L. Raand's Midnight Hunters Series

The Midnight Hunt
RWA 2012 VCRW Laurel Wreath winner *Blood Hunt*
Night Hunt
The Lone Hunt

"Raand has built a complex world inhabited by werewolves, vampires, and other paranormal beings…Raand has given her readers a complex plot filled with wonderful characters as well as insight into the hierarchy of Sylvan's pack and vampire clans. There are many plot twists and turns, as well as erotic sex scenes in this riveting novel that keep the pages flying until its satisfying conclusion."—*Just About Write*

"Once again, I am amazed at the storytelling ability of L.L. Raand aka Radclyffe. In *Blood Hunt*, she mixes high levels of sheer eroticism that will leave you squirming in your seat with an impeccable multi-character storyline all streaming together to form one great read."—*Queer Magazine Online*

"Are you sick of the same old hetero vampire/werewolf story plastered in every bookstore and at every movie theater? Well, I've got the cure to your werewolf fever. *The Midnight Hunt* is first in, what I hope is, a long-running series of fantasy erotica for L.L. Raand (aka Radclyffe)."—*Queer Magazine Online*

By Radclyffe

The Provincetown Tales

Safe Harbor

Beyond the Breakwater

Distant Shores, Silent Thunder

Storms of Change

Winds of Fortune

Returning Tides

Sheltering Dunes

Treacherous Seas

PMC Hospitals Romances

Passion's Bright Fury (prequel)

Fated Love

Night Call

Crossroads

Passionate Rivals

Unrivaled

Perfect Rivalry

Rivers Community Romances

Against Doctor's Orders

Prescription for Love

Love on Call

Love After Hours

Love to the Rescue

Love on the Night Shift

Pathway to Love

Honor Series

Above All, Honor

Honor Bound

Love & Honor

Honor Guards

Honor Reclaimed

Honor Under Siege

Word of Honor

Oath of Honor

(First Responders)

Code of Honor

Price of Honor

Cost of Honor

Justice Series

A Matter of Trust (prequel)

Shield of Justice

In Pursuit of Justice

Justice in the Shadows

Justice Served

Justice for All

First Responders Novels

Trauma Alert

Firestorm

Taking Fire

Wild Shores

Heart Stop

Dangerous Waters

Romances

Innocent Hearts

Promising Hearts

Love's Melody Lost

Love's Tender Warriors

Tomorrow's Promise

Love's Masquerade

shadowland

Turn Back Time

When Dreams Tremble

The Lonely Hearts Club

Secrets in the Stone

Desire by Starlight

Homestead

The Color of Love

Secret Hearts

Only This Summer

Short Fiction

Collected Stories by Radclyffe

Erotic Interludes: *Change Of Pace*

Radical Encounters

Stacia Seaman and Radclyffe, eds.:

Erotic Interludes Vol. 2–5

Romantic Interludes Vol. 1–2

Breathless: *Tales of Celebration*

Women of the Dark Streets

Amor and More: Love Everafter

Myth & Magic: Queer Fairy Tales

Writing As L.L. Raand
Midnight Hunters

The Midnight Hunt

Blood Hunt

Night Hunt

The Lone Hunt

The Magic Hunt

Shadow Hunt

Visit us at www.boldstrokesbooks.com

ONLY THIS SUMMER

by

RADCLY*f*FE

2022

ONLY THIS SUMMER

ISBN 13: 978-1-63679-390-0

THIS TRADE PAPERBACK ORIGINAL IS PUBLISHED BY
BOLD STROKES BOOKS, INC.
P.O. BOX 249
VALLEY FALLS, NY 12185

FIRST EDITION: DECEMBER 2022

CREDITS
EDITORS: RUTH STERNGLANTZ AND STACIA SEAMAN
PRODUCTION DESIGN: STACIA SEAMAN
COVER DESIGN BY TAMMY SEIDICK

Acknowledgments

I'd like to thank my parents for taking me camping in the Adirondack mountains before most of the state campsites even existed. We camped by the side of a small lake, Putt's Pond, every summer beginning when I was five years old. The same half dozen families would return every year and we all became friends, although we only saw each other once a year. We got water from a hand pump down the road and carried it to our tent site. The sanitary facilities were primitive, and we bathed in the lake. I did not understand then how lucky I was to have had those three weeks of careless abandon every year. A forest ranger came to check on us once a week or so, and one of my greatest treasures was a NY State forest ranger emblem he gave me and that my mother sewed on my sweatshirt. I never went to a summer camp like the one in this book, but I have been to the mountains.

Thank you to my editors, Ruth and Stacia, for taking such care with my work. Thanks Eva and Paula for beta reading. And thank you, Sandy, for looking after me and the biz in countless ways, and making the space for me to write.

To Lee, as always, *amo te*.

Radclyffe

For Lee, for all seasons

CHAPTER ONE

With a teeth-jarring thud, the left front wheel of Lily Davenport's BMW coupe dropped into a pothole the size of the Grand Canyon. Emitting an ominous groan that sounded unsettlingly human, the little two-seater convertible bounced out the other side of the chasm and promptly stalled.

"Damn it," Lily muttered, shifting into park to restart the engine. She pushed the ignition button and, in the heart-stopping second of silence, feared her vehicle might refuse to go, in protest over its recent maltreatment. Not that she could blame it. If she was a car, she'd refuse to go any farther on this hellacious path—it could hardly be called a road, considering it was barely wider than the BMW—too. When the engine turned over, she whispered a thank-you and eased forward a few feet, trying to avoid the tree branches that jutted out over the rutted trail, and waited to see if anything vital fell off the undercarriage or exploded beneath the hood.

Despite her open windows, the bit of breeze managing to make its way through the dense underbrush and towering pines offered no match for the early June sunshine, and the inside of the car already resembled an oven. Lily powered down the roof—that was still working—and stared at the hood, waiting for steam or smoke or something equally menacing to seep out.

Why hadn't she listened when Sarah had suggested she might want to lease a Jeep or some other four-wheel-drive vehicle for the summer? Better question—why hadn't Sarah told her that the way up to the lodge, described as a three-season access road—maybe in retrospect she should have asked Sarah what *that* meant—was really little more than a goat path? Or maybe that should be deer path or...some other creature's path. *Road* was being overly generous.

When the engine continued ticking and nothing appeared to be burning or leaking or otherwise malfunctioning, Lily pushed her sunglasses up into her hair and squinted at the nav screen. She loved the little car for its easy maneuverability in the city and speed on the rare occasions she had a chance to get *out* of the city, but the dash was a bit cramped, and reading the map function on the small screen was a challenge at the best of times. At the moment, the monitor showed only a generic regional geographic overview. Thank you, Google, but not helpful when surrounded by forest. Apparently uninhabited forest.

She *must* be on the wrong nonroad.

Mentally reviewing her drive, Lily determined that, at least five miles and what felt like five hours before, she'd been on the right route. She must have turned off the twisting road circling the shore of Lake George too soon. Turning around was presently out of the question. Literally. She wasn't about to risk a ten-point turn and end up putting the rear of her Z4 into a ditch and walking back to civilization.

All she needed to do was slow down and try to avoid any more unexpected road hazards until she found a place to around-turn. Or if she was incredibly lucky—which would be an anomaly—she might actually find the lodge. She hadn't passed a building or another vehicle or any sign of life, human or otherwise, since she'd left the highway and headed off into the Adirondacks.

When all her gauges remained blessedly in the midzone, suggesting she hadn't done irreparable damage to her automobile, she set off once again. Sweat trickled at her temples and misted the back of her neck. She settled her sunglasses into place and squinted into the early morning glare. She'd made excellent time driving north from the city, but that had been open Thruway driving, and at five in the morning, she'd been able to avoid speed traps with the aid of her radar. What should have been the shortest part of her journey was turning out to be the most arduous. Hopefully not a portent for what was to come. Giving up on the GPS, she trusted to fate and continued deeper into the densely packed evergreens.

She swung around a blind corner, hoping the camp would come

into sight any moment or she would at least see a sign saying *Turn Around Here You Idiot*, and slammed on her brakes.

"Oh!" Heart pounding, arms braced against the wheel, she stared at the front end of the vehicle she'd nearly hit. And blinked. Not a mirage. An army-green Jeep with the roof removed and a single occupant in olive-green fatigues sat a foot off her front bumper.

Wonderful. She was alone in the mountains faced with a survivalist, or worse, some private militia playing soldier. She didn't even have cell service. She ordered herself to take a breath. Panic was not her usual response to a crisis—at least it hadn't been, before...

The faint haze that curtained Lily's vision cleared as her pulse slowed, and she got a clearer look at the figure climbing down from the Jeep. The sun was behind them, and in the glare, Lily had a hard time distinguishing the fine details. She could make out that the person striding around the front of her car, headed for the driver's side, was a woman. From her lower vantage point and limited vision, Lily registered tall-ish, lean-ish, in a short-sleeved uniform shirt—nicely defined arms—and matching pants, and yes indeed, a utility belt with a holstered pistol or whatever they were called, along with other paraphernalia.

"Morning," the woman said as she halted by the side of Lily's car, a question in her voice. She wore aviator-style sunglasses...how appropriate, which hid most of her face. Her mouth was sculpted and full above a squared-off chin and angular jaw. *Imposing* was a good word for the impression she created.

A yellow patch on her sleeve indicated she was a member of some kind of organization, but with the sun in Lily's face and her perception still reeling, Lily couldn't identify what branch.

"Who are you?" Lily asked, sounding more abrupt than she intended. The unexpected appearance of the Jeep and its occupant and the surreal isolation of the dense forestland left her mildly disoriented.

"Department of Environmental Conservation," the woman replied in an alto timbre. "Do you know where you are?"

The question of the hour. Lily almost laughed, although the last thing she felt was humor. She didn't intend to admit she'd been asking herself the same question. Somehow the probably innocent implication that she might be lost rankled. *Lost* seemed one step away from incompetent, and she'd just driven five hours to the far end of civilization to escape *that* oppressive, soul-draining sensation. "No. I mean. Yes, of course. Generally speaking."

"I see."

Lily couldn't remember if DEC officers were actually law enforcement agents or not. She thought so, but she wasn't sure what laws they actually enforced. Probably not vehicular ones. Not that she could be speeding on this gods-forsaken, bare excuse for a road, but still. "Is there a problem?"

"We don't see many sightseers out this way."

Lily bristled, certain she caught a faint hint of amusement. "I'm not sightseeing, and believe me if that was my intention, it would not be here. I have permission to be here."

"It's public land, Ms....?" The officer, or ranger, or warden, or whatever the proper term was, removed her sunglasses, and a dark brow lifted over ridiculously blue eyes. Lily had no trouble seeing *that*, or the rest of the very handsome face that went along with them. Younger than she'd thought—twenty-five or six perhaps.

"Davenport," Lily said. "Lily Davenport."

"So, Ms. Davenport, where are you headed?"

"Nowhere, with you in the way."

The ranger laughed. A nice laugh, as if that was the tone she saved for friends. Lily flushed at the visceral surge of warmth. Where had that been hiding all these months? And what a bad time to resurface.

"I'll move unless we have to get you turned around. Mind telling me where you're going?"

"Thunder Ridge Lodge."

"In this vehicle?"

This time the incredulity was unmistakable.

Lily's chin came up. "Do you have something against convertibles?"

"Not in a general sense, but they're not a good choice for whatever you're doing out here."

The hint of a smile lifted the corner of her full mouth, and for half a second, Lily thought she was quite attractive. Irritation chased that thought away quickly enough. Really, she needed condescension and a little bit of arrogance at this point? Not when she was hot, thirsty, and quite possibly on the wrong road. *Not* lost—simply...misdirected.

"You're sure about where you're headed?" This time the ranger's tone held genuine surprise. "There's a Thunder*bird* Lodge off Route Nine another ten miles north of Bolton Landing. Could that be it?"

"I'm quite certain." Lily decided that pride wasn't her best choice at the moment. "Am I on the right…path?"

"You are. You've got a bit of a climb for another mile or so, but if you take it slow, you ought to be all right."

"Wonderful," Lily said, unaccountably relieved. "Um. How do we…" She waved a hand at the Jeep blocking her way.

"I'll back up. There's a spot a few hundred yards back around the next bend where I can pull over. You're sure you want to keep going?"

"Of course," Lily said, wondering, not for the first time, if her decision to leave her apartment, her job, and just about everything else behind for a chance to figure out what it was she really wanted to do with her life was as crazy as everyone thought it was.

❖

Chase put the Jeep in gear and backed slowly uphill and around the curve until she could pull partway off the track, leaving enough room for the Beemer to get by. A minute later the slick little convertible appeared, and Lily Davenport edged past her with a tight nod and continued her slow pace up the mountain toward Thunder Ridge.

Chase shook her head as she continued down the mountain. Lily Davenport was only the first of hundreds of tourists she'd assist in some fashion over the coming months. The season was just starting, and soon the mountains would be filled with civilians—most of whom had little to no forest lore—who flocked to the wilderness intent on camping, hiking, visiting their entitled offspring at camps like Thunder Ridge, or in some cases, engaging in illegal activity. Lily Davenport, in her hundred-thousand-dollar sports car, was probably on her way to interview the staff at Thunder Ridge before foisting her son or daughter off on the counselors for the summer.

Chase shuddered at the thought of being responsible for nearly fifty teenagers of mixed sexes for a day, let alone a summer. Wrangling a bunch of horny, rambunctious, and frequently rebellious teens from one event to another around the clock was her idea of a nightmare. At least most of the counselors had been resident campers themselves once and had volunteered to come back to supervise the latest crop of summer enrollees. Chase couldn't imagine a worse way to spend the summer. Fortunately, she'd be too busy before long to worry about the goings-on at the lodge.

What was vacation time for most people, the late spring into fall, was the busiest time of the year for her. Her duties as a DEC law enforcement officer included not just enforcing the many state and federal environmental regulations but also the local fishing and hunting laws, and investigating crimes associated with those activities in the Adirondack forest. Patrolling her district, a region hundreds of square miles in area, kept her in the Jeep, on foot, or occasionally on horseback eighteen hours a day. She loved every minute of it, even though it hadn't been her plan five years before. Of course, back then, she hadn't thought she needed to make plans.

She wouldn't have time to think about Thunder Ridge beyond her one obligatory introductory session with the campers to review the rules and regulations surrounding hiking and campfire use in the parkland. She likely wouldn't see any of them again unless one of the more adventurous residents managed to get lost.

"Which at least one of them probably will," she muttered, maneuvering the Jeep onto a rocky shoulder off the road. Once parked, she walked down a narrow deer trail to the edge of Cutler Pond to check for signs of illegal fishing. The department had just stocked the lake with trout, and fishing was prohibited until the season started. That didn't keep some anglers from trying for an early catch. Just the morning before she'd issued two citations to a couple of people taking trout illegally. As she scanned the opposite shoreline with binocs, she wondered if Lily Davenport would be one of those helicopter parents who insisted on meeting with her to confirm she was actually qualified to protect their offspring. Funny, the idea of running into her again wasn't all that unpleasant.

The lake looked quiet, and Chase smiled as she climbed back to the Jeep, thinking about her recent encounter with the attractive blonde. Under other circumstances Lily would have been just her type—assuming Lily's tastes ran to women. Self-assured, quick-witted with a hint of a temper—not always a bad thing—and definitely hot. Even the brief glance she'd gotten of Lily in the car was enough to put her into *that* category.

Chase started the engine and sighed. There wouldn't be time for that kind of pursuit soon either, and even if there was, Lily Davenport would be long gone. With a rueful shake of her head, she pulled her radio off the dash to check in.

"Fielder, calling in."

Lieutenant Natalie Evans, her regional supervisor, came back quickly. "Hey, Chase. How's the morning looking?"

"Pretty quiet right now. Cutler Pond is clear this morning."

Natalie chuckled. "Give it a day."

"Yup. I plan a swing-by on my regular tour."

"Good idea. Listen, I need you up at the lodge this morning. Can you make it at nine?"

"I'm just headed out from that area. I was planning to cut over to check the hiking trails around Third Lake. With the rain we've had, we may need to put them off-limits for the coming weekend." Chase frowned. Why the lodge? She flashed on the image of Lily Davenport's BMW headed up the mountain. Hell. Had Lily had an accident? Maybe she should have followed her up. Her chest tightened. "Is there some problem?"

"Not what I'd call a problem, but we need a meeting with Sarah."

"You're the boss." Chase let out a breath. Not an emergency, then. Nothing to do with Lily. "I can still make it out to Third, check the trails, and be back just about ten or a little after. That work for you?"

"Should be fine. See you then."

"Roger that," Chase muttered.

She tried to stay clear of the lodge as much as she could during the summer. Something about the residents brought back memories that seemed a lifetime ago now, of the unfettered freedom to spend every single day in the high peaks, thrilling to the challenges, and never once taking it for granted. Although maybe she had, thinking back. At least she'd taken her place in the greater scheme of things for granted. Maybe now she just envied the kids at the lodge their unlimited view of their futures, as if they could do anything and would.

With a mental curse, she shook free of the anger that still caught her by surprise and took a deep breath of the sweetest air in the world. She let it out along with her ghosts.

Maybe a trip up to the lodge wasn't such a bad idea. Maybe she'd run into Lily. A telltale flare of interest hit her, and she enjoyed the sensation despite the impossibility. Lily was undoubtedly exactly as she'd seemed. A wealthy parent, out of her depth in the mountains but a little too arrogant to admit it. Chase snorted. Not a few people had mentioned that being a little too overconfident might have been a wee problem of hers back in the day. Not so much any longer. Hell, she'd paid the price, after all.

She sighed and let the image of Lily Davenport fade. Fantasies weren't really her thing, and she wouldn't have time for much more than that until September.

CHAPTER TWO

Lily breathed a sigh of relief when a sweeping, three-story log lodge—of course it was log, because what else could it possibly be—loomed into view around the curve of the road, its broad timber front porch wrapping around both sides of the massive structure like huge arms. A dozen smaller log cabins, crouched like baby ducks around their mother, sat tucked within cozy little clearings among the towering evergreens to the right of the main building. The road she'd so laboriously climbed ended in a small turnaround beside a split-log fence. A mud-streaked Kermit-green Jeep and a black pickup truck showing some wear in the rusted-out fenders sat on the hard-packed ground beyond the fence.

Lily edged through the opening in the fence and parked next to the big Dodge Ram. Before she shut off the motor, she closed the top on the convertible and rolled the windows up. Already the seats and the dash were covered by a fine layer of dust, and she could only imagine what it was going to look like in another few days. Not that she planned on driving up and down the mountain any more than she had to. As in not until she was headed…somewhere…in September.

That was a decision for another day.

Lily pocketed the key fob and her phone, climbed out, and stretched.

"Lily!"

Lily's heart lifted, a flood of pleasure she hadn't experienced in so long her throat tightened. Sarah hurried toward her, looking as she always did, a smiling picture of old-fashioned wholesome in a short-sleeved plaid shirt, faded jeans, and hiking boots, her honey-brown hair caught back in a ponytail, her smile so warm and welcoming Lily teared up for no reason she could imagine. Hurrying toward her oldest friend, she blinked the telltale moisture away. Then she was in Sarah's arms, her head on Sarah's shoulder, holding on as if Sarah might suddenly disappear as quickly as the morning mist.

"Oh my God," Sarah whispered, her voice husky. "You're here. You're actually here."

For just a moment, Lily could only nod. Swallowing around the unexpected and slightly embarrassing emotion, she forced her grip to loosen and pulled back to meet Sarah's gaze. "I am. And you look amazing as always."

Sarah held her at arm's length, her hands smoothing down the fabric of Lily's cotton shirt in a steady caress. "And you look as beautiful as ever, except maybe a little too skinny."

Lily knew she was lying. She'd lost fifteen pounds and hadn't been able to get rid of the dark circles under her eyes for months. But she took the compliment and pretended it was true. "I..."

A golden rocket accompanied by a joyous yelp shot past Sarah, and Lily staggered under the onslaught of two paws landing none too gently on her hip. She laughed. "Who are you?"

"Baily," Sarah said, "get down."

"Baily?" Lily rubbed the handsome golden retriever behind both ears. "This can't be Baily. He can't be more than..." She swallowed and looked at Sarah. "The last time I saw him he was three months old."

"He's almost three," Sarah said quietly.

"I remember," Lily said quietly. "You talked me into meeting you at the place you'd rented in the Catskills, and you'd just gotten him. Right before lockdown." She took a tremulous breath. "Sometimes that seems like another lifetime."

"I'm so sorry for everything you've been through," Sarah said quietly, her hazel eyes warm with sympathy.

Lily forced a smile. "Well. Everyone had challenges, right? And we made it out the other side."

Most of us. The words she didn't say brought a barrage of images that she'd gotten better at pushing aside, but could never completely erase. Stretchers jammed head to foot, spilling out of the ER down every adjacent hallway, some holding bodies wrapped in white sheets waiting their turn to be delivered to the makeshift tent morgues in the parking lots outside the hospital. Twelve- to eighteen-hour shifts, understaffed and nearly overwhelmed, for weeks that became months and, unbelievably, years.

Sarah put an arm around her shoulders and squeezed her. "You're here now. Come on, let me show you the place. You'll feel better when you're settled in."

"There *is* one thing I'm going to need," Lily said quietly.

Sarah paused. "What?"

"A Jeep."

Sarah burst out laughing. "Rough ride coming up?"

"Not entirely what I expected." Lily fell into step, grateful she'd packed both pairs of running shoes when she'd left the apartment. The identifiable paths were really just pine-needle-strewn trails studded with rocks, smaller versions of what she'd just driven up. Considering what she'd seen of the terrain so far, she wouldn't be making much use of the sandals she'd opted for that morning in deference to the projected temperatures. Although this far north, under the towering evergreens, the air was decidedly cooler than she'd expected. And...fresh. Another welcome change from the city. Another turn of the wheel between then and now.

"So far, none of this fits the admittedly hazy picture I had of a state-sponsored camp for older teens," Lily added. She hadn't pictured the wildness of the mountains or the remoteness. And she definitely hadn't expected to run into a forest ranger out in the middle of truly nowhere who kept turning up in her thoughts.

"You're smiling," Sarah teased. "It couldn't have been that bad."

"No," Lily said. The ranger *had* been helpful, even if she hadn't bothered to hide her opinion that Lily's choice of vehicle and general judgment were questionable. As annoying as that had been, the encounter had left her energized in a way she hadn't been for so long she'd forgotten the feeling. "No, it was fine."

"Good. Come on, then, let's walk down to the lake while we still have the place to ourselves." Sarah linked her arm through Lily's and led her down a twisting path through the pines. The lodge soon disappeared behind the dense wall of trees, while ahead, sunlight glinted on the mirror-surface of a lake that extended out of sight in every direction. A narrow strip of beach came into view, and flashes of red and orange, bright patches through the green, proved to be kayaks and canoes stacked on metal racks.

"How big is the lake?" Lily asked.

"Several hundred acres," Sarah said. "Nathaniel Wingate, a shipping magnate from New York City, owned twelve thousand acres of forestland with something like six lakes all interconnected by navigable streams. He built the lodge as a hunting pavilion for family friends. The heirs eventually deeded almost all the land back to the state as part of the forest preserve."

"And how much is officially part of the camp?"

"Just shy of five thousand acres, all wilderness preserve under the regulation of the DEC."

"I had no idea how remote the place would feel."

"That's what makes this location perfect as a summer camp. It's not that far from major highways, but we are in the middle of completely uninhabited land." Sarah laughed. "I guess that seems a little daunting to a city girl, huh?"

"Funny," Lily murmured, strolling down to the shore, "it doesn't."

Lily had never been much of an outdoors person. She'd grown up in Manhattan and lived there all her life, but it wasn't hard to appreciate the natural beauty surrounding her. She took in the coffee-colored sand, studded here and there with small stones, that looked nothing like the beaches on Long Island or along the Atlantic where she'd vacationed as a child. Not a cell tower in sight. No rumble of trucks or the ever-present chorus of millions of people filling every street. Being physically cut off from the world as she had known it carried a remarkable sense of relief. Of…freedom.

She dipped a hand in the water. Clean, clear, and…really cold.

"People swim in this?" she called.

"It's June," Sarah said. "There's still snowmelt in the high country feeding these lakes. But it will warm up soon enough."

Despite the absence of sounds she'd grown used to in the city, it wasn't really quiet. Stillness was not the same as emptiness. Looking out over the water, Lily picked out half a dozen different kinds of birdsong, the rustle of tree branches overhead, and even the hushed rippling of the lake against the shore. She glanced at Sarah.

"It's so…different. Beautiful."

Sarah's smile was soft, the sunlight edging her hair in gold. "It is, isn't it."

"And you grew up with this every day."

They turned to walk back up to the lodge, and Sarah said, "We lived only fifty miles or so from here, but at a higher elevation. Longer winters, but glorious springs. My parents made the trek down the mountain a few times a year for essential supplies, but we would go weeks at a time without seeing anyone else. They were busy cataloging animal and bird migrations, and documenting how changes in climate affected wildlife habitats and life cycles."

"And you never thought about doing anything else? Being a naturalist?"

"Not for a minute." Sarah paused in front of the lodge. "Same for you, right? Both your parents are doctors. Family tradition."

Lily nodded. "You're right. Family tradition."

"How are they, your parents?"

"Tired, but for them, the last few years have just been business as usual. They met when they were both working for Doctors Without Borders in Uganda. War—and that's what it felt like when the pandemic hit—was nothing new for them." She glanced away. "I was the one who wasn't prepared."

Sarah's arm came around her shoulders. "No one was. Or at least almost no one."

Lily took a deep breath and forced a smile. "Well, we're winning now, aren't we."

"We are." Sarah squeezed and let her go. "And it's time for R and R."

The sound of laughter, high-pitched, excited, floated down from the row of cabins on the crest above the lodge.

"You've already got campers in residence," Lily said, happy for the diversion. She really didn't want to talk about things that couldn't be changed. Just the opposite. She was so ready for some kind of change. She just didn't know what it would be.

"A few kids arrived last night. Most will be coming in today." Sarah grinned. "Be prepared for a day of chaos."

"Right," Lily said. "I could really do with a cup of coffee. I don't suppose…"

"Please," Sarah said. "Does the sun rise in the east? Come on inside. It was the next stop, anyhow."

Sarah led Lily through the double carved oak front doors into the great room, as large as a cathedral with the soaring two-and-a-half-story-high ceiling, hung in the upper reaches with huge swinging chandeliers. The stone floors held at least a dozen oversized leather sofas and chairs, plus low chunky wood tables gathered into separate seating areas. Two staircases climbed the side walls to a balcony and rooms above. The river rock fireplace, wider than one of the rooms in her apartment on the Upper East Side, occupied the far end of the room. The logs stacked on the hearth were easily a foot in diameter and six times as long. The air smelled faintly and not unpleasantly of woodsmoke, a little bit of lemon, and pine—the real kind, not the cloying scent that came in a bottle or from those horrid things on the dash in the taxis in the city.

"Wow," Lily said, craning her neck to take it all in. "I feel…small."

"Wait until it's crammed with teenagers—you'll wish it was three times as big."

Lily laughed.

"Kitchen's back here—the meal hours are posted on the bulletin board. Coffee, juice, water and the like, plus snacks are always available."

The kitchen, which was really a euphemism for the enormous commercial cooking area at the rear of the lodge, spanned the entire width of the building with two eight-burner stoves, gleaming stainless steel pots and pans hanging from iron hooks above the stone-topped counters in the center of the room. A man and several women who were busy organizing canned and dry goods on stainless steel racks along one wall looked over as they walked in.

The oldest of the three, a fiftyish redhead with a sturdy body and sharp brown eyes, wiped her hands on her crisp white cargo pants and strode over with an extended hand. "Good morning. I'm Clara Maguire, chief cook and bottle washer here. You must be one of the parents."

Laughing, Lily took her strong, wide hand. "Lily Davenport. A pleasure to meet you. And no, I'm not one of the parents."

Sarah said, "Lily's our new camp doctor."

"Ah, delighted to meet you, and an improvement I'll wager over the last doctor."

Lily glanced at Sarah.

Sarah shrugged. "Archie McIntosh was a delight, but a bit of a grump."

"I can't promise anything before morning coffee, but I'll do my best," Lily said with a smile.

Sarah and the other two chefs, who introduced themselves as Juan Ramirez and Nancy Li, laughed as well.

"We're just grabbing coffee, and we'll be out of your way," Sarah said.

The coffee station came equipped with three large stainless steel urns, and Lily helped herself to a white ceramic mug and filled it with, as she discovered, exceptionally good coffee.

"I'll show you our med station first," Sarah said, leading the way out of the kitchen. "We've got a bedroom ready for you upstairs here, but it's only a short walk to the clinic if you have to see anyone at night."

"Does that happen often?" Lily's stomach gave a lurch, an altogether too familiar feeling. The sensation of being awakened after only a few minutes' sleep with yet another emergency washed over her. She wondered when, if ever, that automatic response would disappear.

"Oh," Sarah said, apparently not having noticed Lily's reaction, "we get the usual common ailments—bumps and bruises, contact dermatitis, common colds. Nothing too serious."

Exactly what Lily wanted to hear. Staffing a walk-in clinic for three months should not be too demanding. "I guess we're not really that far from civilization, if for some reason we have a true emergency."

"And we have the rangers, if we need any kind of EMT support."

"The rangers," Lily echoed, instantly picturing the dark-haired officer in the Jeep. "I guess I don't really know what they do."

"Pretty much anything that needs doing in the district. Fire control, search and rescue, land conservation, education." She pushed open the big front doors. "And of course, riding herd on all the hikers, hunters, and fishing nuts."

Lily followed Sarah out onto the wide front porch and slowed as a familiar vehicle came into sight over the crest of the road and pulled around to the front of the lodge.

The Ranger, as she'd come to think of her, stepped from the Jeep and stopped abruptly, locking eyes with her.

"Chase," Sarah called down. "What's the occasion?"

Chase stared up at the blonde on the top step next to her sister. She'd wondered if they'd meet again, and the quick surge of anticipation announced she'd been more than just hoping. She removed her sunglasses and slid them into her chest pocket. "Natalie said there was a meeting."

"Oh," Sarah said. "I expected her and Rob."

Chase shrugged, still watching Lily Davenport, who had narrowed her eyes as if trying to work out some kind of puzzle. Thinking about her, maybe? Yeah. Right. Even *her* ego didn't extend that far. Before Sarah could get wind of her interest in Lily, she got herself moving and headed for the porch.

"Lily," Sarah said, "this is..."

"We've met," Lily said in a tone that gave nothing away. "I'm afraid I never did get your name."

"That would be Chase," Chase said, extending a hand. Lily's was soft and warm and firm as she gripped it for an instant and then let go.

"You've met?" Sarah said with a question in her voice.

Lily smiled. "Yes. On the...the road coming up here."

Chase caught that tiny bit of irritation in her voice again and rather liked it. Far more interesting than the often false notes from women who desired to please or make a good impression.

"Lily—" Chase stopped. "Ms. Davenport was having a little trouble with her BMW."

"Not what I'd call trouble," Lily put in instantly. "Just checking my directions."

Chase didn't bother to hide a smirk, and Lily's brows drew together in a little frown. Definitely still a little irritated.

Sarah looked from one to the other. "I don't know why I expected you might recognize each other. Chase, you must have been, what, ten the last time you saw her?"

Chase shot Sarah a look. "Sorry?"

"Lily is my friend from college. The two of you met at the funeral," she ended quietly after a moment's hesitation.

"Oh," Lily said quickly. "I'm sorry, I didn't recognize you earlier. I never did get a good look—the sun and..." She made an exasperated sound. "I couldn't see your name tag earlier."

"I don't remember you from before either," Chase said, feeling at a loss and unaccountably uncomfortable. Her mother's funeral was fifteen years in the past, but still not something she liked to think about. And finding out Lily and Sarah were friends—hell, too many complications, not that she expected anything to happen, of course. "So you're one of the parents?"

Lily gave a quick laugh. The frown lines disappeared to be replaced by a sparkle in her eyes, the irises that Chase could see now were green, a true green like meadow grass at the first breath of spring. Beautiful.

"Why does everyone assume that? Do I look that motherly?"

"Not even a little," Chase said before she could stop herself. "Not how I would describe you, at least."

A brow arched this time. A light brown, nearly blond brow that set off her eyes perfectly. "Hmm. Now I'm curious."

"Some other time," Chase said. Sarah was watching the conversation with slightly too much interest. She'd gotten pretty good at hiding her feelings, but her older sister had always been able to read her, and she didn't really want Sarah thinking she had any interest in her oldest friend. Sarah made it all too clear how she felt about Chase's love life, or as Sarah called it with a fair amount of sarcasm, her fickle sex life.

"Lily," Sarah interjected, "is our camp medic for the season."

"Dr. Davenport, then," Chase said. "Apologies."

"Lily is fine," Lily said, back to her neutral tone and unrevealing expression.

"I expect I'll see you around, then," Chase said, looking for any hint of interest and not seeing one.

"I was just giving Lily the tour," Sarah said in a way that suggested Chase was dismissed.

"I'll go see what Clara's cooking while I wait on Natalie." Chase bounded up the stairs and paused by Lily's side, close enough she could catch Lily's scent—something citrusy and cool. Lily's eyes widened, and Chase smiled inwardly. "I'll see you, Lily."

Chase disappeared inside, and after a second, Lily followed Sarah down the stairs. "I can't believe that's Chase. She was so skinny and shy."

"She grew up," Sarah said abruptly.

Lily shot her a questioning glance. Sarah was very rarely anything but sunny and optimistic, and the hint of anger in her tone was unexpected.

Sarah caught the look and shook her head. "Sorry. It's been hard. Chase was so young then, and I wasn't really ready to be a parent, and with first Dad going and then Mom just a few years later, she ran a little wild."

"She seems to have turned out pretty responsible. From the way you described it, being a DEC officer is demanding."

"That's true, and for her it's been doubly hard." Sarah shook her head and her smile returned. "That's Chase's story. I'm really happy that she's found her place."

Lily remained silent. There was more to the story, and she wasn't going to hear it from Sarah. She'd heard so many stories, often sad ones, and witnessed so many more tragedies in the past few years that she thought she'd grown immune to them. The sudden desire to know more about Chase Fielder surprised her.

CHAPTER THREE

S o what do you think?" Sarah said.

"Hmm?" Lily said absently, moving around the inside of the surprisingly spacious clinic. Chase Fielder. Of course she wouldn't have recognized her. Chase'd been a child the last time she'd seen her. Not only that, the circumstances had been nothing any of them likely wanted to remember. Sarah and Chase's mother had just died, six years after their father had been killed in a climbing accident. Sarah had been devastated, and Lily could only imagine the impact on a ten-year-old of losing both parents so young. Chase certainly had changed from the pale, withdrawn girl she remembered, replaced by an imposingly confident, exceptionally good-looking woman, radiating no-nonsense vibes and a raw sensuality she obviously made no attempt to hide. And then why should she. Eligible women like Chase probably had all the attention they could want, and more, in a resort area like this. Assuming she wasn't already attached. Big assumption there. Although the vibes said no. And there had definitely been vibes.

Lily smiled. *Vibes.* She hadn't had a sense of those in over two years. Probably because there were none, but even had there been, she wouldn't have noticed them. First she'd been too shell-shocked by the rapidity with which the pandemic had engulfed her, and eventually too numbed to any emotion other than duty to notice the absence of sensation in her life. Why had that suddenly changed?

"The clinic?" Sarah said, her voice rising at the end.

"Oh!" Lily drew herself back into the present. Where she promised herself she would stay, no matter what it took. "It's pretty amazing."

It really was. The cabin housing the clinic—still made of logs, of course, but finished with a sensible tile floor throughout—was at least three times the size of the others on the mountainside, with a waiting room just inside the entrance and an astonishingly well-equipped treatment area with several exam rooms and one procedure room in the rear. The adjustable table in the center of the procedure room could be converted to an OR table. The overhead lights looked like they'd be right at home in any city OR too. Stainless steel shelves were stocked with bandages, slings, splints, and what appeared to be sterile packages of surgical instruments. She turned to Sarah and folded her arms. "This looks like overkill for a walk-in clinic. You're not expecting me to do an appendectomy, are you?"

"That's the state for you," Sarah said with a grimace. "Last year we didn't have enough PFDs at the start of the season. I had to advance my own money to cover life vests for all the campers until the POs from the state came through. *But* we had an unlimited spending budget for healthcare. So"—she waved a hand—"I stocked up."

"It's excellent, and as soon as I have a chance," Lily said, "I'll go through everything, and if I find any shortages, I'll let you know." She frowned and looked around. A red equipment cart with four rows of drawers occupied a spot behind the treatment table. She opened the top drawer, then the next. Epinephrine, lidocaine, bicarb, IVs, bags of saline. Typical cardiac arrest paraphernalia found in every crash cart in every ER in the United States. No analgesics or sedatives. "Is there a drug locker besides that cart?"

"Yes," Sarah said. "This way."

A door on the right side of the room led into a small office set up as an informal consultation room with a leather sofa in the center of a big multicolored braided rug, a couple of matching chairs, and an oak desk against one wall that looked like it'd seen a lot of use in a previous life.

"There's a bathroom in the back." Sarah gestured toward a tall gray metal cabinet tucked into one corner. "That"—she pointed at the cabinet—"contains a limited supply of prescription pain medication, antipsychotics, sedatives, and morning-after pills. You and I have the only keys."

"Oh boy," Lily said. "Will we be needing the morning-after pills?"

"Again, we are prepared," Sarah said with a shake of her head.

"We've got forty-eight teenagers, some of them almost ready to head to college. Pretending they don't have sex is just stupid."

"I agree. Forty-eight?"

"Uh-huh. Six cabins, divided between the boys and girls, eight to a cabin—four double bunks in each."

"What about the nonbinary kids?" Lily asked.

"They chose, along with their parents, which cabins they'll be comfortable in."

Lily did the math. "I thought I saw eight cabins up there."

"You did—one for the four male counselors and RAs, one for the other four females."

"One to six ratio," Lily remarked. "Good numbers. How tight are the restrictions on…mingling?"

"Our people are living among the campers, twenty-four seven. They're not in the same sleeping quarters but take a bed check every night. It's possible, but not easy, for the campers to sneak around after lights out, but we all sleep lightly."

Lily laughed. "Oh, this is going to be fun."

"Told you." Sarah backed out of what would soon be Lily's cabin. "Seen enough? We should head back over to the lodge. Natalie ought to be here any minute."

"Yes, thanks. The setup is great." Lily followed Sarah back outside. "So, um, what's this meeting? Who's Natalie?"

"I'm not entirely sure what's up with the meeting. Nat—she's the district DEC supervisor—called me to set it up with the staff early this morning. You're part of the staff now," Sarah said, "so you, Alisha Miller, and Philippe Santiago—the two head counselors—will need to be present at morning briefing, evening review, and any special meetings, like this one."

"And Chase. Why her?"

"Good question." Sarah grimaced. "Chase usually avoids the lodge."

"Why?"

"No idea," Sarah said, her attention diverted by a green Jeep, a cousin to the one Chase drove, pulling around to the front of the lodge. A trim woman in the familiar green uniform with shoulder-length chestnut hair, a light tan, and a confident stride headed their way.

"Nat," Sarah said. "This is Lily Davenport, our new medic."

Once again, Lily took the extended hand. "Good to meet you."

"Doctor," Natalie Evans said in a throaty alto. "Natalie Evans. Welcome aboard."

"Thanks."

Natalie scanned the small adjacent lot. "I see Chase made it back already."

"She's inside," Sarah said as they climbed the steps to the porch and entered the great room.

A woman who looked about thirty with skin the golden brown of rich oak, in khaki shorts, hiking boots, and a lime green V-neck T-shirt, sat with a pale, thin man with dark wavy hair that draped his high forehead in artfully tangled strands. He had fine features and prominent facial bones that wouldn't be out of place on a Greek statue. They both nodded as Sarah, Lily, and Natalie walked over.

"Lily," Sarah said, indicating the two people on a dusky leather sofa that looked like it might seat a dozen more without crowding anyone, "our head counselors...Alisha and Philippe. This is Lily Davenport, our summer medic."

"Hello," Lily said, returning their friendly smiles and welcoming greetings. Feeling the sudden fatigue of the long drive and the tense journey up the mountain, she leaned close to Sarah and murmured, "Do I have time to grab another cup of coffee?"

"Have at it," Sarah said as Nat chatted with the two counselors. "We're pretty relaxed here, and we're still waiting on Chase."

"I won't be a minute," Lily said and hurried through to the kitchen. She slowed on her way to the coffee station. Chase Fielder leaned with her hips against the stainless steel counter, a mug of coffee in one hand. She looked relaxed and way too young. Not that that was relevant.

"Dr. Davenport," Chase said, lifting her mug in Lily's direction. "Have I mentioned it's nice to know you're not one of the parents?"

Lily flushed. "Lily, please." Lily poured coffee and made a quick decision. Engage, ignore, or deflect? "Why?"

Chase didn't try to pretend she didn't understand. "Because you'd likely be involved."

"A reasonable but not necessarily accurate assumption. I could be a single mother for any number of reasons."

"Are you?"

"Which?"

"Involved or a single mother?"

"No." Lily sighed. "Neither of which is relevant to…anything."

Chase just smiled. "Done with the grand tour?"

"I don't think so," Lily said carefully.

"You see the zip line yet?"

Lily narrowed her eyes. "You're joking."

"No joke. There's a climbing wall…well, it's a rock face. Lots of fun when they get to that."

"Officer Fielder—"

"Ranger Fielder will do," Chase said, "but Chase works better."

"Ranger Fielder," Lily repeated, emphasis on *Ranger*, "if you are trying to somehow worry me, you're wasting your time. I assure you, nothing that might happen here, and I sincerely hope we don't have any reason to find out, will be a problem for me."

"Snakes?"

Lily flinched and forced herself not to look around. "Snakes."

"Yes, as in rattle."

"Endemic?" Lily asked in her best professional, I-will-not-show-fear voice.

"Very much so."

"I'll have to find out about the store of antivenom." Lily couldn't recall seeing any in the clinic. She probably should have researched environmental health hazards. A few years ago she might have. Her curiosity had disappeared along with her joy in medicine.

"We have it."

Lily's attention snapped back to Chase. "We?"

"All the rangers. In my field box in the Jeep. It's best if administered on-site. If by chance one of the campers comes across one of the big guys on their way down to the lake, then obviously you will be closer."

"On the way down to the lake."

"They like to get into the paths when it's sunny." She glanced down. "I would recommend hiking boots at all times."

Lily took mental stock and realized everyone she'd seen, except her, was wearing hiking boots, even with shorts.

"You have hiking boots?" Chase asked.

"I have…running shoes. Sarah said sturdy shoes. I took that to mean, you know, *shoes*."

"Oh boy."

"That won't be a problem," Lily said quickly. "I'll just run down and buy a pair today."

"You don't mean that literally."

"I'm sorry?"

"The run down part."

"Ha ha." The heat was starting to rise in her chest. Chase Fielder was playing with her. And she didn't appreciate it. She wasn't afraid of snakes. Not really. She didn't really know anything about snakes, except she didn't really want to know anything about snakes.

"I'll drive down." Lily turned away. "And now, I believe they're waiting for us in the other room."

"I wouldn't suggest taking that Beemer back and forth," Chase said amiably as she fell in beside her.

"Then I'll take the Jeep down. I saw one out there."

"Probably shouldn't leave Sarah without a vehicle."

Lily blew out a breath. "Well, I'm sure I'll think of something."

"I'll drive you into Bolton tomorrow morning."

"You?"

"I have to take a water sample down to the regional office. Sarah will be busy all day with campers arriving and parents demanding her attention."

"I'm sure I can—"

"Lily," Chase said patiently, "it makes the most sense. And you strike me as…sensible."

Lily gritted her teeth. Sensible. How nice. She could, however, be gracious. "Thank you, I would appreciate that very much. While I'm there, I can rent a vehicle. An appropriate one."

"Good idea." Chase frowned and pushed open the big swinging door between the kitchen and the great room. "Now let's see what's so important at this camp that Nat had to drag me out of the field."

Lily couldn't decide what bothered Chase more—that she'd been pulled out of the field, or that she'd been called to the camp. Something else she wanted to know about Chase Fielder.

❖

"You can't be serious." Chase shot out of her seat and stalked to the twelve-foot-high windows. The view through the trees to Thunder Ridge and the pinnacle above it, High Cloud Peak, sparkling with late snow, was a sight she ordinarily loved, despite the memories. At the moment she had trouble focusing on anything except her new orders.

"It's only for the summer," Nat repeated for the third time.

Chase set her jaw, clamping her teeth tightly together to stifle the angry words clawing their way up her throat. Nat was her boss and her friend, and the small rational part of her mind still working clearly understood this wasn't Nat's call. She was only the messenger. But damn it, couldn't she have done something? Protested?

Fucking politics. How far did she have to go to get away from them? She methodically relaxed the muscles in her neck and shoulders and concentrated on steadying her breathing. Somewhere in the long months of rehab, the value of meditation and biofeedback had finally gotten through to her. The negative impact of chronic anger on her body had registered also, and she'd worked hard to break the links. She'd never totally accomplished it, but she'd made progress. Slowly she turned and let out a breath. "Who's behind this again?"

Nat looked pained for an instant. "State Senator Langford. His daughter is arriving this afternoon."

"And the family is making this request, why?"

Nat shook her head. Maybe she was just as frustrated as Chase. "I don't know. I just got the word to make it happen."

Chase cut a glance at her sister Sarah. "You're the damn camp director. You didn't know anything about this?"

Sarah shrugged infinitesimally. "It's a DEC decision."

"Right, then." No help from the home front. "What about field duty?"

"You'll be on half-time," Nat said. "Just pull your range in unless there's an emergency. I'll alert the other districts to watch our outlying areas."

"But I have to quarter here?" Chase asked. "I can't see why—"

"You'll be working out of this site rather than your home base until further notice." Nat's tone was that of command, and Chase accepted it.

"Right. Is there anything else?"

"No, that's it."

Chase nodded abruptly in the general direction of the people gathered in the sitting area, spun on her heel, and strode out. She braced both hands on the log rail and looked out across the lake. Midday, early summer, in the mountains. A beautiful time. A crystal-blue sky dotted with pristine fluffy white clouds floated overhead. Too perfect to be real, except she knew it was. Knew too just how quickly the sky turned angry with storm clouds rolling over the mountain peaks, sending floodwaters swollen with snowmelt from the high country into overflowing streams, washing out trails and footbridges, and endangering hikers and campers with flash floods and mudslides. All of this land, this beauty, was hers to protect, and in turn the wilderness gave her purpose and a place.

"Chase," Sarah said from behind her.

"Just let me know where I'll be bunking," Chase said without turning around.

"You can have a room in the lodge or take the loft rooms over the equipment facility. There's a decent view from up there, a fridge, and a bathroom. You'll have to get your meals over here with everyone else."

"I'll take the loft." Chase looked at her sister. "You didn't have a clue?"

Sarah snorted. "Hell no. But even if I had, you know there's nothing I could do about it. It's the state."

"Right, and no one argues with the state."

"The state has protected what matters most," Sarah said in the still, quiet voice Chase had heard all her life in times of crisis. "The land. And they put us here to look after it."

"Would be great if they'd just let us do our job."

"Well, everything requires money, and the camp program requires campers. And some of our kids might be scholarship kids, but most of them have families who are paying a pretty hefty tuition."

"And are so used to privilege they don't mind screwing with other peoples' lives. I got it." Chase sighed. "At least you and Alisha will have to deal with the problem child."

Sarah looked away.

"What?" Chase said.

"I'm just guessing here, but the only reason I can see for moving you into Rob's place as the DEC coordinator is that you're female."

Chase stared. "I'm not babysitting. No way."

"Of course not."

"Damn it, Sarah—"

"I'm sure it won't be as bad as you think." Sarah squeezed her shoulder. "I've got some last-minute scheduling to do. The keys to the loft are behind my desk in the office on the keyboard."

"Right."

The door behind Chase opened, and Nat passed her going down the steps.

"It's up to you how you want to balance your time," she said, stopping beside Chase. "Just make sure everything here is covered, and the rest is up to you."

"That's something, I guess."

"For what it's worth," Nat said, "none of us are very happy about it."

Chase watched Nat's Jeep disappear down the mountain and caught a hint of citrus and spice. Lily stepped up beside her. Chase's attention snapped to her, and her anger dissipated.

"I didn't really follow all of that," Lily said, "but I did gather that being assigned to the camp is not high on your list of coveted positions."

"It's a soft job for the most part," Chase said. "Organizing the outdoor activities, supervising the away excursions, instructing the campers on wilderness survival. It's not a bad gig if you've spent twenty years on patrol, and that's why I'm not interested in it."

"This is too tame for you," Lily said. "You like being on patrol."

Surprised, Chase nodded. "I do."

Lily nodded. "Why?"

Chase answered without thinking. "I like the solitude. I like... never mind. I'm sure you'd find it boring."

"On the contrary. I'm curious. I don't have a very good idea of what it's like for you. Working alone like that every day."

"It's peaceful, and beautiful. And challenging. Always something different happening."

"Always something different happening," Lily murmured. "You know, I think we are completely opposite. Because the thing I'm really looking forward to this summer is the routine. No surprises."

Chase leaned her shoulder against the porch post and studied her. For the first time, in the slanting sunlight, she realized that Lily Davenport looked tired. Not tired from lack of sleep, although maybe there was some of that, but weary. Literally worn thin. The urge to brush the shadows away constricted her chest, and she pulled in air. "Why?"

Lily didn't expect the question and struggled for a few seconds to answer. "I'm an ER doc. I chose the specialty because I loved how different every minute of the day was. Different cases, different challenges, different tests of just how much I knew. I loved the fast pace, I could teach as well as treat, and I could beat the odds—most days at least. And then"—she rubbed her eyes, as if that would erase the images—"well. The pandemic changed everything almost overnight. Different challenges every day still, but not any that I could solve. Hundreds, then thousands, of patients we didn't expect and didn't know how to treat. Supplies we couldn't replenish, space we didn't have for those who needed it. Every day brought a new problem I couldn't solve."

Lily stopped, hearing herself. "I'm sorry. I'm whining about my problems, as if that mattered when people were dying."

"People you wanted to save," Chase said matter-of-factly. "Must've made you a little crazy."

Lily almost laughed, the relief was so unexpected. How refreshing, not to hear the sympathy she'd gotten so often from so many. "It practically did. After a while I just got numb to the frustration."

"I don't believe that," Chase said. "If you did, it wouldn't still be eating at you."

"It isn't," Lily said quickly.

"Okay," Chase said softly, as if she didn't believe her. And of course, she was right not to.

Lily appreciated she didn't push, didn't try to make her feel better. "I'm sorry that you're getting saddled with a summer that you're not looking forward to."

"There are some positive aspects," Chase said. "I'll get to see more of you, for example."

Engage, ignore, deflect. The last two were impossible. Chase was too persistent, too direct, too damn attractive. "I'm flattered. But—"

"It wasn't meant as flattery," Chase said. "I don't expect you need it or like it. It was a statement."

"And one I appreciate," Lily said. "And in the spirit of directness, you should know I'm not interested."

"In women?"

"In anyone. The only thing I'm interested in this summer is…" If she actually knew what she wanted, she could've said so. But the pictures wouldn't come. "Something…not what I had before."

"So it's not that I'm female."

"No," Lily said and couldn't help but laugh. Really. Did Chase really not know she exuded sexy with every breath? "Very much not that."

"Then, like I said, there are definitely some positives."

"Are you always this tenacious?" Lily said.

"Yes," Chase said instantly. "When I set my mind to something."

"I'm afraid you'll be disappointed."

Chase shrugged. "I've been disappointed before, but so far it hasn't kept me from trying."

Engage, ignore, deflect.

Lily said, "Is our trip into town still on for tomorrow?"

"Yes. Are you an early riser?"

"Always."

"Good. I'll be by around seven, if that works for you."

Engage, ignore, deflect.

It was only a bit of shopping. Lily smiled. "I'll see you then."

Chapter Four

Lily, alone and at loose ends after Sarah disappeared to her office and Chase drove off, decided to drag her luggage to the second floor of the lodge and find her room. Someone must know which was hers. She hadn't packed all that much, considering she was going to be away for an entire summer, but she'd covered everything on Sarah's list, including a rain poncho. She'd considered substituting a raincoat and then thought better of it. Sarah was the meticulous type. She'd said poncho, she must mean poncho.

Somewhat like sturdy footwear did not equal running shoes.

Smiling to herself at the sound of Chase's voice teasing her about that, she lugged her new canvas duffel up the broad stairs. She hadn't been teased about anything for a very long time. That must be why she enjoyed it—that awakening of a little humor in her life. Not that Chase actually had anything special to do with it. Besides, there was the part about the snakes. Chase wouldn't have made up *that* part. Of course, she didn't know Chase at all. Odd, that someone she'd met so recently could occupy so much of her thoughts.

And the next thing on her to-do list was to check the antivenom stock.

"Excuse me," she called to a young man in the ubiquitous attire of T-shirt, khaki shorts, and of course, hiking boots, who looked like he knew what he was doing. The fact that he was pushing a cart loaded with linens and other household-type items was something of a give-away.

He turned, his dark eyes alight. "Yo. Help you?"

"I hope so. I'm Lily Davenport. I'm supposed to have a room up here somewhere."

His thick dark brows drew down a little over heavy lids, edged with ridiculously long, gorgeous eyelashes.

"We've got a Dr. Davenport coming."

"That would be me."

"Ha, right. Sorry about that."

"No problem. The room?"

"Middle one down there on the right," he called as he pushed his cart in the opposite direction. "Nice to meet you, Doc."

The middle one. There were six doors on the right side of the hall. Which one was the middle—the third one from the near end, or the fourth? Might as well try the third. The door opened, the room showed no signs of occupancy, and the windows across from the door let in air so fresh she could taste it as it blew her hair away from her face. The bed, a queen against one wall, was a simple affair with a plain oak headboard and a three-drawer bedside table on one side and a partially open closet on the other. A small chair and desk sat against the fourth wall with a bureau of oak to match the other furniture crouching nearby, and a closed door beside that. Lily's pulse thudded.

Please let that door lead to a bathroom. She hadn't even considered that she might be sharing communal bathroom facilities. She dropped her duffel by the bed and opened the mystery door…that blessedly led into a small but efficiently arranged bathroom with all the necessary items, including a reasonably spacious shower stall. No tub. But then there was the lake. She could always swim, her favorite form of exercise—something else she'd stopped doing.

Of course, there were the snakes. Did they swim? She shuddered. Not something she wanted to think about or even know the answer to. Why did freshwater lakes have to be populated with so many unsavory things? The ocean was so much more…anonymous. She snorted. Thunder Ridge camp did not afford anonymity in any fashion—not with communal eating, shared lodgings, and *people* everywhere. She hadn't been surrounded by so many people who didn't resemble exhausted automatons in months. Her world was suddenly taking on color and…life.

Her heart twisted. After so much death and despair, she wasn't sure she was ready for all of this. She took a deep breath. But she was here. So she'd do what had always worked—she'd attack the task in front of her, and then move on to the next.

She unpacked, filled the bureau with her mostly newly purchased camp clothes, and arranged her bathroom articles. Now she needed a plan. After endless days of barely having enough time to eat and shower, facing an afternoon without responsibility seemed foreign. She'd start with checking the supplies in the clinic. She paused at the door, turned back, and put on sunscreen.

After she'd checked the supply list neatly printed and left on the desk in the waiting area against their inventory, and found the antivenom serum in the undercounter fridge in the treatment area, *and* checked Medline as to indications and dosages, she closed up, making a mental note to get the keys from Sarah.

The only other area she hadn't seen much of was the cabins for the campers, and she headed up the dirt path that connected all the buildings. All the cabin doors stood open, and she climbed the porch to the first one she came to. The porch was wide enough for four canvas-backed camp chairs and a couple of small wood tables painted in jaunty red and yellow. A quick peek inside revealed a common room with an L-shaped, dark leather sectional and a pair of matching recliners that faced an open-hearth fireplace, a heavy oak table tucked into a window nook off to one side, and a door at the rear that probably went to a bathroom. A narrow staircase against one wall led to a short loft balcony and several open doors—likely the bedrooms. The furniture sat on colorful braided rugs, giving the place a cheerful air. All in all, the place had a rustic but homey kind of vibe.

"Oh good," someone with a lilting soprano said from behind her, and Lily turned.

A lithe blonde teen wearing a tight white Lycra tank and black running shorts with white running shoes—not hiking boots, Lily noted—climbed up to the porch and continued, barely glancing at Lily, "My luggage is in the black Mercedes SUV parked in the lot. I'd like to get a shower, if you can bring it up as soon as possible."

"Hello," Lily said, holding back a laugh. Oh my, this *was* going to be an interesting summer. "I'm Lily Davenport, the camp medic. I don't believe there's any kind of porter or maid service. You'll have to bring up your own things."

The teenager snorted, not bothering to give her name. "You can't be serious. These…rooms…are a five-minute walk from there."

"Not quite—once you get used to the trails, there are a few shortcuts. I've only just arrived myself, so I'm still exploring."

"There must be some mistake, because I don't plan on doing…" Her voice drifted away, and her expression suggested she couldn't even put into words the impossibility of what she was imagining.

"First time at camp?" Lily asked.

The teen shot her hip and folded her arms, regarding Lily with a mixture of curiosity and disdain. "I can't imagine why anyone would do this *once*, let alone more than that. Usually, I'd spend the summer sailing."

"What kind of boat do you sail?"

A flicker of interest, quickly extinguished, crossed her long, lean, and decidedly pretty face. "A Jeanneau Sun Fast. Why, do you know anything about sailing?"

"I've done a fair amount of sailing off the Hamptons. Not much long-range ocean sailing, though."

The teen glanced toward the lake, visible through the treetops. Her expression morphed from disgust to a second of sadness. "There won't be anything like that around here."

"No, freshwater sailing is a lot different. Fun, though. I've done a little of that."

The girl's face closed down as if she suddenly realized she was having a conversation that she hadn't intended to have. "What am I going to do about my things?"

"If you need a hand, I don't mind helping. I'm not doing anything else right now."

"Oh good. There should be someone with the car. Just tell them Ford sent you."

"Oh, not what I meant," Lily said. "I'll walk down with you. I can help you carry some things back up."

"I see," the girl said with a sniff of annoyance. "Never mind. My security will just have to take care of it."

"Right," Lily said slowly. "It was nice meeting you, Ms.…?"

"Ford," she repeated, and stepped into the cabin.

Lily looked after her but saw no point in following. She ought to find Sarah. If she wasn't mistaken, this was their high-profile camper, and if Ford was supposed to have security, shouldn't someone be around somewhere? Were state senators' families automatically assigned security? She had no idea. And if that was the case, where were they?

The parking lot came into view at the bottom of the winding trail leading down from the cabins, and Lily picked out the large black SUV pulled up beside her BMW. The license plate indicated it was a government vehicle, as if the appearance itself wasn't enough to suggest it. A woman with short dark hair in black tailored pants, white shirt, and dark blazer, despite the heat, stood by the driver's side. Lily headed that way. Looked like she'd found security.

"Are you with Ford, by any chance?" Lily said.

"Yes. Are you Sarah Fielder? Ms. Langford is waiting with her mother for you at the main building."

"No, I'm Lily Davenport, the camp medic." Lily judged the brunette to be late twenties or early thirties, a bit above average height, and athletic looking even in the suit. Probably a job requirement if she was the security Ford had mentioned. "And Ford isn't at the lodge. She's up at the cabins. I just spoke with her."

A look of irritation quickly flashed across the woman's face. A muscle jumped at the angle of her jaw. "I see. Thank you."

"Well, good to meet you, Agent…?"

"Sergeant Latoya. New York State Police."

"Oh. I see."

"If you'll excuse me, Doctor," Latoya said and strode off toward the trail Lily had just descended.

Lily watched her go, yet another person not enjoying her summer assignment.

❖

A few hours later, Lily followed the hum of conversation and the scent of something tantalizingly savory to the communal dining room, which, as it turned out, occupied an entire L-shaped extension off the great room. Banks of windows on two sides provided sweeping vistas to the lake below and upward to the mountains for which the lodge was named. The snowcapped crests of Thunder Ridge formed a gap-toothed line against the sky, with dense evergreens marching down the mountainside to the lodge and the cabins. She wondered what was on the other side of the ridge, feeling overshadowed by the sheer magnitude of the untouched forest in every direction. She mentally transposed the skyscrapers of NYC on the skyline. There, not so very different after all.

Smiling to herself, she carried her tray with a few helpings of vegetables and sliced turkey to a table by the windows where Sarah sat with Alisha.

"Room for a third?" she said.

"Please," Sarah said, indicating one of the two empty chairs.

Campers filled a third of the room, boys and girls mostly segregated, likely by choice, into adjacent tables, many of them surreptitiously eyeing one another. Lily flashed back to what those obligatory school and family social affairs had been like where her girlfriends would be watching the boys, and she more likely would be watching them. She shook her head. "I would not want to be a teenager again for anything."

Sarah and Alisha both laughed.

"How is everyone doing?" Lily asked.

"About half the kids are returners," Sarah said as she sipped a carbonated water. "They're helping the newbies get acquainted and oriented, and so far pretty much everybody's happy to be here." She laughed. "It's the young ones who usually panic the first night away from home—along with their parents. These are teenagers and far too cool for that."

"They might act cool, but I'm not sure everyone is pleased to be here," Lily said. "I ran into Ms. Langford—who said to call her Ford—this afternoon. What is her first name, by the way?"

"Giovanna," Sarah said. "And she is definitely not happy to be here."

"Is it some kind of disciplinary thing?" Lily asked.

"Not according to her mother," Sarah said. "Mostly, I think, from a few veiled references her mother let slip, her family is concerned she's been moving outside her social circle, and they wanted to break those connections."

Alisha sighed. "As if that ever really works. Trying to keep people away from their chosen friends generally just makes them work harder to see them."

"I suppose if she's here, at least, that's not going to be possible," Lily said.

"Unless she goes AWOL," Sarah muttered.

"What about her security? Is she staying?" Alisha asked.

"That remains an open question," Sarah said. "I think Julia Latoya and Chase will have to work that out. Or their bosses will. Technically, they're all part of the same law enforcement department, as the DEC falls under the banner of state police."

"That might explain why the change in assignments to base Chase here," Alisha said. "Giovanna's father probably wanted female security for her."

Sarah sat back in her chair, her expression resigned. "That would make a lot of sense. I feel sorry for Chase. It's an assignment she definitely is not going to want."

Lily nodded in sympathy. "I got that feeling too."

Sarah looked at her quickly, and Lily flushed. Why she didn't know. "I talked with her a few moments after the meeting earlier."

"I see," Sarah said in a way that made Lily wonder what Sarah *thought* she understood. "Chase isn't one to do a lot of talking."

Still not sure what Sarah meant to imply, Lily said neutrally, "She mentioned she much prefers being out on patrol to anything else."

"Of course she does—she's always been a child of the mountains." This time the faint censure in Sarah's tone was clear, and surprising. Lily had never known Sarah to be judgmental about anyone's life choices—but then, they'd all changed in the last few years. And sometimes with family, one's attitudes were different.

"Can't say I blame her there," Alisha put in. "Riding herd on a pack of kids is exhausting." She grinned. "But then, I get to sleep in a nice cozy cabin and eat great food at every meal. So—worth it."

"Chase'll adjust—she's had a lot of practice at that," Sarah said quietly. In a lighter tone, she added, "You're not doing justice to our very fine cuisine there, Lil."

Surprised, Lily said, "Oh. It's great."

"We do have an excellent chef," Sarah said. "The mountain air will probably ramp up your appetite soon enough."

Lily heard what she wasn't saying—that she'd lost weight and looked the worse for it—and appreciated that Sarah wasn't nagging about it. She hadn't really thought about food as anything other than essential fuel that she grabbed whenever she could for the last year. So many changes and she'd only been here a day. No schedule, no line of critical patients waiting, no constant clamor of emergency sirens and alerts. People who weren't fighting to survive, but who were actually enjoying life. And most surprising of all, a woman who kept darting into her thoughts at unexpected moments. Lily hardly recognized herself. She'd lost so much of her old resiliency, everything was a challenge. But at least here, any missteps wouldn't lead to disaster.

When the meal finished, Alisha headed off to see that the campers were getting settled into their accommodations, and Sarah left to untangle a snafu with a delivery that had gone missing. Upstairs in her room, Lily showered, changed into a light cotton shirt and loose drawstring shorts, and pulled up a book on her iPad. She'd left the window beside her bed open, and a pine-scented breeze drifted in. An hour later the room had darkened, and the air had chilled. She set her iPad aside, exchanged her shorts for lightweight gray sweats, and headed downstairs. She wasn't used to going to bed so early and sometimes didn't get more than a few broken hours in a twenty-four-hour period.

The sun had dropped almost completely beyond the mountains, and twilight settled over the camp. The great room was empty, and just a few lamps on side tables provided enough light to see by. Lily wandered out onto the front porch and contemplated the path leading down to the lake. The moon was high and, in places where it reached through the trees, nearly as bright as day. The trees gleamed silver.

"Beautiful," she murmured. The lake beckoned, and then she thought about what Chase had said. Snakes slept at night, didn't they? Still.

"Thinking about a walk?" Chase said quietly from the darkness.

Lily jumped as Chase rose from a chair on the far end of the porch and walked toward her. "Hello."

"Couldn't sleep?" Chase asked. She wasn't in uniform now but wore a dark T-shirt with no logo tucked into tapered jeans and, of course, boots.

"It's too early, and too quiet," Lily said. "Not really quiet. I can hear things making noises. Chipmunks or something."

"Squirrels probably, raccoons maybe."

"They're not afraid to come around? The wildlife?" Lily swallowed, her throat dry. The moonlight shimmered on Chase's face. She was beautiful too. More than that—magnetic. The pull stirred an unfamiliar longing in Lily's chest.

"A lot of them keep their distance," Chase said, "but the scavengers, the smart ones, they know if they're lucky they'll find a loose trash bin lid or bit of luggage to get into."

"Um, I left my window open."

"They're probably not gonna scale the walls."

Feeling foolish, Lily laughed. "Right."

"Want to take a walk?"

The pull grew stronger, and Lily tensed.

Engage. Deflect. Ignore.

"Is it safe?" Lily asked.

"Depends on what kinds of things scare you," Chase said softly.

Lily's breath caught. What indeed. She answered without thinking. "Facing the unknown."

"People or things?"

"Situations I can't control, disasters I can't fix—God, what am I saying." Lily took a step back from the edge of the porch, as if something out there in the silvery night had torn open a door to places inside her she didn't want to explore. "Let's forget I said that."

"Why?"

"I must sound terribly controlling."

"You sound like a doctor to me—or a law enforcement officer or any number of people who try to help in a crisis." Chase grunted. "And it sucks when you can't."

"Yes, it does," Lily said softly, oddly relieved to hear her struggles summed up with such simple truth. "In this case, I was actually talking about...creatures."

"You're close to camp, so you're not likely to run into anything that won't run from you. You should have a flashlight, though."

"I don't have one."

Chase patted her side. "But you're in luck."

Lily saw the head of a slim flashlight sticking out of Chase's front pocket.

Chase laughed, a deep warm sound that nevertheless caused Lily's skin to tingle. "Something to get with the boots tomorrow."

Lily sighed and rubbed her arms to dispel the distracting sensation. "I think I'm going to need a longer list."

Chase grinned. "Could be."

"I'd like to see the lake," Lily said impulsively. "I can see little bits of it from my window, and it looks so serene—so magnificent—in the moonlight."

Chase nodded. "It is. Come on, we'll go see."

And just like that, Lily followed her down the stairs into the night, guided by the thin beam of light on the ground and Chase's solid presence by her side. Engaged, and not even questioning what that might mean. So unlike her, and yet, somewhere inside, feeling exactly right.

CHAPTER FIVE

"A re you sure about this?" Lily asked. "I mean, I know you're sure we won't run into Bigfoot—oh, that's in the Rockies, isn't it—but can you see all right?"

Chase laughed. The trails around the lodge were so familiar, she could traverse them with her eyes closed, and nothing about the mountains at night concerned her. "I have excellent night vision—in fact, I wouldn't ordinarily use a flashlight unless I was hunting for something, or someone, in the scrub. Night is my favorite time, really. Growing up, I'd sleep outside whenever I could, no matter the season."

Lily slowed. "Really? I mean, what about snow?"

"Winter nights are when the sky is the best, usually—black and clear—and the constellations are closest. Some of the best ones, anyhow. Warm enough in a decent sleeping bag, as long as you get out of the wind. In the summer, when the nights got steamy, I'd just toss an old blanket on the ground. Still do, whenever I can."

"Why night?" Lily asked. "Why is it your favorite?"

Chase hesitated. How could she explain how the night was tied to her best memories? How listening to the night sounds and watching the stars revolve overhead brought her back to a time before loss taught her to be wary of trusting joy. One of the first things her father had taught her about the beauty of the night was the constellations. Reclining beside her and pointing out the formations, he'd told her the stories, the ancient myths, behind each one. With the dark close around them and his quiet, sonorous baritone turning the night sky into a canvas of wonder, she'd been happy without ever realizing how precious the moments were until he was gone.

Avoiding the answer, Chase slowed at the crest of a moderate decline and reached out for Lily's hand. "It gets steep here, and with the dew on the pine needles, it can be slippery."

She felt more than heard Lily's gasp of surprise when their fingers touched.

"Thank you," Lily said, clasping Chase's hand. "I came down here this morning with Sarah, but everything seems different now." She laughed quietly. "Bigger, somehow. And I feel a lot smaller. In fact, every time I look out anywhere, I'm reminded just how insignificant I am out here."

Chase smiled. "Once you get used to feeling part of what's around you, that might change."

"You don't think you have to be born to it to belong?"

"Not if you're willing to really look," Chase said. "It's not much farther now."

"Oh," Lily exclaimed as, suddenly, the trees gave way to the shoreline. "The lake is so…perfect."

"That's a good word for it," Chase murmured, watching Lily, who was far more enchanting to look at than even one of her favorite views. Lily's face shone as if lit from within, her lips faintly parted, her eyes, normally so green, flickering like firelight now. Seeing Lily's pleasure was a pleasure in itself, a new experience for her. She'd always enjoyed pleasing women physically, finding unique satisfaction in the intensity of the moment, even as she felt safely apart. But she'd never shared a moment like this—when Lily's appreciation of something so precious to her felt like a gift.

"It's as if it's sleeping," Lily whispered, "totally at peace."

"If you're up for it," Chase said quietly, careful not to break the spell, "there's a spot a little farther up the beach that I think you'd like."

Lily turned to her, and for a second, that expression Chase doubted she was aware of settled over her face—calm and impenetrable as she made her decision. Chase didn't know what she was thinking or how she decided, but she'd seen it several times that day. Lily's eyes would come alive as soon as she'd charted a course.

They sparkled now in her direction, and Lily said, "Lead on."

Under other circumstances, with another woman, Chase might have interpreted that as an invitation, but she knew this wasn't. Lily Davenport did not strike her as the kind of woman who made roundabout innuendos. Chase had been looking for—hoping for, more than she wanted to admit—some signal of interest from Lily but hadn't seen one. Now she could accept the reality there was none or keep hoping that Lily was very good at not showing her intentions. Since she wasn't anywhere close to giving up, she'd hold out for the latter.

As they walked along the shore, she could have released Lily's hand, as the going was much smoother, and she'd already clicked off the flashlight so only moonlight illuminated the path, but Lily made no move to draw away, and she didn't want to let go. Lily's hand was smooth and warm and firm, and her fingers curled around Chase's as if they liked being there. Chase took her around the bend into the little cove where a wooden dock, long and not much wider than she was tall, stretched out into the placid lake.

"Come on out here," Chase said and led Lily out to the end of the dock. Water lapped gently against the pilings, and the dock swayed softly like a woman dancing in her arms. "Take your shoes off."

"What?" Lily actually croaked, and Chase stifled a laugh.

"Take off your shoes and socks." Chase unlaced her boots and pulled them off along with her socks and sat on the end of the dock. After a few seconds of hesitation, Lily removed her running shoes and socks and sat down beside her.

"Now put your feet in the water."

"Oh no. No way," Lily said adamantly. "It's dark down there. There could be *anything* down there. In fact, there is anything—many anythings—down there. No."

Laughing, Chase nudged Lily's shoulder teasingly. "Okay, I'll go first."

She dangled her legs over the side, and the warm water came up to the middle of her calves. "Nothing down there but my toes."

Lily peered down. "I can't see a thing. This close, the water is black."

"I know you're not afraid of the dark."

"I'm afraid of quite a lot of things," Lily said softly in that tone that told Chase she was thinking of those moments when the crisis had been at its worst. Moments Chase could only try to imagine and knew she couldn't even come close.

All the same, she ached to reach out, somehow touch those memories, and smooth away the sharp edges that still caused Lily to bleed. She knew that wasn't possible but wished it still. Instead of offering empty words, she offered what she could. Silence. Slipping an arm around Lily's waist, she pulled Lily a little closer against her side and watched the moonlight skim the surface of the lake like a lover's hand.

Slowly, Lily lowered her legs until her feet dipped into the water. She caught her breath. "It's so warm! It was freezing this morning."

"It happens at night, because of the reversal of the thermal currents," Chase said. "The cool air pulls the heat from her depths—kind of like a kiss."

Lily leaned away until she was facing her and laughed into her eyes. "That might be the most romantic thing I've ever heard."

"Go ahead, laugh. I can take it." Chase grinned. "But it is pretty relaxing, to sit here like this and look at the stars."

"Mmm, no doubt." Lily braced both hands behind her on the dock and tilted her head back, gazing up at the sky.

Chase mimicked her position.

"You know all of them?" Lily asked.

"Yes," Chase said quietly.

"Tell me."

"Just one tonight," Chase said, pointing up to Polaris. "There. Ursa Minor—the little bear. That one will always be up there, all year round." She told Lily how in Greek mythology the big and little bear constellations represented the two nymphs who protected Zeus when he was small, and how, as a reward, he placed them in the heavens.

"I can actually see that one," Lily said. "You'll tell me the other stories?"

"Next time we have a chance to stargaze," Chase murmured. "Although many of the most romantic stories involve ones that are seen best in the fall."

"That's too bad," Lily said. "I'll be back in the city by then, and stargazing, even if I had time, would be impossible. Too much light and God knows what else in the air."

The swift shaft of disappointment caught Chase by surprise. Of course Lily would be leaving when the camp closed after Labor Day. The kids would be gone by then, and Lily's job would be over. Not that it mattered, really. Even with women she actually dated, three months was a long time.

"You'll probably be happy to get back to civilization by then," Chase said.

"Yes. Probably. I should get back to the lodge, Chase," Lily said abruptly, as if mention of the future had broken their spell.

"Of course." Chase rose and pulled off her T-shirt, leaving her in the tank she wore underneath, her jeans, and barefoot. She quickly wiped the water from her lower legs and tops of her feet and handed the damp tee to Lily. "Use this before you put your shoes on. Otherwise you'll end up with sand and pine needles stuck everywhere."

When Lily didn't answer, Chase realized Lily was staring at her.

"Something wrong?" she asked, but she knew the look. Lily was taking in her body, and she liked it. Chase liked her looking too, a pulse jumping low in her belly.

"Not in the slightest," Lily said, her voice throaty. She took the shirt, still looking at Chase. "Thank you."

"Sure."

"Do you do this often?" Lily asked.

"Do what?" Chase held back, cautious with her reply. If Lily only knew all the things she'd been doing since they'd left the lodge— marveling at the softness of Lily's skin, being mesmerized by the way the moonlight set Lily's face aglow, wishing she could read Lily's mind, and wondering if any kind of overture from her would be welcome.

"Come down here at night like this?" Lily said, pushing into her running shoes.

"Ah," Chase said.

"What did you think I was asking?" Again, no playful note to suggest flirtation. Direct, interested.

"Could have been a couple of things," Chase said as she pulled on her boots. "To all of which I would've answered, no, this is a first."

"Oh," Lily said, her voice caressing the word.

Aha. Lily liked that, being the only one, and Chase enjoyed a rush of satisfaction. She'd answered truthfully, but she'd learned something too. Lily was interested.

"I'm not usually at the lodge at night," Chase said.

"Oh," Lily said, this time sounding a little disappointed.

Chase chuckled and laced her fingers through Lily's. Lily didn't pull away. "And I've never walked along here in the moonlight with anyone."

Lily laughed softly. "Obvious, was I?"

"Anything but. I have a hard time figuring out what you're thinking."

"Why try? You could ask."

"Maybe I'm afraid of being disappointed," Chase said.

Lily stopped and tugged on Chase's hand until they faced each other, the lake water lapping against the shore a few feet away, moonlight streaming through the trees, focusing on them like a pale spotlight on nature's stage. They were almost of a height, but Chase had to look down just a little to find Lily's eyes. Her hair, shimmering gold by day, was like an afterglow of sunlight at night, delicately pale. The bit of a breeze blew silky strands against her cheek, and Chase caught them with her fingertips and brushed them back along the line of Lily's jaw. She let her fingertips drift downward to Lily's throat where a pulse fluttered like bird wings, fragile and swift.

"I've never kissed anyone out here either," Chase said. Her voice was hoarse, the hunger rising swift and hard from deep within her, clamping urgent fingers around her throat.

Lily's hands came up to her shoulders, and she tilted her head ever so slightly to the side. "Neither have I."

"Would you like to?" Chase whispered.

"I believe I would."

As hard as the want beat within her, Chase whispered the kiss against Lily's mouth, a brush of her lips over Lily's, a fleeting taste, sweet as honeysuckle. Her breath came hard and fast, and she held herself carefully apart from Lily's body, even when every instinct bade her to touch. Lily's hands cupped Chase's shoulders, fingers digging a little bit into the muscles of her back. Chase's pulse trip-hammered as if she'd been climbing for hours, the muscles in her arms and legs trembling, breath burning through her chest, sweat streaming into her eyes, exhausted, exhilarated, so very much alive. She shuddered.

"Chase?" Lily murmured. "What?"

"Nothing," Chase said gruffly and kissed her again, driving away the memories with the heat of Lily's mouth. Lily kissed her back, a hungry kiss, the slide of teeth over her lower lip, the flick of tongue that sent heat streaking low between her thighs. She slid an arm around Lily's waist and pulled her closer until the darkness between them disappeared and their bodies met.

"Damn it, you feel amazing." Chase explored and teased and lost herself in the scent of her.

Lily pulled away, her breasts rising and falling swiftly against Chase's chest. "Time-out."

"What?" Chase muttered, her head clouded with everything Lily—her scent, her taste, the soft heat of her breasts against Chase's.

"I don't usually do that," Lily said, her words breathless.

"What?" Chase repeated, struggling to focus.

"Invite a woman I barely know to kiss me."

"Did you now? Invite me?" Chase kissed the angle of Lily's jaw before tugging the lobe of Lily's ear carefully between her teeth. "Forward of you."

Lily arched into her, her head dropping back with a moan.

"I believe…I did. I was…I…God, that feels good, Chase."

"*You* feel good," Chase whispered, her mouth against the beating pulse in Lily's throat. "I can't get enough of kissing you."

Lily laughed, a sound as light and fleeting as a breeze. "I think we'd better stop. Considering…"

Chase raised her head and blinked. "Why?"

"We don't really know each other," Lily said, "and…mmm, right there, you have *such* a gorgeous mouth…and you're my best friend's sister, and—"

"My sister has nothing to do with this, and I know enough." Chase kissed the base of her throat. "I know you like fast cars, and cream in your coffee, and see beauty in silence…" She unbuttoned the top button of Lily's cotton shirt and kissed the spot she'd exposed. "I—"

"If we keep going, it will be harder to stop."

"So?" Chase went back to kissing Lily's throat, and Lily wrapped both arms around her neck, her body gently surging against Chase's. Lily's fingers stroked through her hair, setting her skin on fire wherever she touched.

"We're standing on a rocky beach in the middle of the night," Lily said. "It's stop or go insane."

"I'm already insane."

Lily laughed and gently pressed both hands against Chase's shoulders and pushed herself back. "You make me forget."

Chase tried to catch her breath and couldn't remember the last time she'd been senseless with need, if ever. Her stomach twisted with urgency, and her muscles twitched with the relentless pressure to touch her again. "Forget what?"

"Everything, Chase. Everything."

"Is that bad?"

"I don't know. But I think I need to."

"I…all right. Enough for now." She brushed the back of her knuckles gently along Lily's jaw. "But I want to do this again."

"I can't promise that," Lily said quietly.

"You don't have to."

The night grew steadily cooler as Chase took Lily's hand, and they walked in silence back to the lodge.

"Thank you for that," Lily said at the foot of the steps.

"Which part?" Chase asked quietly.

"Every minute of it. It was wonderful."

"It was." Chase closed her hands into fists or else she would've touched her again. "Good night, Lily."

"Good night, Chase," Lily murmured and waited a few moments as Chase walked away into the night. She took a deep breath. "Well."

A cold nose rubbed against her hand, and she jumped. "Baily! You have to stop surprising me like that."

"He thinks everyone loves him," Sarah said, coming to the edge of the porch, her loose, blue-and-white checked flannel pants and a shapeless, long-sleeved T-shirt just visible in the faint light from the windows behind her. "Somewhat like my sister."

"He's right," Lily said, scratching the ecstatic dog behind the ears and ignoring the unexpected comment about Chase.

"Have a nice walk?" Sarah asked.

"Yes. The lake is even more gorgeous at night," Lily said, climbing the stairs, Baily glued to her side. She stretched and sighed. "And it's later than I thought. Are you headed inside?"

"Mmm. I was just getting ready to turn in when Baily wanted to come out for one last sniff around. He's always hopeful he'll find the squirrel, but he never does."

Lily laughed.

"I'm sorry," Sarah said as she held the door for Lily, "but in all of the rush this afternoon, I forgot to mention that sick call is from six to seven every morning. Any campers who won't be participating in the day's activities can be seen then and given a medical excuse to exempt them from the day's events."

"That's not a problem," Lily said. "I'm used to being up early. Besides…"

"Besides?" Sarah asked.

"Oh, nothing." Any other time, Lily would have confided her plans to her best friend, but the hint of censure every time Sarah mentioned Chase made her reluctant. She hadn't seen Sarah in years, and she didn't know Chase at all, beyond the obvious. Blushing and glad Sarah couldn't see it in the dim light, she vowed to resist Chase's charms before she did something she would regret.

❖

Lily should've been tired, but she lay awake strangely energized by a day like none she'd ever experienced. She'd driven two hundred miles to leave behind a life that had grown gray and hopeless, without the passion and joy that had always given her purpose. She knew all the explanations for the weariness, the mental and physical exhaustion, the emotional deprivation that had taken its toll over so many months. But understanding was different than feeling.

What she felt now was not just the absence of that gray pall, but the excitement of reawakening passion for the world…and the people in it. Of course, she knew what that was all about too. In this new place, with the burdens lifted from her shoulders, surrounded by a sense of serenity that was completely different than anything she'd ever known, she could imagine herself a different person in a different place. That would pass, probably quickly, and along with that, whatever impulse had motivated her to invite a kiss from Chase Fielder. Even lying alone in the dark, she closed her eyes and shook her head. Whatever had she been thinking?

Of course, that was the entire explanation. She hadn't been thinking. She'd been seduced—by the newness of walking through the wilderness in the moonlight, by a woman who was at once charming in an oh-so-unpolished way and quietly sensitive in unexpected moments. All that without even mentioning how utterly and unabashedly sexy she was.

And, surprise surprise, she wasn't so far gone that she hadn't noted Chase's interest from almost the moment they'd met. The appreciative glances, flirtatious smile, the gentle but not-too-subtle innuendos. No, she hadn't lost so much of herself in the last two years that she hadn't noticed that. She would've said it was impossible a few days before that any woman could have her acting so unlike herself, but then Chase was like no one she'd ever met before either.

Lily turned on her side and hugged her pillow, watching the moonlight flicker through the trees outside her window. They'd shared a kiss, a few moments of human connection, something universally, intrinsically human. And that's all it meant. She was human, and surprisingly, she was still alive.

She must've drifted off to sleep, because she woke with a start and, for an instant, couldn't place her surroundings. An on-call room? A cubby in the ER? No. The air was too fresh. No alarms blared. No beeper at her waistband trilled a warning. She took a deep breath, stilling the racing of her heart.

She wasn't in the hospital. She was in the mountains. Far away from all that.

Then what?

The rumble of an engine cut through the silence, and Lily rose up in bed in time to see headlights flash for a moment outside her window before they disappeared into the forest. Someone leaving. The quiet returned, and she settled back down, pulling the light blanket up against the unexpected chill, and let sleep come.

CHAPTER SIX

L ily woke a little before five after only a few hours' sleep, but those hours had been deep and restful, her dreams only vague shadows that left her mercifully unhaunted. She showered quickly in her little bathroom and pulled on a favorite pair of jeans that were too loose now, along with a long-sleeved, button-up cotton shirt. She smiled as she laced her running shoes, thinking about new boots. Maybe she needed to add new jeans to that list, if Chase had time and didn't hate shopping. Lily wasn't wild about shopping, and hadn't been in so long her wardrobe—excluding her new camp clothes, of course— was probably hopelessly out of style. Chase didn't give off born-to-shop vibes, but people could be surprising. She laughed aloud. She'd surprised herself just accepting the mad invitation to hide out here for the summer, and what did she do to disturb the peace and quiet she was after but practically jump the first attractive woman she met. Although, in her defense, Chase was a pretty extreme example of attractive, like a 10 on the Richter scale.

And she really needed to stop thinking about Chase every spare minute. She'd see her in a little over two hours, not that she was clock-watching or anything.

Determined to keep her mind off Chase, she headed downstairs in search of coffee.

"Good morning," she called to Alisha, who sat curled up at one corner of the leather sofa in front of the fireplace in a gray hoodie and jeans, her boots on the floor in front of her and her sock-clad feet tucked up on the seat. A fire burned low in the hearth, embers glowing red and the lingering scent of pine in the air.

"Morning," Alisha called back, looking and sounding wide-awake and energetic.

"Did you start the fire?" Lily asked, hoping it wasn't something she'd need to do—maybe she should have asked if there was some kind of chore list she'd have to volunteer for. Not that she'd have any facility for much that would need doing around the lodge. Coffee making, yes. Log burning—no.

"Not me. Sarah most likely," Alisha said. "I'm an early riser, but somehow she always beats me to it."

"It's nice," Lily said, enjoying the heat and subtle, smoky scent of the burning wood.

"Mmm. Mornings are still pretty crisp around here, so we'll probably have a morning fire until the end of the month."

"I've never started a fire," Lily said.

Alisha laughed. "I won't tell anyone. If you ever need help with anything, come find me."

"Thanks, I will. Okay for me to hit the kitchen?"

"Absolutely. Coffee is always on, and you'll probably find some other kinds of treats. They start cooking around three."

"Morning," Lily called to Juan and Clara as she helped herself to coffee and the best-looking blueberry scones she'd ever seen. Sarah came in just as she was adding cream to her coffee.

"How did you sleep?" Sarah asked as she poured coffee.

"Wonderfully," Lily said. "And you're right, the mountain air definitely does something to the appetite. I'm starving."

Sarah smiled, a distracted expression on her face.

"Problem?" Lily asked.

"What?" Sarah looked surprised and quickly shook her head. "No, no. At least as of right now everything is quiet."

"Oh good. I know I have walk-in clinic hours at six. What about after that? I was going to go into town with Chase to—"

"Chase isn't here," Sarah said abruptly.

"Sorry?" Lily thought she'd misheard. She'd said good night to Chase barely six hours earlier.

"She left sometime in the middle of the night. Must've gotten a callout. No telling when she'll be back."

"Oh," Lily said, a flare of disappointment coursing through her. "I guess that happens a lot."

"The district is about nine hundred square miles," Sarah said as if she was reading from a brochure, "and there are only three rangers to cover it. In an emergency, they'll all get called out." She grimaced. "Although knowing Chase, she picked up something on the radio from some local dispatcher and just went to lend a hand." She shrugged. "Whatever it is, she'll probably be out for a while."

Lily's stomach tightened. Even here, the emergencies managed to shatter her brief illusion of calm. "They must be spread pretty thin with so few people and such a huge area."

Sarah gave her a long look. "They're all trained for it, but yeah—could be anything from retrieval of an injured hiker to an unrestricted burn somewhere or a multijurisdictional operation to apprehend poachers."

"I never had any idea the rangers got involved in things like that."

Sarah shrugged. "They're police officers. They just have a different kind of district than most."

"I see," Lily said quietly.

"Chase is—" Sarah blew out a breath. "Chase is happiest when she's out there somewhere. She never was one to want to stay in one place, even home, for very long."

"Then she has the perfect job," Lily said quietly, watching Sarah, who was sending some kind of message here, but she wasn't sure exactly why Sarah thought it was important for her to know that.

"She's not likely to settle down, Lily."

Lily couldn't help but laugh just a little. "Sarah, if you're worried that I have any intentions toward your sister, you don't need to be."

"I wasn't thinking about your intentions," Sarah said. "I was more thinking about Chase's. She…enjoys women…briefly."

"I see," Lily said, tamping down on her irritation. Really, she didn't need a lecture from Chase's sister about who she should or shouldn't date—even if she wasn't planning to *date* anyone, and even if Sarah was her very good friend. But Sarah had practically raised Chase after their mother died, and that probably made her overly protective. Creating an issue over something that didn't even exist was foolish. "If you're worried about my tender feelings, you needn't be. I'm not twenty, Sare."

Sarah pursed her lips. "Right. I'm being an ass, aren't I."

Lily shook her head, fondness erasing her pique. That was her friend Sarah, always willing to call BS on herself if she deserved it. Maybe sometimes when she didn't. "No, you're just being a big sister and a good friend, and the two of them in this instance are probably giving you fits. You don't have anything to worry about."

"Not even after the moonlight midnight walk last night?" A bit of teasing had crept into Sarah's tone.

But still.

"Not even after that," Lily said, refusing the bait. She wasn't about to talk about her personal time with Chase, or any other woman for that matter. Good friend or not. She glanced at her watch. "And since I'm on duty in half an hour, I'm going to go enjoy my coffee and this delicious-looking scone. Coming with?"

"I've got a few minutes before I need to make some phone calls. And I promise not to nag anymore."

Lily looped an arm through Sarah's. "Fair enough."

If Sarah's gentle warning was intended to prevent her from thinking about Chase, it hadn't worked. As she sat with Alisha and Sarah, half listening to their casual chatter about camp business, she thought about Chase. About a hand guiding her down the trail in the dark, a kiss so tender she'd felt precious, and desire so strong she ached. Even knowing she was probably the farthest thing from Chase's thoughts, she couldn't stop wondering when she would see Chase again.

❖

Lily unlocked the clinic front door a little before six and picked up an envelope just inside the door with her name on it. She opened it and pulled out the single sheet of folded paper as she turned on the lights in the treatment rooms.

Lil, she read, in Sarah's neat block printing. *Here's a roster of campers by name, age, and cabin. Files in computer by folder dated this month have pertinent medical history as provided by parents. The campers may or may not know or be willing to tell you if they have any health-related issues. Parents did not flag any health concerns on prelim applications. Only Marty Riley, cabin 8, and Canto Kim in 2 take Rx meds—parents signed waiver allowing camper to bring and take their own meds.*

Sorry I couldn't go over this with you in person—usual first day snafus. Text me if you have probs – S.

The password to the computer is TLR!#mtn10

Lily scanned the list. Not a great start to her first day. She should have thought to ask for the campers' medical profiles yesterday afternoon. Just because they were young did not mean they were illness free, mentally or physically, and she was responsible for their well-being. She hadn't thought about primary care in forever, and not cutting herself any slack, she hadn't really thought very hard about what this job might require. She'd fallen a little too comfortably for Sarah's hard sell of no stress, no emergencies, and no unpredictable hours for three months. She'd needed so badly to get out of Manhattan, to get away from the ER and leave the pressure and self-recriminations behind, that she hadn't prepared for her new job.

Had she really drifted so far from who she once was and every-thing she prided herself on? Only if she let that be true. With a long breath, she settled in the chair, typed in the password, and pulled up the folder with the health forms. She needed to see all the information for herself. Predictably, not all the campers had routine health histories.

Giovanna—Ford—Langford was allergic to bee stings. She should be carrying an EpiPen at all times. Lily, who'd never given up the habit of jotting notes to herself on paper, found a pen and made a list on the back of the roster. She'd track down Ford after clinic and ask her about that. Jeremy Ridgefield had a history of asthma, although he didn't take any medications. Another note—did she have a nebulizer, albuterol, Decadron, and the other meds she might need for an acute attack? Who knew what lurked in the forest that might trigger an attack—mold, or moss—was moss a mold?—and likely all kinds of other pulmonary irritants. Canto Kim took Imuran for control of pediatric Crohn's disease. No note on special diet for him, but she'd check with him. And Marty Riley, cabin eight, took Prozac.

A red flag flew up Lily's mental flagpole and snapped in the breeze. She knew from the psych consultations she'd gotten for troubled kids in the ER that Prozac was generally prescribed for serious depression in teens. Damn it—the parents didn't think *that* warranted a health alert on the application? She found no indication in the past medical history section of any in-hospital treatment, but these health forms were only as complete as what the families supplied. And many patients, or parents of patients, did not want to disclose mental health problems.

She scanned back up to the beginning of Marty's application form—age seventeen years, seven months. Under gender—nonbinary. Pronouns: they/them/their. Connected to the depression? Certainly possible, but not a given. Lily squeezed the bridge of her nose. Double damn it. From the driver's license photo, an average-looking kid, sandy brown hair cut in casual layers, dark brown eyes, height and weight average also.

She made her last note: get to know Marty Riley.

By six forty she'd made it through all the files and felt much more comfortable, having at least begun to think of the campers as her new patient practice. She'd never considered anything other than emergency medicine, family practice seeming too tame, too ordinary. Right now tame and ordinary was very appealing.

The door opened and a boy came in wearing a camp T-shirt, loose sweats, and high-top sneakers. She recognized his face but not his name from the files.

"Morning," Lily said as she rose and came around the desk to greet him.

"Um, I came to see the doctor."

"That would be me," Lily said with a smile and held out her hand. "Lily Davenport. And you are…?"

He looked surprised and a little chagrined. "Uh. Manuel. Manuel Lopez."

"So," she said indicating the hallway behind her, "do you want to come on back here and tell me what's going on?"

"Oh," he said, shuffling his feet, "it's kind of personal."

"We'll talk in private, how's that?"

He hesitated for just a second, then said, "Yes, okay."

Once in the treatment room, she gestured for him to climb up on the treatment table while she sat at the small shelf provided as a desk and opened her iPad to the medical records she'd downloaded from the clinic computer. "So what's going on?"

He said, "Nothing really."

"Okay. Did you just want to talk?"

He grimaced. "Um, yeah, so, I have…I think…a rash?"

He said it as if it was a question.

"How long have you had it?"

"Just since last night. But"—he grimaced—"it really itches, and I think it's spreading!"

"Maybe I should take a look at it."

He flushed, and then said, "Yeah, okay, it's"—he gestured to his thigh—"down there."

"Right. Were you out in the woods, maybe wearing shorts?"

He nodded. "Yes, gym shorts. Some of us new guys, we went with Jeremy—he's been here before—on this shortcut to the lake. To, um, swim."

Translation—a bunch of boys found some spot to go skinny-dipping, and Manuel either sat in, on, or otherwise tangled with some allergenic plant resin. "Let's have a look."

He jumped down and pushed his sweatpants down to his knees. A string of angry-looking red bumps trailed over his thigh and disappeared under the edge of the navy underwear. Lily did a very deep dive into her long-ago derm rotation. One did not see much contact dermatitis from foliage in Manhattan. Fleas, lice, bedbugs—yes. Leaves and stems? Not so much.

"How high do they go?" she asked, googling derm images.

He winced and indicated his groin.

"Right," Lily said. "Looks like poison ivy. I bet it itches, doesn't it."

"All the time."

"We've got something you can put on there to stop the itching and quiet down the inflammation, but it's going to have to get better on its own. I think if you're going to be in the...woods like that again, shorts are not a good idea."

"I won't again," he said vigorously. "Thank you, thank you."

She smiled. "Once you get dressed, wait for me out front and I'll bring you the ointment with instructions. You can shower like normal. It's not contagious."

"What about swimming?"

"You can swim in the lake." She managed not to smile.

"Thank you, Dr. Davenport."

She smiled as he left. "That part went well."

❖

The rest of the morning was filled with the usual orientation-type discussions, with all the campers congregated in the great room while Sarah went over things like meal schedules, the daily roster of events and where to find them, quiet hours, and reminders that the counselors were available twenty-four seven, and if there was anything urgent, campers could always find her or Lily. Lily stood in the back, mostly watching the teens, who for the most part seemed to be paying attention, with a few notable exceptions. Ford Langford sat on one of the leather sofas with another girl, a redhead Lily remembered being named Shannon Kelly. The two of them spent the entire time heads close together, talking. Lily picked out Marty Riley sitting with several other campers on a bench off to one side of the room. She couldn't tell if Marty was actually with the others but didn't see them talking with anyone. Natalie came in toward the end of Sarah's presentation and made her way over to Lily.

"Good morning," Natalie said.

"Hi."

"Getting settled?"

Lily smiled. "Most of the shock has worn off."

Natalie chuckled. "That's right. Sarah said you came up from New York City."

"Yes."

"Quite a change?" Natalie asked.

Lily laughed softly. "A little bit. But I have to say, I'm kind of excited and looking forward to the summer. It's beautiful here."

"It is."

"Are you doing one of the sessions?" Lily asked as Sarah told the campers to take a break before meeting at the shore in swimsuits.

"And don't forget to stop at the facilities building and get a PFD," Sarah called as the campers crowded toward the door. "No vest—no kayaking."

Natalie said, "I'm going to talk to them about general water safety. We have an entire series of talks on how to get along in the wilderness that we work in with the skills they're learning. So it's a little bit of education and hopefully a little bit of fun."

"Yes," Lily said, "I saw that kayaking drills were scheduled for today."

"Ever do any kayaking?" Natalie said as they walked out onto the porch.

"No, I'm a sailor."

"You'll like it."

"*I* will?" Natalie smiled and Lily appreciated how attractive she was. "Why am I going to enjoy it?"

"It's probably a good idea that you're able to handle a kayak, just in case for some reason you need to go out on the water. And if you're going to be in one, you need to know what to do when you're not in one anymore."

"As in, being in the lake."

"Uh-huh."

Lily imagined the scenario and nodded. "Thanks for the heads-up, Natalie. That does sound like fun. I think I better go get into a suit."

"Don't forget your life vest. And it's Nat."

Natalie seemed to hold her gaze for just a second longer than ordinary, and Lily wondered... She mentally laughed. Obviously something in the mountain air stimulated more than an appetite for food. Not that she minded, entirely, but she wasn't prone to thinking every new woman she met was flirting with her, either. Which of course brought Chase instantly to mind. *That* had gone quite a lot farther than flirting, and all on her initiative too. Not that she really had to worry. She wouldn't be taking any moonlight walks with Chase or Natalie, so she could put the issue of flirting *or* kissing safely aside.

"I'll get the life jacket," Lily said. "See you soon."

"Good," Nat said.

Lily changed into a plain, two-piece black suit, grabbed a towel and a cover-up, thought about sandals, and opted for her running shoes. She'd be walking down that trail again. And...snakes. Which, of course, made her think of Chase all over again.

CHAPTER SEVEN

Lily rose at five for the second morning of walk-in clinic. This time she was alone downstairs in the lodge except for the kitchen staff and carried her coffee outside to the porch along with an apple muffin, still warm from the oven. A glance toward the parking lot showed no sign of Chase's Jeep. The emergency must be serious if Chase was still out on the call. The nagging worry blossomed again, and she pushed it aside. Chase was an expert and equipped to handle whatever she faced out there. She was the one out of her element, which no doubt brought on the anxiety over what Chase might be dealing with. Not every emergency led to a disaster like the first deluge of infections that caught her and every other doctor in the country unprepared. This wasn't the same. She needed to find her balance again, that was all.

But she'd feel better when she saw Chase again.

At six when she unlocked the clinic, she found another note on the floor and smiled. This was obviously Sarah's favorite mode of communication, which struck her as sweet and very Sarah. Her smile disappeared as she unfolded the note and scanned the unfamiliar tight, precise script.

They tell you to say something to someone if you see something wrong. I think there's something wrong in cabin 8. A couple of the girls are saying Marty doesn't belong with the rest of them, and trying to get some of the others to go along. This isn't fair and I thought someone should know. Thank you.

"Ah, hell," Lily muttered. She wasn't surprised cliques formed among the campers—they did in most social situations where some people needed to seek out the like-minded to feel safe. Often at the expense of others. Wasn't that the norm for high school and even college? Bullying, though, took that natural like-seeking-like behavior and injected a toxicity that was far more common now, or at least far more overt. Maybe this hadn't reached the point of outright bullying, but she certainly didn't want it to. She wondered who'd left the note.

Marty?

Someone else in cabin eight?

Lily pulled out the roster sheet again and opened her computer to match names with faces. She already knew Ford Langford was in eight—they'd met on the porch that first day. Marty Riley. She focused on each face, linking it to a name, and paused when she came to another familiar face—the redhead Ford had been with the day before. Shannon Kelly.

Lily closed the files. She'd learned as a med student not to jump to conclusions, even when the answer seemed obvious. She needed more information, and she needed an expert consultation. Or two.

She texted Sarah first, then Alisha, to ask to meet as soon as they could. Before she got a response from either of them, a knock sounded at the door and a pretty brunette came in.

"Hi," she said, "I'm Dee Murphy from cabin six. I think I did something to my arm yesterday because it hurts every time I lift it."

"Well, let's have a look. Come on in," Lily said.

While Lily counseled Dee to use OTC anti-inflammatories and a cryosleeve, which she provided—because Sarah had ordered everything with the state's generous health budget—for Dee's tennis elbow, Lily got a text from Sarah.

Meet us when you finish in my office

When Lily arrived, Sarah was behind a big cluttered oak desk, a cup of coffee in hand. Alisha sat in a navy camp chair in a damp T-shirt. Her hair, a mass of inky curls, looked wet too.

"Were you swimming?" Lily asked. "Sorry to call you away."

"Not a problem," Alisha said.

"What's up?" Sarah asked.

Lily showed them the note. "Marty Riley identifies as nonbinary. They also have a history of clinical depression."

Sarah winced. "That's a flaw in our system I'll have to address. We didn't get a flag there."

"Probably because Marty's parents didn't identify any outstanding heath issues on the intake form. I only saw it because I read through them yesterday."

Alisha said, "We have to assume there's something going on, even though it could be one of those transient power plays with some girls staking out their territory. Then once everyone sorts themselves out, it quiets down."

"It's also possible," Sarah said, "that Marty has been bullied before."

"We can't be sure unless we talk to Marty," Lily said. "I wanted to meet with them anyhow. I think a one-on-one is the best first step, and then I can refer them to you, Alisha, if they want to talk to someone in the future."

"That's fine," Alisha said. "Just keep me in the loop. Marty should be at breakfast about now."

Lily rose. "Thanks. I'll go find them."

❖

Lily had waited until Marty had finished breakfast to ask them to come by the clinic for a few intake questions.

"My office is this way," Lily said, leading Marty to the informal room adjoining the treatment area. When Marty settled on the chair that matched the worn leather sofa where Lily sat, she said, "I routinely review everyone's medical history to be sure I'm prepared if anyone needs me for any reason."

Marty nodded, their brown-eyed gaze direct and serious. Like all the other campers, they wore the casual uniform of T-shirt—this one with the logo of a band Lily didn't know, khaki cargo shorts that came down to their knees, and substantial-looking hiking boots with tall, heavy gray socks. Their sandy hair was cut in a floppy shag.

"Your form says you'll be bringing your own meds. Are you all set there?"

"I'm fine," Marty said, shifting subtly on the chair.

"Good. If you need refills, let me know. If you want to talk to anyone at any time, I'm available, as is Alisha."

"Okay."

Lily leaned forward. "I have to ask you something, and I'm sorry if it seems intrusive. Are any of the other campers in your cabin making you uncomfortable in any way?"

"Why?"

"Because someone suggested that might be happening."

"Who?"

"I don't know. Someone left a note."

"It wasn't me."

"Okay. A friend, I guess."

Marty's brows drew down. "That's weird. I don't really know anyone here. It's my first time at this camp."

"So no problems?" Lily asked again. "I don't really know what prompted the note. All I care about is that you're not being harassed or made to feel uncomfortable in any way."

"I'm fine."

Lily nodded. Not an answer, but that wasn't surprising. Kids often didn't want to bring authority figures into their interactions, fearing that would make them even more of a target.

"I want you to know that any kind of bullying, even verbal jabs, is not okay. We will address it and put a stop to it. No exceptions."

Marty regarded her a long moment. "That's not always so simple."

"I know in school there are lots of ways kids can gang up on other kids, especially with social media, but that's not the situation here. If there are campers causing problems for other campers, we'll send them home."

"You'd do that? Even if they're, like, important?"

"You're important, Marty."

"I'm okay," Marty repeated.

"All right, then. I'll be here, anytime, night or day," Lily said as she walked Marty out. Now all she could do was keep watch and hope she'd made a connection Marty would trust.

The rest of her day passed quickly as the morning schedule of activities kept everyone busy, and as the hours went by with no sign of Chase, she tried to ignore her disappointment. Even Natalie didn't show up for the afternoon introduction to wilderness campsite setup, with Alisha and Phillipe filling in for her. Lily had half decided to ask Nat about Chase's whereabouts and probably ought to be grateful she hadn't the chance. Everyone, including Chase, made it perfectly clear Chase would rather be anywhere else, doing anything else, than here at the lodge.

Lily's relationships, when she'd had time for them, were always mutually compatible arrangements that worked for both parties—low-key, nondemanding, convenient. She did not spend time wondering or worrying about when she might see someone next.

Now was definitely not the time to start. As evening came and went, she kept busy until she could slip away to bed. Where she absolutely did not think about Chase much at all.

❖

Just shy of dawn, Chase slowed at the turnoff for the lodge, hesitating. If she traveled another ten miles up the road, she'd reach the off-road trail up to her cabin, and she could sleep in her own bed for the first time in three nights. Any bed, for that matter. But she'd already missed the first two days of camp, and Sarah wouldn't let her forget about it for a month if she missed much more. And then, there was Lily. She'd broken their date. Maybe not a date, exactly, but she'd been looking forward to taking Lily into town. Lily'd interested her from the first time they'd met, with her slightly prickly facade, quick wit, and drop-dead sexy...brain. Chase chuckled. Yeah, and the great body, the amazing kisses, and the sadness that crept into her eyes all too often. The sadness more than almost anything else got to her, made her want to know why, made her want to wipe it away.

When the callout came, she hadn't had any way to tell Lily she was leaving or how long she'd be gone, because she hadn't known, and once she was out in the mountains, there was no way to communicate with anyone except the base station, and she wasn't about to ask one of the other rangers to give her friend an update on her schedule. Couldn't even call her *girl*friend, and even if she could, that's the last thing she would've done. She wouldn't hear the end of it for a year. Probably more. Long after Lily had disappeared.

So now she wanted to see her. And if she wanted to see her, she'd have to go back up to the lodge. Grab an hour or so of sleep. Maybe see if Lily could work in that trip to town. But she was damned if she was gonna crawl into bed in the clothes she'd been wearing for two and a half days, and feeling like she'd been beaten all over for most of that time. A shower wasn't gonna be enough. She eased the Jeep as quietly as she could into the parking lot as the sky lightened, dug around in the back until she found a clean set of clothes and a fairly clean towel, and headed down to the lake. Like most nights this time of year, the air was a little crisp, but she needed the refreshing.

She was tired, bone-deep physically, weary from climbing up rocky escarpments and rappelling down sheer rock faces, worn down by the strain of searching for almost forty-eight hours over rugged terrain still muddy from snow runoff, into areas that would be off-limits for hikers even at the height of the season. The dogs had led them through it, and the rest of the team'd followed as quickly as they could without risking someone breaking a leg or worse. Her stomach tightened. She knew what worse could mean. The weeks of pain, wondering if you'd ever be able to move the way you had before, the rehab where the progress was so slow it was hard to believe there'd ever be an end to it. And then when you finally reached the end, discovering you'd never be who you were before. What you were before.

Exasperated, she threw off the melancholy that came with exhaustion. She knew what it was about. Lack of sleep, not enough food, and an outcome that she'd never get used to. She reached the dock and stripped off, leaving her dirty clothes next to her boots in a pile, and set her clean clothes and towel within reach at the end of the dock. She dove in and let the water, warmer than the air around her, start to loosen some of the tension in her muscles and the aches that were deeper than that. She swam out a distance and then flipped onto her back, eyes closed, shadows dancing across her eyelids as the first whisper of dawn crept over the mountaintops. In another half an hour, the lodge would come to life. She ought to sleep, but her stomach rumbled. Coffee, some kind of sandwich, and she'd have enough energy to get through whatever headache of a schedule Sarah had waiting for her. She stroked leisurely back to the dock, reached up with both hands on the edge, and pulled herself up and out of the water.

"Oh!" Lily said. "Oh. Sorry."

Chase flipped the wet hair from her face with one hand and blinked away the water from her eyes. Nope, not a mirage. Lily in a loose white shirt and shorts that stopped just above her knees, spinning around at the foot of the dock, putting her back to Chase. From where Chase was standing, she could tell Lily had folded her arms across her chest as if warding off a chill. The air was a little cool, but she didn't think that was the problem.

Grinning to herself, she reached for the towel. "Morning."

"I didn't think you'd be here. I'm very sorry to disturb you."

"I'm not disturbed. Are you disturbed?"

"I'm…" Lily still hadn't turned around. "Are you decent?"

"Haven't been accused of that recently."

Lily's hands came to her hips. Back stiff. "You know what I mean."

"It's just a body, Lily," Chase said quietly as she finished drying off.

"Well, is the just a body covered up yet?"

"Working on it." She pulled on jeans and reached for her T-shirt. "All good."

Lily turned and Chase grinned, pulling the T-shirt over her head a second later.

"That was juvenile," Lily said.

"Are you mad?"

"No. That would be juvenile too." Lily came down the dock toward her, and Chase's stomach tightened. She'd been playing with her a little bit, but she liked Lily looking at her. She'd like it a lot more if Lily touched her. She stuffed the tail of her T-shirt into her jeans as if that would somehow erase her desire for more. It wasn't working.

"Did you just get back?" Lily asked.

"Yeah," Chase said with a sigh. "How's things been around here?"

Lily lifted a shoulder. "I don't know if I could say routine or not. I don't think there's any particular problem."

"Is Ford Langford causing any trouble?" At Lily's questioning look, she added, "Her parents obviously thought she needed watching— since they angled for more on-site security."

"Not that I've seen." Lily sighed. "She happens to be in the cabin where there might be some trouble brewing, but it could just be teenage drama. I don't know why I didn't expect that."

Chase shook her head. "See, that's why the camp makes me crazy. Too many hormones, too much drama. Who needs it?"

Lily laughed. "How old are you?"

Chase smirked. "Why?"

"Because you sound like you're ninety."

"I'm twenty-five."

"You can't have forgotten what it was like to be a teenager, then."

"I wasn't like that," she said quietly.

Lily cocked her head, the dawn light bright enough now for Chase to see her clearly. She'd pulled her hair back with some kind of hair tie, and her eyes were clear and bright. She looked great in that loose shirt that still managed to cling in all the right places, and the shorts left a lot of leg to admire. Still those damn running shoes.

"What were you like?" Lily murmured.

Chase ran a hand through her hair. She was too tired for this conversation. "I didn't have any questions about who I was. I knew exactly what I was gonna do." She laughed shortly. "I just needed to grow up fast enough to do it."

"Be a ranger, you mean."

"No," Chase said, "that was not my plan." She leaned down and bundled up her dirty clothes.

"What was your plan, then?" Lily asked.

"Some other time, Lily." Chase sighed. "Sorry, just…long story."

"You're tired, aren't you," Lily said.

"No, I'm fine," Chase said quickly.

"Have you had any sleep since you left here the other night?"

"Did I wake you up?"

"I didn't realize it was you," Lily said. "I heard a vehicle leave. I guess I should've known it was you, but I wasn't used to things around here. No one else seems to stir between sundown and dawn, except Sarah. I think she's always up late."

"I end up going out most nights," Chase said. "We get a lot of calls, and in the summer, it's pretty much all the time. Sometimes I don't even get to the messages until midnight."

"Not a job for the fainthearted." Lily walked beside Chase back to shore. "What was it?"

"Missing hiker," Chase said. "She was twenty-four hours late for check-in, but her friends kept expecting her to show up at any time, because she always did, and then they finally let us know."

"Solo hiker?" Lily asked.

"Yeah." Chase let out a long breath. "Not unusual up here at all. I always used to go out alone."

"Yes, but you were born climbing, I'll bet."

Chase gave her a quick look. "Why do you say that?"

Lily looked surprised. "I know that you grew up in the mountains, and I've seen you look at them. They call you, don't they?"

"They do," Chase said flatly. "They won't be calling this girl anymore. We needed the dogs to pick up her trail. She'd been making a serious climb, probably got onto a muddy patch that looked solid and wasn't. She went into a ravine."

"She was gone?" Lily asked.

"Yeah. We couldn't get the chopper in when we found her, and we needed to rappel down. Carry her out. It just took us a while."

"I'm sorry. That's horrible."

"It happens more times than you think every year."

"That doesn't make it any easier, I know." Lily slipped her hand around Chase's forearm. Her grip was warm and comforting, and Chase's body hummed as if Lily was infusing her with strength.

"It helps that you understand without me explaining," Chase said.

"What you need is something to eat and a few hours' sleep."

"I definitely need the food. I'll have to look at today's schedule, but I don't think there's gonna be any sleep in my future."

"I imagine we can figure out how to fill the campers' time without you. The last two days have been nonstop orientation, boating- and water-safety instruction, and I believe today has something to do with survivalist camping—knowledge I sincerely hope I never need to utilize."

Chase groaned. "That's definitely going to be me, then."

"Maybe Natalie can fill in again."

Chase shot her a look and quickly covered the totally out-of-nowhere spurt of jealousy. Totally not her thing. "Has Nat been here?"

"She came by the first morning for the orientation because you were't here. Since then, she hasn't been around. She wasn't out with you?"

"No, there was an unscheduled burn in another part of the district, and she was on that. She doesn't usually go out on search-and-rescue unless we need multiple teams to cover the search area. We've got the dogs, and we're all SAR rated."

"It's an amazing job that you all have."

"No more amazing than what you do." Chase laughed a little. "We just have a better place to do it."

Lily laughed with her, a lightness to her tone that Chase hadn't heard before and that struck her with another surge of energy. Lily brought a light into the dark places.

"How would you like to have breakfast with me?" Chase asked.

Lily stopped and searched Chase's face. When their eyes met, she smiled, and Chase felt the punch all the way to the pit of her stomach. Oh yeah, the heat was still there.

"I would like that very much."

"Good," Chase said around a knot of desire in her throat. She wanted her, more than she'd realized.

❖

Lily thought about the way Chase had looked climbing out of the water, the way the droplets had gleamed on her skin as the first rays of sunlight banished the night. When Chase had bent down for the towel, Lily had caught a glimpse of her back, right before she'd turned her own. The scar down the center of her spine was impossible to miss, and she knew what it meant. A major trauma of some kind, and she could only think of a few ways it might've happened. But she couldn't think of a way to ask.

And then she'd been too busy trying not to keep seeing the muscles in Chase's shoulders, the curve of her breast as she leaned over, the sweep of her flank, and the power in her backside and thighs. She'd felt some of that body against hers when she had her arms around Chase, when they'd been kissing. She'd imagined it in her mind more than once since, but she'd been far from the mark. Chase was young and strong and beautiful. Looking at her made Lily ache to run her hands down the smooth length of her arms, over the muscles in her chest, and over the fullness of her breasts. Okay—deflection was clearly off the table now—Chase was too hard to ignore and just as impossible to deflect. Especially, Lily admitted ruefully, when *she* wasn't working very hard to ignore or deflect her. But engage? That way lay danger— and she'd have to be very careful not to be pulled in by the charm and the grin and the outrageously sexy that streamed off Chase like the clear, cool lake water on a sweltering day.

She had to stop thinking about that right now, or anything else that had to do with Chase Fielder, because she was about to walk into the kitchen, and undoubtedly Sarah would be somewhere nearby.

Sarah had always been good at reading her mind, and today everything about her was probably an open book. She'd rather not start the day having Sarah know she was lusting after her sister.

CHAPTER EIGHT

Chase noticed she and Lily earned a hard stare from Sarah when they walked into the dining room together, and she pretended to ignore her sister's scrutiny on her way through the breakfast line. Usually she laughed off Sarah's not-too-subtle commentary about her less-than-serious approach to relationships, but this time a surge of protectiveness mixed with annoyance had her directing Lily to a table by the windows out of Sarah's sight line.

"Okay over here?" Chase asked.

"It's great." Lily off-loaded her plate of eggs and waffles and cup of coffee onto the table and sank down with a sigh. "Every time I look out the window, I'm a little astonished to realize I'm here."

"Miss the city?"

"Not yet." Lily smiled. "Other than the shopping, of course."

Chase winced. "Sorry about the change of plans—I promise we'll get into town as soon as there's a free couple of hours."

"Oh, don't be silly. I know—at least I'm coming to understand—what a demanding job you have. Trust me, I get not being able to make plans with any certainty."

"Thanks," Chase said as she took her first blessed sip of decent coffee in two days. "But I really do want to make it into town with you. And I don't make a habit of standing women up."

Lily regarded her over the top of the coffee cup she held in both hands as if it was a precious object. "I wasn't thinking of a trip to buy boots as a date."

Chase laughed. "How about if I add lunch—or dinner. Or, hell, breakfast?"

"How about we decide what to call it if we actually ever manage to get out of here."

"I plan to make that a priority," Chase said steadily. "I've been looking forward to it."

Lily blushed. "So have I, but we both have work first."

"So, how are you liking things so far?"

"The medical work is pretty straightforward," Lily said pensively. "It's a lot like family practice. Nothing urgent most of the time, just the usual common problems in a place like this. Rashes and bug bites and sprains, the things active kids always run into. Not that I'm complaining—I'm perfectly happy not dealing with much in the way of serious problems."

"Big change from what you're used to," Chase said.

Lily nodded. "Even before the last couple of years, big-city ERs were pretty much trauma units twenty-four seven, even when the cases weren't actually traumas. Patients presented with more and more serious problems, mostly because there were fewer and fewer primary care physicians to see them, and the health care system forced them to do less and less. The ER has become the only source of care for many people, so it was pretty much nonstop." She shook her head. "And then the pandemic hit and everything came to a screeching halt. The work turned into something…unrecognizable."

"And all of you in the city were really the first in the US to get hit in a big way."

"Yes. We had no idea what was happening at first—a trickle of cases turned into an avalanche practically overnight."

That haunted look appeared in Lily's eyes, and Chase reached for her hand. "I'm sorry I brought it up."

Looking surprised at the contact, Lily nevertheless turned her hand over until her fingers brushed Chase's palm. The sensation shot through Chase like lightning, leaving her just a little breathless. She sat very still to avoid breaking the tenuous connection.

"No, you shouldn't be. It's just there isn't very much to say. None of us had ever experienced anything like it before, had no idea from one day to the next how bad it would get or when it would stop, and there was just this constant…lack. Lack of everything. Knowledge of what to do, understanding of the disease…" She gave a bitter laugh. "Believe me, there's nothing much worse for a physician than not understanding what they're up against. Except failure." She looked away. "And there was a lot of that."

"I'm sorry," Chase said, "that you went through it, and that I brought it up today."

"It's part of us all, now, isn't it?" Lily said. "But we're here, and we're moving on. Even if it takes longer for some of us." She moved her hand from Chase's, but her smile was bright and her eyes clear again. "Besides, I'd rather hear about what you'll be doing in the next few days."

"I've got a list of messages that will take me an hour to get through, the session with the campers to go over what they'll need for their first wilderness outing tomorrow, and then seeing to any callouts along with my routine patrol."

Lily sat back with a head shake. "I'm not hearing the part where you get some sleep."

Chase grinned. "I'm an expert napper."

"In your Jeep?"

"Sometimes. Mostly, though—"

"A blanket on the ground," Lily finished.

"You remembered." Chase registered the odd pleasure over such a small thing that somehow didn't feel so small.

"I won't criticize, as I've been there myself plenty," Lily said. "Tell me what's in store for the kids on this wilderness thing."

"You mean when I take them out into the woods and plop them down somewhere and tell them I'll be back for them tomorrow?"

"You're kidding about that, right?"

"I'm actually kidding about it *today*, but we are going to do that at some point. It's called wilderness survival training for a reason, and this camp is designed to impart serious outdoor skills. That's really clear in all the info provided before campers apply. So it's part of the experience. It's why they come here and not somewhere else. We actually teach advanced wilderness skills."

"You're really going to leave them out there somewhere?"

"Eventually. Of course, we're not gonna go very far away. The only real danger is if someone decides to cut out and head back on their own or the occasional predator wanders too close to camp."

"*Occasional* and *predator* do not seem compatible."

Chase laughed.

Lily shook her head. "I have to say that some of these kids do not look to me like they want to be left out in the woods overnight."

"True," Chase said. "There are always a couple who never really absorb the message or who end up here for the summer because their parents think it will be good for them or they just wanted a supervised environment for them for the summer. Those kids tend to resent any part of what we do here."

"Recipe for revolt," Lily observed.

"Totally agree. Those are the kids who are probably here under moderate duress."

Lily quirked a brow. "Are you talking about anyone in particular?"

Chase glanced around to be sure no one was close enough to overhear. "Julia Latoya pretty much confirmed that Giovanna Langford is here because her parents didn't like her choice of friends and wanted to make sure she was tucked away somewhere remote *and* secure until they could ship her off to college."

"I know her father's a state senator," Lily said, "and I gather he's a pretty extreme conservative."

Chase smiled. "That's summing it up a little too nicely. He's anti just about everything that isn't white, Christian, heterosexual. I suppose if he didn't have a wife and a daughter, he'd be more vocally anti-woman too."

"Can't be fun growing up in that household, especially if there's security around all the time."

"No, I'm sure it isn't." Chase finished off the last of her food and slid the plate away. "And I feel sorry for the kid that she's here when she doesn't want to be, but there are worse places she could be. Worse things that she could be experiencing."

"Do you know anything about the nature of her parents' concerns?" Lily paused. "It's not just idle curiosity. If she's into drugs or something potentially self-destructive, I ought to know, so I can keep an eye out. We might have a zero-tolerance policy for drugs and alcohol here, but that doesn't mean it's impossible for the campers to have access. They're not prisoners, and I suppose they're going to have a chance to go into town."

"Oh yeah," Chase said. "There's an outing planned every week for shopping, sightseeing, that kind of thing. And there's the big Fourth of July celebration with a night tour of the lake on one of the historic paddleboats. We have the whole thing to ourselves."

"That sounds like fun."

"It is, actually. It's beautiful, and you can see the fireworks really well from the lake."

Lily said, "I haven't seen fireworks in years."

"It is one of those things that never gets old." Chase smiled.

"Simple pleasures?" Lily said.

"Sometimes they're the best." Chase paused. "Like stargazing." She couldn't quite keep the desire that surged with the memory from showing in her voice.

"I haven't forgotten," Lily murmured.

"Neither have I." Chase almost confessed she'd spent a lot of time reliving various moments of that moonlight walk—especially the kiss—and wondering when and how she'd manage another, but she didn't want it to come off as a line. Lily deserved more than that.

"So," Lily said in a tone that signaled she was intentionally changing the subject, "what do you do when you're not patrolling, out there in the wilderness by yourself?"

"Work out, read, do a little gardening during the summer."

Lily laughed, her eyes sparkling. "You garden?"

Chase drew herself up and feigned affront. "I'll have you know I not only garden, I cook."

Lily stared. "You cook."

"I do," Chase said just a tad smugly. "I grow lots of vegetables, obviously, because they're great fresh and a lot of them keep well in a root cellar. I've got some raspberry bushes, and blueberries grow wild everywhere up here. Stock up on dry goods—beans and pasta—and you've got a good assortment for most meals."

"Pleasure or necessity?"

"Both. I live where I work, we all do—it's a job requirement. So a forty-minute drive from anywhere that offers takeout, and I can't really afford to be in the middle of dinner in Lake George when I need to be fifty miles in the other direction, chasing a bear away from somebody's campsite."

"Is it where you grew up—where you live now?" Lily asked.

"My parents' land, yes. The homestead is Sarah's—she gets up there a few times a year. I built a cabin not far from there a few years back."

"You built…as in had it built, or…"

"I built it. Log and stone."

"I'm impressed."

Chase shrugged. "I had some time on my hands, and I needed something to keep me in shape. Sarah helped."

"So you built your own home, grow your own food, and what else? Do you hunt?"

"No. My parents were naturalists, and every form of life, animal or plant, was a miracle to them. I don't kill animals for food, but I also understand that the world is populated by people who eat animals, and others raise animals for food, and their livelihoods depend on it. So if I want to eat meat, I buy it. I do like to fish, and I catch and release almost everything. But during the season when the lakes and streams are stocked, if we don't fish them down a little bit, they'll be overpopulated. So now and then, I'll take a bass or trout if I get one and cook it up."

"That's fascinating."

"You don't cook?"

Lily smiled. "Does heating up leftover pizza count?"

"Not even close. But I do *make* a mean pizza."

"When do you have time?"

Chase lifted a shoulder. "This time of year I don't have much, but I don't have a wide variety of interests. What interests me"—she glanced toward the windows and, beyond that, the mountains—"is out there. There's always something to see, something to discover."

"I can imagine. Do you get much chance to climb?"

Chase jerked back. "No."

"Oh," Lily said, reaching for the dish of raspberry jam for her last piece of toast. "I'm surprised, it seems like a natural—"

"I don't climb anymore," Chase said flatly.

Lily looked up. "I'm sorry. Not my business."

Chase let out a breath. Not the direction she expected the conversation to go. From easy and casual to raw and too damn close. Not Lily's fault. "I used to. Then I fell."

Lily had heard every tragic story of loss imaginable, but she never grew immune to it, and this time the barely concealed pain in Chase's eyes struck her hard. "Then I'm sorry for mentioning it."

Chase grimaced. "It's the morning for treading on tender spots, isn't it."

"It doesn't have to be." Lily put down her knife and took Chase's hand the way Chase had taken hers. "I want to get to know you, the parts you want to show me, but we all have our secrets and places we'd rather not go. The last thing I would want is to bring up past pain."

"It was seven years ago—I'm...I *was* a free-climber. That's—"

"I know what it is—no ropes or safety lines, right?"

"Yes. I started when I was a kid, and by the time I was eighteen I was a ranked competitive climber. I planned to climb a few more years and then open a climbing school." Chase's voice turned to gravel and misery darkened her eyes. "I missed a handhold—a simple thing I'd done ten thousand times. I fell, broke my back, and my climbing days were done. I ought to be over it by now."

"Why?"

"I'm lucky," Chase said, her grip on Lily's hand tightening. "I healed, I can do what I need to do for my job—I just can't climb anymore. Not the way that counts for me."

"I don't know if there's any time limit on grief. Or anger."

Chase stared. "It's the anger I mostly feel now. How did you know?"

"You lost something important to you—I don't need to hear the story to know that. I can hear the mountains in you when you talk. I sensed them in you when..."

"When, Lily?" Chase murmured, her fingers closing around Lily's. "When?"

"When we walked by the lake," Lily whispered, her gaze searching the depths of Chase's eyes, the deep blue of the sky. The dark clouds of old pain had passed, for now, and a weight lifted from Lily's heart. "When I watched you swimming at dawn." She took a deep breath. Too much had been said already to pretend nothing had passed between them. "When we kissed."

"See?" Chase rubbed her thumb over Lily's palm. "Told you I was lucky."

Lily smiled around the sadness for Chase's loss. "I—"

"Sorry to interrupt," Sarah stated in a tone that suggested she wasn't sorry at all, "but Nat's on the radio looking for you. Says they need you up at Crandall's trailhead—some dogs have treed a bear, and Fish and Wildlife are requesting an assist."

Chase frowned and pulled her phone from her pants pocket. "Hell, it's dead. Never got a chance to charge it." She rose and glanced at Lily. "Sorry."

"Of course, go," Lily said.

Chase hurried away, and Sarah said, "When did you run into her? I didn't know she was back."

Lily reached for her coffee. "She was coming back from a swim." Technically true. "I was up early—it's so quiet here at night, I can't sleep."

Sarah frowned. "I told Nat she'd just gotten back, but that's what it's like this time of year."

Lily had an anxious moment, thinking about the physical toll of Chase's job after what Chase had told her about her injury, and then just as quickly reminded herself that Chase was fit and healthy or she wouldn't have gotten the job in the first place.

"She loves it," she said quietly.

"She tell you that?" Sarah asked, an odd curious note in her voice.

Lily rose and smiled, thinking about moonlight walks and kisses. "She didn't have to."

CHAPTER NINE

Lily glanced up from the computer where she was finishing a notation on the last of four teens who'd presented to the walk-in clinic that morning with complaints of intestinal distress. Apparently they'd decided to pick their own blueberries the afternoon before. After she'd determined what they'd eaten was a close relative of a blueberry, not quite as well-tolerated by the human intestinal tract, but fortunately, not poisonous, she'd prescribed some symptomatic relief and given them all a pass on the day's activities.

Expecting to see another of the group, she half rose behind the counter in surprise. "Chase!"

"Morning, Lily."

"Did you just get back?" She'd looked for the Jeep out her bedroom window as soon as she'd risen and hadn't seen it. Chase looked surprisingly awake after what Lily presumed was a night of work. And Lily's morning took on a new dimension of expectation. Chase.

"Got in a few minutes ago," Chase said. "Sorry, I thought you'd be done by now. I just need to grab some antibiotic ointment and a couple of four-by-fours. My med kit needs restocking."

Lily tilted her head, feeling as if she'd missed a step. Her first thought had been that Chase had come to see her. Apparently not the case, which was embarrassingly disappointing. "Sure, but do you usually restock from here? Because I'll have to adjust my threshold for reordering inventory if that's the case."

"Not usually, but Sarah doesn't mind if I top off in an emergency."

Chase shrugged and then winced. "I've got a full day here and don't have time to get down to the station to resupply."

"I thought you were out on a call about a bear," Lily said, coming around the front of the desk. "Did someone get injured? Is that why you were out all night?"

"No, just took us all night to track the bear, get her back to her home territory, and track down the asshat owners who were running hunting dogs on restricted public land."

"Long night. So, the bandages?"

"Big bear, restless sleeper. While we were getting her strapped in, she rolled over and took a swipe. No malice intended." Chase grinned, a crooked grin that would've been charming if Lily's antennae hadn't already been reading high on the BS meter.

"Who got injured, Chase?" Lily repeated slowly.

Chase averted her gaze for a second and then sighed. "I might have a scratch on my shoulder. It's damn hard for me to reach back there by myself."

"A scratch," Lily said coolly. "I see. Let's go on back to the treatment room, and I'll take a look at it."

Chase glanced at her watch. "I don't really have time, and it's just—"

"I haven't tested the extent of my authority here, but I suspect if I called Nat and told her you aren't fit for duty, she'd have to find someone else to take your calls."

Chase narrowed her eyes. "You wouldn't."

"Try me."

"Come on, Lily," Chase muttered, but dutifully trudged toward the hall and the treatment rooms.

Lily got a good look at her back as Chase walked in front of her. "Chase, your shirt's shredded, and there's blood on it."

"The shirt looks worse than me. My turnout vest got the worst of it."

Lily was still processing. She'd handled rat bites, dog and cat bites, even horse bites. This, as with so much with Chase, was new territory. "You were mauled by a bear, and you didn't go to the emergency room?"

"Lil," Chase said, glancing over her shoulder, "we field-dressed it. It's fine. Like I told you, we had to track down and deal with the dog runners. We've been trying to catch this particular crew for the last six weeks." She grinned, something of a feral grin that struck Lily as extremely sexy, which seemed totally inappropriate in the moment. *Was* totally inappropriate.

"You went off to arrest…miscreants…while you were injured."

Chase stopped walking so abruptly, Lily nearly bumped into her. Chase slid both hands to Lily's hips and cantered her head as she whispered, "It's a scratch."

Lily's heart thundered beneath her ribs. A familiar scent clung to Chase's skin, something sweet and tangy that she finally recognized as the way that the air smelled first thing in the morning. Mountain air, clean and pure, dense with life. Chase teemed with the energy of life. Just being near her stirred Lily's blood the way nothing ever had, even before the soul-numbing last few years. She swallowed, aware that Chase's mouth was a fraction of a breath away from hers.

"I'll be the judge of whether it's a scratch or not," she murmured.

Chase eased back a little, and that mouth, so sensuous and so tantalizing, slid into the smile that told Lily Chase knew exactly what she was feeling.

"You're the doctor."

Lily pressed both palms to Chase's chest and gently gave her a little push. "So nice of you to notice. Treatment room. First door on your left. Go."

"I know where it is." With a chuckle, Chase turned, walked in, and, even though Lily was only a few steps behind her, somehow had her shirt unbuttoned and was shrugging it off.

By the time Lily closed the door, Chase's back was to her. A white bandage covered a quarter of her back beneath a black tank top, extending from her trapezius to below her shoulder blade and almost to the edge of her latissimus beneath her arm. Four parallel streaks of blood showed through the white dressing.

"You'll need to take off your tank."

"I could use a little help with that," Chase said. "It's a little hard raising my arm."

"How fond are you of this tank? Because cutting it off is going to be a lot simpler."

"Good thought. I've got others."

Lily pulled the bandage scissors from the top drawer of the

equipment cart that stood next to the treatment table, walked around behind Chase, and cut the tight support tank up the back, well away from the lacerations. "Are you allergic to any drugs?"

"Nope."

"Did you have any antibiotics administered in the field?"

"I took two 500 mg capsules of cephalexin."

"I'm going to take off the dressing," she said, pulling on gloves. "I'm sorry, it's probably going to hurt."

"Go for it."

With the dressing removed, Lily got a good look at the four surprisingly neat gouges in Chase's back. She bit back an oath. "Whoever saw this and didn't send you to the emergency room needs to be written up for—"

Chase turned and rested her hips against the edge of the stainless steel table. "It's okay, Lily. It's been treated. We do things differently out in the field."

"Oh, don't give me that. You weren't in a war zone. You could've left."

With exaggerated patience, Chase said, "No, I couldn't. We had a three-hundred-pound mother black bear, with two cubs out there somewhere alone, who'd been chased out of her territory by three dogs. She somehow decided to lure them away rather than kill them, and we needed to get her tranqued, on a sled, into the back of the transport, and home where she belonged. And then, like I said, I had to deal with the guys who set those dogs loose on her."

Chase was angry and Lily could hear it. Furious, in fact. She gave up arguing in favor of treating her. She laid out gloves, a bag of sterile saline and a sterile basin, Betadine, and the dressing she'd need to rebandage it. "How did you know who they were?"

"Their dogs were wearing GPS collars—that's how the guys follow them through the forest. The bear was tagged too. So we knew her home range and that she had cubs."

Lily sighed, defeated. Of course Chase would have stayed until the call was finished. "Up on the table so I can get this cleaned up. These are deep—at least one is down to fascia. God, Chase, how did you function after this?"

"I've got some numbness in that area. That probably took the edge off."

"I see," Lily said, and she did, as the surgical scar that ran from the base of Chase's neck down the middle of her back, and likely the injury beneath, would have damaged some of the sensory nerves. Her stomach churned as she assessed in her mind's eye what the damage must've been, and the level of pain and fear, and a recovery as painful as the injury. "What level was your break?"

"T-four five," Chase said.

"God, you were lucky," Lily murmured.

"Yeah," Chase said in a flat tone. "They kept telling me that. Took me a long time to accept it."

Lily laid a hand gently on Chase's uninjured shoulder. "I'm sorry. I know what you lost, and you must've worked mercilessly in PT to recover the way you have. But you're here, moving, doing what it seems to me you love to do."

The rigid tension in the muscles beneath her fingers drained away. "You read that right, Lily. I was lucky. I know it."

Lily removed her hand and straightened. "Well, you were lucky again last night. If I'd seen you right away, which I should have," she said, her voice hardening with exasperation, "I could've cleaned this out and possibly sutured it. Now, this long after the injury, that's not a good idea. The risk of infection is much higher with delayed closure of contaminated wounds like this."

"I hear you. Got a look at it with a mirror last night. Ought to close all right."

"Yes, it should." Lily worked as they talked, irrigating away the few clots with a dilute Betadine solution before irrigating with saline again. "And if you're careful, you don't have to go on the injured list."

Chase swiveled on the table to face her head-on. "You weren't even thinking of that, were you?"

"Yes," Lily said with asperity, "given that you've been mauled by a bear, that had crossed my mind."

"*This* was not a mauling. You have to trust me to be the judge on this."

"Really? Because you are not prone to take chances, or consider yourself superhuman?" She was angry too, and not doing a very good job of hiding it. The injury could have been so much worse. What if the damn bear had swiped six inches higher and a little more forward? It would have severed Chase's carotid. She could have—probably *would* have—bled out right there. And Lily would not have known. Could not have helped. Would have lost someone else—someone whose face, whose laugh, whose stubborn strength and gentle touch had emerged from the mass of faceless hundreds she'd tried to save and couldn't to awaken her soul. Lily's stomach churned.

To her surprise, Chase grinned. "My sister has been talking to you again, hasn't she? She's always accused me of being an adrenaline junkie. Undeserved, I have to say."

"As a matter of fact, no, Sarah is innocent. That conclusion was relatively easy for me to come to on my own."

"I know my limitations, Lily, and this is not a problem. I'll take my antibiotics, I'll keep it clean, I'll be careful to avoid any undue physical strain, and it'll heal up in a week. It's no more of a problem than a bad sunburn."

Lily laughed, she couldn't help it. "I don't think we can equate a second-degree burn with a little blistering to being clawed by a bear!"

"Just as annoying."

Lily shook her head. "I'm starting an IV and giving you an intravenous dose of cephalosporin. Then you report here every twelve hours for the next two days for a wound check. If you're not willing to do that, then I'm getting on the phone to Natalie right now."

Chase gave her a long stare, and Lily's chin came up. She'd had a lot of practice dealing with difficult patients, and even though this one annoyed her more than most, she was willing to go to the mat to see that her orders were carried out. Chase was a classic risk-taker. From everything Sarah'd said, and the things Chase had revealed about her childhood and her free-climbing, Chase was into extreme physical challenges. Now, deprived of her natural outlet of climbing, she answered any emergency call, even when it wasn't her primary responsibility. She either lived on the adrenaline rush, which was pretty typical of extreme sports or risk enthusiasts, or she had something to prove.

Right now, Lily didn't care which. Her only concern was to see to Chase's safety and health.

"Well?" she asked when Chase only smirked. Definitely a smirk, not a smile.

"I have to check in with you every twelve hours. Take my shirt off, alone with you somewhere?" Chase's eyes glinted. "Not a hardship, Lily."

"Not personal, Chase."

"Whatever you say."

"God, you are so annoying."

Chase laughed. "You say that to all the patients who irritate you?"

"As a matter of fact, no, I do not. You are an exception." Lily waved a hand. "Now turn back around so I can get this dressed."

"Go ahead, get this done. I want to get the day started."

"I'm serious—you need to take it easy."

"All I'm going to be doing is walking. I won't even carry anything heavy, I promise."

"I'm going to keep an eye on you today to make sure you follow through on that."

Chase laughed softly again, and the sound brought heat to Lily's midsection. "That's not going to be a problem either, Lily."

❖

After all the other campers in the cabin left for breakfast, Marty sat on their bunk, opened their backpack, and took out all the items one at a time to double-check they had all the required gear for the day's hike and would be able to find it when needed. Mentally reviewing the list they'd gotten the day before, Marty put their water bottle in the side pocket, already filled with fresh cold water, their field first-aid kit, snakebite kit, compass, waterproof box with matches, flashlight, and MREs inside, and strapped their heat resistant thermal blanket and individual pup tent—compressed into its own go-bag—onto the back of their twenty-five-liter backpack. The tent wasn't strictly required, but they'd never set out on a hike without it, so it seemed they should take it along even if this was just an exercise. Since Marty hadn't backcountry camped since the fall before with their dad, this was a good refresher. They slipped on the pack, adjusted the straps, checked that the load was evenly distributed, and had just swung it off again when the cabin door opened.

Ford and Shannon bounded in on a storm of laughter, accompanied by a strong waft of weed. Marty hadn't seen either of them earlier and had just assumed they'd gone to breakfast. Maybe not.

Shannon halted abruptly and cocked her head as if discovering something strange in her path. Weirdly, Ford looked chagrined.

"Oh, look who it is," Shannon said in that tone of voice that could be construed in any number of ways, from mocking to just trying to be friendly, "it's…oh, who is it today? Would it be Martha? Or Martin?"

"Come on, Shannon," Ford muttered.

Shannon shot her a look, her red eyebrow perfectly arched as if to say *What? Did I say something wrong?* She smiled, and it wasn't a smile Marty could possibly misinterpret. They'd never really known before what the phrase *cruel smile* referred to, but they recognized it now. Disdainful and angry, for some reason. Which was weird too, because they didn't even know these girls.

"So?" Shannon said, her gaze swinging hard to Marty. "What are you feeling today? A little bit boy or a bit more girl? Because, you know, I don't want to misname you, or *whatever*."

"Marty's fine anytime." Marty headed toward the door, swinging wide of the pair who stood just inside. For just an instant, they thought Shannon might sidestep and block their way. That was new—until now, name-calling and snide remarks were the worst Marty'd had to deal with. But they knew enough to be wary of possible physical encounters. They slowed, their heart racing. Everyone else was probably already down at the lodge, a good quarter of a mile away.

"I have to get my things," Ford said, crossing between Shannon and Marty, as if interrupting the line of fire. "Come on, Shannon. You haven't even started to pack."

"Like I care about some stupid hike," Shannon snapped, but she stomped over to her own bunk and out of Marty's way.

Marty hesitated, watching as Ford swept a number of loose items lying on her bed into a backpack. Ford didn't take the EpiPen but seemed to intentionally push it aside.

"I'm good," Ford said, straightening. "You ready, Shann?"

"I suppose," Shannon said scornfully. "Like, there's no way out of it, is there?"

The two of them turned in unison and walked past Marty as if they'd suddenly become invisible, another familiar occurrence. They had no idea why Shannon didn't like them. Well, they *knew* why Shannon didn't like them, but not the reason beneath the dislike. From the minute they'd introduced themself and said their pronouns, Shannon had had issues. The *why* didn't really have anything to do with them.

But there it was. When Marty was alone with just Ford and Shannon, or Shannon solo, Shannon's comments were even nastier. Marty sighed.

Not like they hadn't heard it all before, and sometimes worse. They glanced back at their bunk to make sure they had everything and then, for some reason, back at Ford's, the bottom bunk across from theirs. They picked up Ford's EpiPen, slid it into their back pocket, and walked out the door.

CHAPTER TEN

Chase rounded the corner to the facilities building and paused. Sarah sat on a plain wooden bench adjacent to the staircase leading up to Chase's temporary sleeping quarters, which she'd yet to use.

"Morning." Chase sat down beside her, cradling the cup of coffee she'd snagged from the kitchen, and waited for Sarah to say her piece. She'd been a player in a scene like this, in various forms, since her mom had died and Sarah had changed her life to come home and take care of her.

"I saw your Jeep," Sarah said, "when you came in an hour or so ago."

"Yeah," Chase said, wondering which direction Sarah was about to go in. Reminding her that she'd been notably absent for the first week of camp? Even though she had good reasons for it, Sarah might consider it suspiciously convenient. Then again, there might be other topics on Sarah's mind.

"Nat said you had a run-in with a bear last night," Sarah went on in a quiet voice that didn't give a hint as to where she was going.

Chase let out a breath. Why did she ever think anything would get past Sarah with her network of informants? Okay, maybe informants was a little strong, but really, she wasn't ten years old anymore. "I wouldn't call it a run-in. More like she was just running in her sleep."

"You can't always laugh away the things you don't want to talk about," Sarah said, staring down toward the lake.

"Why don't you say what you have on your mind, Sare—it's been a long night." Chase held on to her temper, barely. No one could get to her like Sarah, and she ought to know that by now.

"I don't suppose you had it checked out at the hospital."

"Jerry Malloy was out with us," Chase said, although Nat had undoubtedly told Sarah that also. "He's a paramedic, remember? He looked at it."

"Right, in the field. Wounds like that—"

"Sarah," Chase said gently, because after all, her sister was just worried about her, "I'm fine. But if it makes you feel any better, Lily checked it out a little while ago. Shot me full of antibiotics, and she'll keep an eye on it."

"Lily." Sarah slowly turned her head and met Chase's gaze. "Lily seems to be your first stop whenever you turn up here."

The reins on Chase's temper unraveled just a little more. "Right. Lily. You know, the camp medic. The emergency room physician from the big New York City hospital with credentials probably as long as both my arms? She's more than qualified to handle a big scratch."

"I won't even point out that bear claws leave more than a scratch," Sarah said with the first hint of a bite in her voice, "and I know all about Lily's credentials. She's a superstar, you're right. Top of her class, every class. Destined, I'm sure, to head the ER at that big city hospital. She's also…fragile right now."

If Chase had had hackles, they would've been standing up three inches high along her spine. A red cloud of anger suffused her. She'd heard this kind of thing from Sarah before. Keisha's a nice girl, don't lead her on. Josie's on the rebound from a nasty breakup and she's likely to fall hard for the next person who pays any attention to her. Juanita is a lot more sensitive than you think, and…

"I don't think Lily needs anyone to stand up for her, Sarah," Chase said before Sarah could include Lily in that long list of warnings.

Sarah said, "Lily is one of the smartest, strongest, most accomplished women I've ever met. And she wouldn't be here if she didn't need healing of some kind."

Chase shot to her feet. "I'm not going to discuss Lily with you. And maybe it's time you started giving me a little bit of credit. I'm not the kid you came home to take care of anymore."

She expected Sarah to shoot back at her, but instead, Sarah just shook her head. "I know that. But sometimes, Chase, your ten-year-old is awfully close to the surface. Like every time you head out on a call that isn't yours because you don't want to miss out on something.

Whatever the action might be, it's never enough for you. Just like none of the women has ever been enough."

"You only know what you see, Sarah. That's true for all of us." Chase tossed the dregs of her coffee out onto the grass. "Lily sees something else."

"I wouldn't be surprised. Lily is good at taking care of other people's wounds." Sarah rose. "Maybe not so good at taking care of her own. That's what I was trying to tell you."

"And you think I'm going to hurt her."

"I think one of you will get hurt if you keep heading in the direction you're going. If one of you doesn't walk away."

Chase had to walk away right then. "I'm scheduled to take kids up the mountain this morning. I'm going to grab a couple hours' sleep."

"I wouldn't say anything if I didn't love you both," Sarah called after her.

"I know," Chase said and kept going. Nothing she could say would ease Sarah's worry, and anything she *did* say would only make it worse.

Because Lily would have to be the one to turn and walk away. It wasn't going to be her. Lily pulled at her like a magnet, dragging her closer with every breath. No matter where she was, she thought about Lily, replayed every conversation, no matter how ordinary, looking for any sign that Lily wanted her the way she wanted Lily. Remembered every single touch, even the ones that Lily would have given to anyone. Lily's hand on her shoulder that morning was consoling and warm, but that's not what Chase's body had registered. Lily's scent had been all around her, the timbre of her voice and the gentleness of her touch had wrapped her in arms that were anything but comforting. Hell, she was still vibrating, still turned on. She needed a shower because she was too tired for anything else.

Maybe if she was lucky, she'd dream of Lily. Again.

❖

The campers were supposed to meet on the parade grounds, at least that's what Marty called the common area in front of the lodge, at oh-ten-thirty hours. They were one of the first to arrive, but most of the other kids showed up soon too. Of course, Ford and Shannon were the last to arrive a couple of minutes after everyone else. It was like they had to be late, and Marty couldn't figure that out either. Their dad always said being on time showed you were prepared and fit for duty.

Chase Fielder came out of the lodge along with the counselors and Dr. Davenport.

"All right," Chase said, "let's everybody gather around."

Marty hung back just a little while everyone shuffled into a loose circle, then found a spot in the crowd with a good sight line to the leaders. They'd learned—after needing to change schools a lot when their dad got assigned to a new base—how to fit in without really drawing much attention. That really helped recently—until they got here. Marty shrugged off the distracting thoughts they couldn't do anything about and concentrated on the briefing.

"So today," Chase said, "we'll take a short hike up to Blueberry Pond—it's about three miles. Temperatures are projected to be in the low seventies. You're not going to feel particularly hot, but you will be sweating, so you need to drink every fifteen to twenty minutes. Once we get there, we're going to set up camp using only what you brought in your backpacks."

"What's the point of that," one of the older guys from cabin two said with just a hint of derision in his voice. A few of the other campers laughed. "If you're gonna camp, you'd bring everything you needed."

"If you planned to camp," Chase said calmly, "you're right. Although chances are you'd forget something."

A couple of other kids laughed. Marty smiled, because that's what lists were for. You didn't forget things then. That was another thing they'd learned early—their dad always posted lists all over the house, lunch lists, grocery lists, first day of school lists, checklists for camping. Lists just made sense.

Chase went on, "But this isn't about the planned outing. This is to show you what to do if you find yourself out overnight without having planned to be there."

One of the younger girls from cabin seven squeaked a little and blurted, "We aren't staying out overnight, are we? Because I don't think I have the right things."

Chase shook her head. "No, not this time. This is just a trial run, so you can learn how to do this if you have to with just what you have today. We'll be back by dinner."

The younger girl looked relieved. A few campers grumbled, but most everyone looked excited. Except not Ford or Shannon, who both had the same bored expressions. Marty'd overheard them talking about how their parents had forced them into coming. Blackmailed into it, Shannon had said—camp or no new car for college. Ford had announced she'd had to choose between this and the summer with her grandparents on a *farm*. Shannon and Ford seemed to want everyone to know they thought the camp was definitely *not* lit.

Marty focused on the ranger and put Shannon and Ford out of their mind.

"All right then," Chase said, "first, gear check. Let's make sure you've all got what you need to start out with. Anyone who doesn't have all their gear will have to go back for it and come up with the rearguard. Which means you will have all the cleanup detail when we get ready to leave."

Quite a few campers grumbled, mostly good-naturedly, though. Marty laughed.

Alisha called out, "Let's line up by cabins. Shouldn't take long."

Reluctantly, Marty joined the other campers from cabin eight, some of whom, they noticed, sent wary glances in Shannon and Ford's direction and shifted away from them in the newly forming line. The staff spread out, each one taking a cabin to check on what the campers had packed.

Dr. Davenport came over to their group and stopped in front of Marty.

"Want to show me what you've packed?"

"Sure." Marty pointed out the items in the outside pockets and then opened the top. They held it open and verbally ran down everything inside.

"Good. Nice job."

Someone snorted.

"Thanks." Marty didn't look around. They shouldered their bag and waited. They were used to that too.

"Shannon?" Dr. Davenport said, moving down the row. "Ready?"

Shannon, looking bored, held out her bag. "Whatever."

After a minute, Dr. Davenport said, "I think you might have forgotten a couple of things."

Shannon sighed. "Really?"

"Your water," Dr. Davenport said, "which you'll definitely need, and the snakebite kit. You have one, don't you?"

"Why should I have to worry about that?" Shannon said. "You're the doctor. Isn't that what you're here for? In case one of us gets a mosquito bite?"

Marty took a quick glance at the two of them. Other campers were watching too. They wondered if Shannon liked the attention. The doctor seemed unbothered by Shannon's snide tone.

She said, "I will be carrying emergency supplies, yes, but should you be separated from the group, or if for some reason *I* am, and you need any of the gear, especially the snakebite kit where time matters, you would not want to wait to find me. You'll have to go back to your cabin and get that and your water bottle."

"Oh, for fu—" Shannon almost snatched the bag back from Dr. Davenport, spun around, and stormed toward the trail leading back to the cabins.

Ford, who was next, held out her open backpack expressionlessly.

Dr. Davenport waited while Ford pointed out all the items, and then said quietly, "You've got everything on the list, but where's your EpiPen? Remember we talked about you needing to always have it with you."

"I don't really need it," Ford said quickly. "There was only that one time, and all I had was a little rash."

Dr. Davenport shook her head. "When you have any kind of allergy, the reaction can vary from one time to the next. No matter where you are, it's not something to take a chance with, and definitely not when we're in the mount—"

"Oh," Marty said, "sorry to interrupt, but I think I saw you put it in the side pocket of your backpack back at the cabin."

Ford frowned at her. "I…" She spun her pack around, slipped her hand into one of the many exterior pockets, and came out with her EpiPen. Her eyes narrowed on Marty before she quickly said, "I guess I did stick it in there."

"Good," Dr. Davenport said and moved on.

Ford muttered, "What the fuck, Marty," but just then Chase called out, "Let's form up in twos and head for High Meadow Trail."

Marty hesitated, expecting everyone to pair off with friends. Ford glanced toward the trail where Shannon had disappeared, and sighed. "Um. So, I guess we should go."

"Okay," Marty said.

As they fell into line, Ford said, "Why did you do that? Take my pen and stick it in my backpack."

"I don't know," Marty said. "I saw it there after you left, and I figured it might be something you should have with you. I just grabbed it."

They didn't know how to explain that they'd been taught that everyone on the team had to look out for everyone else. Ford, for sure, wouldn't think of Marty as any kind of teammate.

"You could've said that instead of bailing me out."

"That wasn't much of a bailout."

"Well…thanks."

"You're welcome," Marty said softly.

They walked on in silence, but Ford didn't hurry off to join any of the others when she had the chance. Marty trod along enjoying the views, the scents of pine and fertile soil, and the unexpected company.

❖

Lily enjoyed herself more than she'd imagined she would. She'd learned more than she'd ever need to know—Fates willing—about finding shelter, constructing a windbreak, preserving body heat if temperatures dropped unexpectedly, and finding safe sources of drinking water if she ever found herself lost in the wilderness. Mostly she'd enjoyed watching the campers tackle the challenges of solving those problems. Some formed teams and divvied up tasks—others, like Marty Riley, worked alone, efficiently establishing a neat little area where Lily could envision Marty comfortably riding out a long night or even more in the wilds. Shannon, she also noted, showed no interest in participating, although Ford watched several others, including Marty, and eventually did a reasonable job. Now that they were all on their way home, Lily registered a pleasant hum in her muscles along with a nearly forgotten sense of contentment.

"How are you doing?" Chase asked as she joined Lily in the line wending down the trail in pairs and small groups.

"It's been fun," Lily said, then laughed. "And I really do need to get hiking boots. Three miles didn't sound like very far this morning, but you didn't mention it was three miles straight uphill over a goat path strewn with boulders."

Chase chuckled, an amused sound that for some reason stirred a tremor in Lily's chest.

"When's the last time you hiked three miles?" Chase asked.

"That would be…precisely never? I spent my free time on a sailboat."

"What the hell made you decide to spend the summer up here?"

"Your sister."

"Yep, that would do it. She's always been persuasive," Chase said with just a hint of long-suffering in her voice.

"That's true," Lily said, "but she balances it out with a generous heart."

Chase nodded, her expression serious. "That she does. And lucky for me."

"It seems that Sarah has done well by both of us. She was a great friend to me in college and ever since. And this job, I think, is exactly what I need."

"Just the job? Because, you know, all work and no play…"

Chase gave her a look that Lily couldn't possibly misinterpret. She glanced around, but the kids were either trudging wearily along in silence or chatting. No one appeared to be paying attention to their conversation.

"I'm flattered, but—"

"I haven't made an offer yet."

"Haven't you?" Lily wasn't about to be put off with that line. "I may not have had a lot of practice recently, but I can still read signals."

Chase grinned. "Not rusty a bit? Because the mountain air is great for getting everything back in working order."

"You do really like to live dangerously."

"That's what they've always said about me."

Lily shot her a look. "Some things you never forget, but that's not the point."

"What is?"

"I'm here to work, we're surrounded by teenagers, not to mention your sister, and…" She frowned. "That's enough."

"Could I offer a counterargument?"

"Could I stop you? Something tells me you're not used to hearing no either."

Chase held her eyes and shook her head. "Lily, if it's a definite no, it's a definite no, and I won't bother you again."

Lily should've said no instantly. She'd just made all the arguments why it was a no. Instead she said nothing.

After a few seconds, Chase said, "I happen to think you're an extraordinarily attractive woman, and I like your style."

"My style?" Annoyed to be drawn in, Lily couldn't help repeating, "My style?"

That little flicker of a grin again. God, she was good-looking.

"You're intrepid, or else you wouldn't be here. You're obviously smart, considering what you do. Sarah's a good judge of character, and if you're her friend, that automatically spells loyalty and honesty. And"—she paused and her gaze darkened—"I like the way you look at me, Lily."

"I don't…" Lily was not in the habit of lying to herself, and she certainly wasn't going to start now. "All right, I'm living and breathing, and you are…"

Chase's brow rose and, again, that little smirk Lily was beginning to find amusing as well as sexy.

"You know damn well you're attractive."

"I'm only interested in being attractive to you."

Lily laughed out loud. "That is a terrible line. And *I* know damn well you like being attractive to women. Plural."

"All right, I'm only interested in being attractive to you, singular, right now."

"Better."

"And," Chase went on, "to continue why I want to see you…as in spend time with you and that includes sexually, I find you attractive and you find me attractive and we're both single, I believe we've established, and adults, so why shouldn't we enjoy each other? It's only one summer, Lily."

"That's being optimistic. How do you know it wouldn't only be for one night?"

Chase lifted a shoulder. "Fair enough. I don't, but I can hope."

"You are terribly smooth for someone so young."

"Come on, I'm not that young."

"A decade at our age is young. And what we experience ages us too," she said more quietly.

"I know what you've been through, Lily," Chase said, "and I know it was hell. But do me the favor of not assuming that you know all there is to know about me."

Lily took a slow breath. "You're right, and I'm sorry. I don't know a lot about you, and that's maybe the point."

"Do you always know a lot about the women you sleep with?"

"I usually know them well."

"Friends first, sex later?"

Lily paused, thinking about it.

"Friends, yes, but not friends like Sarah."

Chase flinched. "Hell, hope not."

Lily laughed again. "No. And as to the other women in my life... they were women I respected and enjoyed. Not all of them, or even most of them, are close now."

"I don't want to be your friend," Chase murmured. "I want to be your summer love."

"Don't you mean summer lover?"

"Could be the same thing," Chase said offhandedly, and Lily surprised herself with an unexpected surge of disappointment.

What had she expected? Chase was playing with her, and she'd invited the casual. Casual relationship. Casual sex. A fling. She'd never had anything close to what she'd call a fling. And if she was honest, she was enjoying every second of Chase's unapologetic pursuit, and she didn't have an argument against anything Chase had said. She couldn't deny the attraction and couldn't conjure a rational reason not to take the next step. Except...she couldn't banish the memory of the voice whispering in the quiet of the night *You'll want her, and you'll regret it. She'll hurt you in ways you didn't think you could be hurt. Don't let her in.*

"Lily?" Chase murmured with a question her voice. "What is it?"

The lodge came into view, and Lily said quickly, "Let's just say we'll see what happens, how about that."

"I'd call it progress." Chase slowed. "I've got to check my calls and go over a few things with Alisha and Philippe, but what do you say about a drive into town tonight for dinner and hiking boots. We ought to be able to find a place that's open for the boots."

Lily considered it. She had to eat, and she really needed boots. Chase was good company, and the idea of an evening away from four dozen teens and Chase's older sister was hard to resist. "I could definitely work that into my extraordinarily busy schedule."

Chase grinned. "Outstanding."

CHAPTER ELEVEN

Lily grabbed a quick shower and went in search of Sarah. She found her going over the food lists with Clara.

"How was the hike?" Sarah asked.

"I think of it more as a trek," Lily said, "but it was fun. The kids seemed to really like it, even the ones who started out doubtful." She paused. Shannon had been the noticeable standout who'd refused to even pretend to be trying to master the solo set-up exercise. When Alisha had pointed out that all the camp activities had a larger purpose in preparing the campers for actual wilderness experiences, Shannon had merely smirked and wandered off to talk to several of the boys from cabin one. "Most of them, at least."

Sarah shook her head and Clara snorted. "There's always a few just putting in time. Something else up?"

"I was wondering how you wanted me to handle being off-site. Do you have a beeper or anything for me to carry, or will the cell phones be reliable?"

Sarah put the clipboard she'd been carrying down on the counter and moved a few steps away from the kitchen staff. Lily followed.

"Going somewhere?"

"Into town," Lily said, not feeling the need to explain any further.

"Tonight?" Sarah asked mildly.

"Yes," Lily said, also not feeling the need to hide anything. "Chase and I are going to have dinner, and I'm finally going to get the hiking boots I should have gotten to begin with. Today definitely convinced me I needed them."

"How is Chase doing?"

The question wasn't surprising. Of course Sarah would know that Chase had been injured. Chase was Sarah's sister, but also Lily's patient, and now Lily was about to go off on what even she had to admit was a date with Chase. Murky boundaries everywhere, but none that she saw as compromising anything personal or professional—yet.

"She looked pretty comfortable out there today," Lily said, "but it's Chase. I suspect she doesn't let much in the way of physical discomfort show."

"You seem to know her pretty well," Sarah said. "That's kind of surprising, seeing how she almost never shares anything that really matters with anyone."

Sarah's frustration was hard to miss. Lily could only imagine how terrifying Chase's accident must have been for Sarah. They'd been each other's only family for more than half their lives. Shutting Sarah out, if that's what Chase did, had to have been unconscious. Lily could never imagine Chase hurting Sarah intentionally.

"I don't know about that," Lily said. "Chase lets people see what she wants them to see. That goes for everyone, I imagine."

"She seems to think that you see more than that."

Lily felt heat rise to her face. She was both pleased and intrigued. "Really?"

Sarah's eyes were probing, and Lily wasn't sure if she was reading criticism or curiosity.

"I don't think I've ever seen Chase really serious about anyone she was involved with," Sarah said mildly.

"We're not going over this again, are we?" Lily asked. "Because it's really not—"

"No, actually." Sarah spread her hands and smiled wryly. "I've given up on relationship advice for the rest of the summer."

"Well, that should cover things, then, as far as I'm concerned at least." Lily said it lightly, even as the idea of Chase giving Sarah some reason to be concerned about *another* woman ignited an unexpected and totally unreasonable flare of…annoyance. Because she didn't get jealous—never had—and had absolutely no cause to start now.

Sarah raised a brow. "Anything's just temporary, right?"

"At the moment there's nothing to really even consider in that regard, but my stay here does have an end date."

"I suppose if that's the situation, there isn't really much to say. I hope you enjoy dinner."

"I plan to," Lily said, happy to move on to safer ground. Anything to do with Chase seemed to catch her off-balance. Not a comfortable or common place for her to be. "I like being here, but it's…remote."

Sarah laughed. "That would be the definition, yes. What do you miss?"

"Shopping," Lily said instantly and then laughed herself. "Although, goodness knows, I haven't had a chance to do that in forever."

"Then you should go and…shop."

"The beeper?"

"We really rely on the radios, since cell service is so spotty up here. If you're going to be with Chase, I can contact you that way."

"If you're sure," Lily said.

"Go, and have a good time." Sarah smiled. "Really."

"Thanks," Lily said, relieved that Sarah recognized there was nothing to worry about. After all, how much could happen in one summer?

❖

Chase waited on the front porch and, when five minutes went by, began to worry that Lily might change her mind. She appreciated how Lily considered a problem from every angle before coming to a decision—most of the time. She'd rather Lily didn't have too much time to rethink her verdict on dinner. When Lily appeared and smiled at her, Chase's tension ebbed and a buzz of anticipation took its place. "All set?"

"Yes. Sarah said she would contact you by radio if they needed me for any reason."

"Good enough. Let's get out of here before Sarah remembers something I need to do."

Lily bumped her shoulder. "Stop. She's not that bad."

"Okay. You're right—but I still don't want to take any chances. I've been trying to make this happen for two weeks."

As they walked off the porch, Chase rested her hand in the small of Lily's back. The contact was casual, and Lily found she liked it very much. "Considering you've been working every night for most of that time, maybe you should be taking the night off."

Chase gave her a slow-lidded, heavy look that caught Lily in between breaths with a wave of arousal that made her heart lurch.

"That's the first inane thing I've ever heard you say," Chase said.

"Consider the statement retracted," Lily murmured and threaded her arm around Chase's waist as they walked. She'd already done it before she could catch herself, and the solid feel of Chase's body beneath her hand felt so right, she kept it there.

Chase lightly stroked Lily's back as they walked. "Anything special you'd like for dinner?"

"Something I can't get here."

"That covers a lot of ground," Chase said with a laugh. "How does Thai sound?"

Lily paused by the side of Chase's Jeep. "Seriously?"

"Yep. There's a good place on the lake not far from the sports outlet where we can get you some boots. And we can walk around town a bit if you like."

"I would like very much." Lily looked forward to the evening far more than she'd imagined she would. A night where she wasn't taking care of sick or dying patients, where the air was clear, the sky was bright, and the company was exciting? She couldn't ask for anything more.

The ride down the mountain with the sun setting behind them and Chase driving was a completely different experience than what Lily'd experienced driving up. That day seemed part of a different lifetime. Despite the clear blue sky and brilliant sunshine, her world had been tinged with gray. Without her noticing, the gray had disappeared. She studied Chase, her profile a study in light and shadow as the sun sank low and lanced at an angle across the open-topped vehicle. Chase was a study in contrasts too—fiercely independent and self-sufficient, but not without human attachment or needs. She loved Sarah as deeply as Sarah loved her. And she wanted Lily. To pretend otherwise would be to lie to herself. The wanting might be a physical one, but the need for touch—to give and receive physical pleasure—was as basic a human need as breathing. Lily had forgotten that need for a long time and welcomed the awareness of it now.

Chase glanced at her and smiled quizzically. "What?"

"I need a Jeep," Lily said. No reason for Chase to know just how much she enjoyed her attention.

"You would if you're going to go back and forth yourself," Chase said, "but you know, I'm happy to chauffeur."

"Right. In your free five minutes once a week."

"I could probably squeeze in a few more minutes for you, Lily." She reached across the space between them and took Lily's hand.

Startled, Lily shifted to face her.

"You mind?" Chase said, her other hand on the wheel and her eyes on the trail.

"No," Lily said truthfully. She liked the warmth and strength of Chase's hand in hers. She liked the contact. She liked the connection. And she wasn't going to look more closely than that. "You can really do this one-handed?"

Chase laughed. "I've been up and down this trail five hundred times. I know every rock."

"Then I don't mind a bit."

"Good," Chase said in that low, sexy rumble. "Neither do I."

❖

"Boots, walk around town, or dinner first?" Chase asked as she parked in a small lot between a touristy gift shop and a pizza parlor on the main thoroughfare through Lake George. The village, as it was still called, although Lily suspected it was larger in population than the designation implied, hadn't changed much since the last time she'd been there, which had to have been more than a decade before. Perhaps even the last year of college. The resorts still looked the same, mostly low-slung motor courts interspersed with newer condos and individual freestanding units on either end of the village. Once outside the commercial area, every free bit of roadside property was developed until reaching the million dollar mile, a stretch of road bordering the lake, so named for the early twentieth century mansions of the wealthy families who had once flocked from New York City to Lake George in the summer. Many still privately owned by those families, they stood as reminders of the historic past, multistory stone edifices overlooking sweeping lawns that led down to private beaches with docks and boathouses and pavilions. Curving drives and stone patios sat framed by meticulously manicured gardens. Lily had the fleeting thought that she'd rather spend the summer in the mountains than behind some of those constraining walls.

She said to Chase, "Let's walk, pick up the boots, and be done with everything before we eat. Then we won't have to rush the meal."

"I can get behind that," Chase said as they walked along the beach in the center of town where the big tour boats docked. Long lines of tourists snaked out into the street waiting for the next departure.

"Ever been on one of those?" Chase asked.

"No," Lily said, "but I gather we'll be doing that on the Fourth."

Chase pointed to one of the paddleboats, slightly smaller than the largest triple-decker tour boats, with two decks having areas of open seating fore and aft, and an enclosed section in the center for the less intrepid passengers. "That's the one we'll be taking, the *William Henry*."

"Did you spend much time in the village when you were young?" Lily asked as they strolled past T-shirt shops and arty boutiques offering handcrafted ceramics, paintings, and sculptures interspersed with eateries and a few designer clothing shops.

"Not often. A trip into the village was a real outing for us. I looked forward to it for weeks. But then when I got here, everything felt so strange. So noisy and busy, and there wasn't really all that much I really wanted. Except ice cream."

Lily laughed. "I suppose that was hard to come by where you were living."

"Pretty much nonexistent," Chase said. "My father did most of the cooking but my mother baked. So we never went without treats, but ice cream was a little tough to conserve."

Lily pointed to a line of people in front of an ice cream stand. "Still think it's a treat?"

Chase grinned. "I do. But you know, there's the problem of spoiling our dinner."

"I'll risk it if you will."

"You know I love a challenge."

Lily laughed, the timbre of Chase's voice striking a chord in her, as if hearing the opening of a melody she'd forgotten. "I *have* gotten that impression of you, yes. Come on then. My treat."

They got in line, and Chase predictably ordered a cone with three different kinds of chocolate ice cream. Lily went for the cherry and blueberry cheesecake mix.

"How is it?" Chase asked as they walked back to the pathway that wended along the shore.

Lily held out her cone. "Excellent. Want to try?"

Chase stopped walking, cupped Lily's hand in hers, and, her eyes on Lily, leaned down and slowly licked a circle around Lily's cone.

Lily found her breath coming faster. "Well?"

Chase straightened. Her gaze never left Lily's. "Delicious. I can't wait for another taste."

Lily laughed. "Chase, you're shameless and obvious."

"Guilty and guilty as charged. But"—she slid her arm around Lily's waist as they began walking again—"is it working?"

Lily could never remember a moment like that in her life. She'd been on dates, she'd held hands with a woman or two in public, but she'd never felt so physically connected to another person, so comfortable, and so aroused. The evening somehow seemed fresher, brighter, and her blood pulsed to a beat that echoed deep inside her. "You know it is."

"Just hoping so," Chase murmured.

Lily glanced up at her. "We should go shopping for boots."

"I'd almost forgotten about them."

Lily finished her cone and, using one thumb, wiped a smudge of chocolate off the corner of Chase's mouth.

"Chocolate," she said.

"Lily," Chase said, her gaze liquid heat.

Lily quickly shook her head. "No. Boots."

"They'll be there tomorrow."

"And I'll be back in camp tomorrow doing my job." She summoned all her willpower. Resisting Chase when the pull to say yes to what Chase suggested, to what she wanted, was nearly overpowering. "Boots."

Chase sighed and took her hand. "This way."

Half an hour later, Lily tucked the package under her arm. They dropped the boots off at the Jeep and walked the opposite direction away from the crowds and the traffic to a small, unassuming restaurant that sat on the water. Its outdoor patio extended to the shoreline, and the view of the lake was uninterrupted for miles. Still so early in the season, they were able to get a table without any trouble, and they sat beneath an umbrella at one corner of the deck as the sun set over the chain of islands that ran north in the middle of the lake.

"Does anyone own those islands?" Lily asked.

"A few of them," Chase said. "Others are actually part of the parkland, and we patrol them by water."

"Do you spend any time on the water?" Lily asked.

Chase shook her head. "Not unless there's a rescue. Too far for me to come down, and I'm not a boater. I don't mind it, but…"

"The mountains are your thing," Lily finished for her.

Chase nodded solemnly. "You got it. How about you, Lily," Chase asked as they drank the sweet Thai coffee. "You said you sailed. What else? What calls to you?"

Lily blinked. And blanked. She was silent, searching for an answer. "You know, I don't really know anymore."

Chase reached for Lily's hand. Her thumb caressed the top of Lily's knuckles. "Maybe you'll rediscover it. What that is."

"Maybe I'll find it for the first time," Lily said musingly.

"So," Chase said after a quiet moment, "sibs?"

"No," Lily said. "Only child."

She told Chase the story of how her parents had met, both having spent all their lives training and then traveling around the world with Doctors Without Borders.

"Sarah was kind of a sister for me," Lily said, thinking back. "I never really had anyone near my age to share things with. Those three years in college were just about the happiest of my life."

Chase looked out over the water. "Sarah gave that up to come back home and take care of me. She had to finish up her degree going part-time and commuting."

"I don't think, for one single second, she regrets doing that," Lily said. "I've known her half my life, and one thing I know for certain. She adores you."

"And I've been nothing but a huge headache," Chase said, only half laughing.

"Well, she's never *said* that," Lily said and laughed lightly, happy to see Chase smile back.

"She giving you a hard time about me?" Chase asked.

"No, not at all." The last thing Lily would ever do was come between the two of them.

"That is a very diplomatic answer."

"If you're worried about how Sarah feels," Lily said carefully, "we don't have to—"

"Whoa," Chase said instantly. "I love my sister. And I'd never intentionally do anything to hurt her. But that does not extend to my personal life. Especially not where you're concerned."

"Well, I might be getting ahead of things, but—"

"Lily, you know you're not. You want to tell me you haven't thought about that kiss? A single time?"

Lily laughed, astounded that her voice was shaking. "You know damn well I can't do that."

"Neither can I. And there's nothing I can do to stop thinking about you, either. To stop wanting another kiss, and more."

"And do you think that will take care of it? Another kiss, and more?"

"I doubt it," Chase said. "But we'll never know until we try. There's a very nice private little motel about five miles up the road. I thought we might go there after dinner."

Lily swallowed and shook her head. "I didn't bring a toothbrush."

Chase nodded. "Let's enjoy dinner, then."

Dinner came and went, and Lily enjoyed it as much as she could while struggling not to second-guess herself. Not to let her rational, reasonable self be overshadowed by the instincts clamoring for her to just let go.

When they'd finished their meal and walked back to the Jeep, Chase took her hand again. "It doesn't have to be complicated, Lily."

"I never was the most spontaneous person in the world," Lily said slowly. "Maybe I never had a chance to be, but I pretty much always knew my direction and didn't give a lot of thought to anything else."

Chase held the door of the Jeep open for her and regarded her steadily. "A *no* will do it, Lily. You don't owe me an explanation."

Lily braced an arm on the door. "Oh, but I do. I know what's been going back and forth between us, unsaid, since the first time I saw you climb out of that Jeep, all tall and lean, and dark and mysterious with the sun behind you. I couldn't see your face clearly and I didn't know a single thing about you, but I was intrigued even then."

"This might be the nicest *no* I've ever heard," Chase said, softly running the backs of her fingers along the edge of Lily's jaw. Before

Lily could lean into the caress the way she wanted to, Chase drew her hand away and slid it into her pocket. "And you make it really hard for me not to push a little bit."

"I know, and that's on me, and I apologize."

Chase laughed. "Really, you've got no game, Lily."

Lily took a breath and drew herself up straight. "I beg your pardon?" Chase grinned, that devilish grin that Lily was coming to adore, not only because it made Chase even more handsome, but because it stirred that excitement in her middle that was so pleasant. Maybe that's what she didn't want to lose. "That is *not* the way to win my heart."

"Then don't apologize for making someone, who you know wants you, crazy. If that's what you were intending."

"Not in so many words," Lily said softly. "I'm not a tease."

"No, you're not, or you wouldn't be talking about it. And I don't for a second think you're playing with me—at least not in any way I don't enjoy."

"This is not helping," Lily said.

"I never said I was gonna help."

"I feel like…" Lily huffed. "It's a step toward something I can't see or understand very well, and I don't want to misstep."

"I understand," Chase said, more seriously than Lily had heard her before. "But what I said earlier still goes. It doesn't have to be complicated. And one night will not obligate you to anything else."

Lily knew Chase meant it, and that fueled her reluctance. What she wasn't going to tell Chase was that she wasn't certain that one night would be enough for her. And that was somewhere she didn't want to go. She'd already had more emotional hits than she could take, and she wasn't about to let herself in for another one.

"I've never actually had a one-night…thing."

"I'm not surprised. But the thing is, Lily," Chase said, running her index finger down the top of Lily's bare arm and leaving goose bumps behind when the warmth of that small, solitary touch drifted away, "it's not a one-night stand, not between you and me. Because I won't disappear in the morning, and neither will you. And it won't be just sex."

Lily's chest tightened again. No, it wouldn't be just sex, and she only wished she knew what it would be.

"I'm sorry I'm probably overthinking this," Lily said, "and that's totally the antithesis of sexy."

Chase threw back her head and laughed. Her laughter always drove away Lily's uncertainty and strengthened her resolve to say what she felt, even when she couldn't completely define it. Chase's acceptance set her free.

"Lily, baby," Chase said with that rumble in her voice again that spoke to the part of Lily that had nothing to do with reason or sensibility, "everything about you is sexy. And if we're going back to camp, we should go, because I can't promise not to keep trying."

Wordlessly, Lily slid into the Jeep before she could change her mind. Again.

The ride back from town was quiet and oddly restful. They talked sometimes, were quiet others, and when they stood in the moonlight in front of the lodge, Lily pressed her hand to Chase's chest and kissed her gently. "Thank you for a wonderful night."

Chase's heart thundered beneath Lily's palm, and her breath was warm against Lily's mouth.

"You're welcome, Lily. Pleasant dreams."

Lily smiled to herself as she climbed the stairs to her room. She didn't need pleasant dreams when the evening had already been one.

CHAPTER TWELVE

Chase made a quick detour away from her temporary quarters and headed down to the lake. No way was she going to be able to sleep now, not with yet another kiss from Lily still burning on her lips. Just a little good night, thank you for a nice night kiss that had her tied up in knots. Not altogether unpleasant knots, for sure, but way too tight and tangled for her to ignore. She'd been teasing when she'd said Lily had no game. The woman had game in caps—precisely because she didn't play at anything. Lily didn't pretend she wasn't interested in Chase or that she didn't want something to happen between them—instead she looked at Chase with a hunger she didn't bother to hide. Lily said no and said why, right up front. And Chase couldn't argue. Lily felt what Lily felt. And anything between them was destined to be short-term— only this summer. But a night, a week—hell, a month—with Lily? Chase knew in her bones even the least of it would be unforgettable. And that left her waiting for Lily's next move. Not her usual style at all.

Usually she did the chasing—yeah, she'd heard all the jokes there were about that, but truth was she liked the hunt maybe more than the eventual catch. Probably why none of her affairs—couldn't call them relationships—went anywhere. Fan the flames, ride the fireball, and move on when the heat cooled. No hurt feelings and definitely no broken hearts. She was good at it, even if lately the whole routine had become *so* routine, she'd lost interest in playing. Mostly.

Until Lily. When she'd first seen her, she'd had that immediate, *Oh yeah, she's definitely worth getting to know* reaction. Gorgeous and sexy, plus challenging and unpredictable. Still, she'd met other women with those attributes, and none had kept her awake at night. None had her on edge and simmering twenty-four seven. Lily was like no one she'd ever known—self-contained, self-aware, deliberate, and direct. She wasn't afraid to let Chase see her desire, and she wasn't afraid to walk away from it. That elusive sexuality hooked Chase deep. Okay, Lily might have said *no, not tonight*, but she hadn't told Chase to walk away. She'd told her *not yet*.

Not yet.

Chase's stomach clenched, and everything a little lower pulsed, full and tight. Her head joined in, and images of Lily naked beside her, beneath her, above her, kaleidoscoped through her brain. The pounding in her belly amped up a few hundred beats per second. "Fuck."

Lily had all the power, and she didn't even know it. If she didn't decide soon, Chase would probably go down in flames. Or just plain incinerate. She wanted Lily that much.

She strode down the dock, shedding clothes on the way, and dove into the lake as the moon crested the mountains. She swam until the pain of exhausted muscles replaced the ache of lust. Back on the dock, she wearily pulled her jeans and shirt back on and trudged up the trail. Halfway up, the sound of muted voices caught her attention, and she stepped off into the cover of the pines. No one appeared on the trail she'd just taken back from the lake. Must have been someone on one of the adjacent trails that circled the ridge and the cabins. Couple of campers out after hours—not unheard of. She'd had quite a few stolen moments with a girl or two when she'd spent summers at the camps where Sarah oversaw the summer programs. She shook her head and continued up to her room. She'd let the counselors know that their bed checks might need to be doubled.

"Good swim?" Sarah asked from the shadows by the stairs to Chase's room.

"Always is." She eased down on the bench beside her sister. "I'm kinda old for you to be waiting up for me."

Sarah laughed. "True. And I wasn't. I saw the Jeep come in and figured I should catch you while I could. You *have* been pretty scarce around here since the season started."

Chase sighed. "Not intentionally. You know we're spread thin, and this extra duty doesn't help."

"I know. Peace." Sarah stretched an arm along the back on the bench and tapped Chase's shoulder. "So, how was dinner?"

"Nice," Chase said noncommittally.

"Not big on the details," Sarah said casually.

Chase let out a breath. "Let's see, we got Lily the boots she's been needing."

Sarah chuckled. "Very practical."

"Walked around a bit, stopped for ice cream, had dinner at the Thai place. Just, you know, casual." Chase hoped she sounded casual. Remembering the ice cream brought a little tightness to her chest and the buzzing back in her belly. Lily had liked watching her. Lily watched her a lot, and she liked that. That's all it took really, was knowing Lily liked looking at her. If she thought about it too hard, she'd know she was in big trouble. Especially right now.

"That does sound nice," Sarah said. "Do you think Lily is doing okay here at camp?"

"Yeah," Chase said, "she seems to be enjoying it. Why, are you worried about her for some reason?"

"No, not really, but you know, I have a tendency to push people into things maybe they don't actually want to do."

Sarah shrugged, a motion Chase could make out even in the moonlight and shadows. Her sister tended to worry, and if she wasn't, she'd worry about what she should be worried about. Chase draped an arm around Sarah's shoulders. "You know, that's not really true. You might be a little pushy *sometimes*, but a lot of the time you just show people the way they really want to go before they're quite ready to admit it. I guess you could call that foresight."

"Sometimes I think…"

"What?" Chase said gently. "What's going on, Sarah?"

Sarah shifted to face her. "Maybe I shouldn't have kept you here with me, when Mom died. Grandmom—"

"What the hell, Sarah?" Chase shot upright. "*Grandmom* lived in Chicago, and we never really saw her. You know she didn't like Dad. I would have been on the road back here in a week."

"You were ten."

"So?"

Sarah laughed. "You're right. Crazy idea."

"And just what do you think would have been different?" Chase said. "Do you think you would have kept me off the mountain? Because if it hadn't been Casson Peak, it would have been another one, somewhere. Until someday—"

"I'm sorry," Sarah said urgently. "Don't go there. I wanted you here. I would have been lost without you."

"Same here," Chase said gruffly. "So can we leave the past where it belongs?"

"Can you?" Sarah asked,

Chase hesitated. She'd had dreams and she'd lost them. She'd been bitter for a long time—even to the point, she realized, of resenting the clueless campers who, like her at that age, had thought they could do anything and be anyone they chose. Some of them probably would. And...good for them.

She had a different life than the one she'd imagined, but she wasn't ten now, or even twenty. And she had something else—someone else—she wanted now.

"Yes."

Sarah must have heard the conviction in her voice and, in the way she'd always had of reading between the lines, probably heard what Chase didn't say. She let out a breath. "Sometimes I just think I ought to keep some of my opinions to myself. Lily might be a tad annoyed with me."

"Lily knows you come from a good place." Chase leaned over and kissed Sarah's cheek. "And so do I. And now, I'm going to bed because I have to take the angels...sorry, *campers*, to the climbing wall tomorrow. And won't that be fun."

"Are you sure you can handle it?" Sarah asked.

Chase bristled. "Why wouldn't I?"

"Now *you're* making assumptions," Sarah said. "I'm talking about your shoulder. And come to think of it, how is it?"

"To tell you the truth, I've practically forgotten about it. But I promise I'll get the doctor's seal of approval in the morning."

Sarah laughed. "Now why doesn't that surprise me."

"Can't imagine," Chase said as she rose to go upstairs. "'Night, Sarah."

"'Night, Chase," Sarah called softly after her.

Chase let herself into the plainly furnished but serviceable apartment, shucked her clothes, and stretched out naked on the narrow bed below the window. She could see the moon above the trees when she turned on her side. She smiled to herself. She'd started out the evening with plans that didn't include sleeping alone. But rather than be disappointed, she felt weirdly content. She'd see Lily in the morning, and for right now, that was all that mattered.

❖

Marty tensed as the cabin door opened and closed softly behind them. They'd made a bet with themself as to who it might be, and won when Ford dropped down on the top stair beside them.

"Hi," Marty said.

"What are you doing out here?" Ford said, drawing her knees up toward her chest and wrapping both arms around them.

At just before midnight the night was cool, the sky clear, and the stars a billion flashing points of brilliance scattered across an inky sky. The moon played hide-and-seek behind clouds that raced by as if on their way to some other world. Why wouldn't they want to be out here instead of in a twenty-by-twenty-foot dorm with seven other people and a couple of windows that barely let in a pathetic breeze? That didn't sound like something they could say, though. Just something else to make them seem weird.

"I was finishing a book," Marty said, pointing at the closed e-reader beside them. "It was nice out here, and more comfortable than the bunk."

"You got that right," Ford muttered. "I can't believe my parents even *knew* about this place."

"Couldn't sleep?" Marty ventured to ask, not really sure if Ford would welcome conversation, but they were sitting out there together, and pretending otherwise seemed silly.

"Oh, it was hot in there and..." Ford's voice drifted off, and after a second she said, "What are you reading?"

"A book about an alternate ancient world with sorcery and dragons."

Ford snorted softly. "Really? A fantasy."

"Yep."

"Kind of surprised. You don't strike me as the fantasy sort of girl." Ford hesitated. "Guess that's not really right, is it, the girl part?"

"Well," Marty said slowly, wondering if the question was serious or just snark, "I don't really identify with being a girl or boy."

"Yeah, I got that part. So, are you bi?"

Another unexpected question, but Marty didn't detect the usual condescension or ridicule. "No." They decided to take a risk. "Ace. How about you?"

"Cis and straight." Ford paused. "Mostly."

Marty laughed. "Fluid, right?"

"That. Yeah."

"Do you really hate being here?" Marty asked.

"Yeah," Ford said. "Not really as much as I thought, though. But jeez, rock climbing?"

"It'll be fun," Marty said. "I'm pretty sure we'll do the climbing wall first, before we actually, you know, do some bouldering."

"Do some bouldering," Ford said very slowly. "You are really weird."

"I've been told."

Ford huffed. "Oh, not because of that. I'm not meaning sex or whatever."

Ford shifted and her knee lightly brushed Marty's. That felt weird, and Marty slowly eased away until the contact broke.

"So why then?" Marty couldn't seem to stop asking questions they knew they'd regret. But Ford was actually talking to them, and that made the risk worth it.

"You're all over this outdoorsy stuff. Do you want to be a ranger or something?"

"I'm not really into the law enforcement part of rangering," Marty said, "but I've been wilderness hiking and camping for as long as I can remember. With my dad."

"That's cool, I guess," Ford said, sounding like nothing could be less cool.

Marty laughed. "You'd rather be sailing, right?"

"How do you know that?"

Even in the moonlight, Marty could tell Ford regarded them suspiciously.

"I heard you talking to Shannon. I wasn't trying to."

"Huh. Yeah. I've been sailing since forever. I just never figured my summer would be anything else."

Marty nodded. "I guess maybe we love what we learn to love, you know, when we're little."

"You're being weird again, Marty," Ford said.

"Right."

"So how come you're not off somewhere, you know, doing wilderness stuff with him?"

"He's active duty," Marty said flatly. "Right now he's in Africa."

"Oh. He's a soldier."

"Army."

"So you live with your mom when he's not around?"

"No, my grandmother. She lives in Huntington, so that works out for the school year. But I wouldn't want to spend the summer there."

"Boy, we couldn't be more different."

"I noticed," Marty said flatly.

Ford laughed again. "True—"

Alisha emerged from the trailhead and ambled over to them. "Late night. What are you two doing up still?"

"Sharing our life stories," Ford said sarcastically.

Alisha looked between the two of them. "Everyone else bedded down in there?"

"Yeah," Ford said quickly.

Marty tensed. Shannon's bunk was empty.

Alisha said, "Probably a good idea to get some sleep. Busy day tomorrow."

Marty stood up quickly. "I'm headed inside."

Alisha moved off to the next cabin, and Ford stood up and looked at Marty. "What?"

"Why do you cover for her?" Marty asked softly.

"Because she's my friend," Ford said sharply. "Something you might not understand."

"No," Marty said, "I guess not."

Ford didn't follow them inside, but a few minutes later Shannon and Ford came in together and went to their bunks.

Marty lay awake awhile, thinking about friendship and what you would do for your friends. Their dad would say you would die for your friends. But would you lie for them? Would they expect you to? Marty had to think about that.

❖

Lily hadn't dreamed, but in those few moments between sleep and waking, she'd drifted in a half-aroused memory of the previous night and the latest kiss she'd been unable to contain. With a sigh she rolled onto her back and opened her eyes. Kissing Chase was becoming a habit, one she enjoyed. It didn't have to be complicated—Chase's words, and true. Chase had been clear—no obligations, no expectations. One day at a time, no regrets in the morning. Lily'd left New York, but she really hadn't left the feeling of impending chaos and imminent failure behind, and she needed to. Wanted to. And couldn't think of any better way to spend a summer than enjoying time with a woman she enjoyed. For the summer, at least, she could live a day at a time.

After a quick shower, she grabbed a cup of coffee and headed over to the clinic. Chase sat on the steps, a cup of coffee in her hand.

"Good morning," Lily said.

Chase rose. "Hi. How was your night?"

"My evening was terrific, and I slept very well. I hope this is a professional visit."

"Hey. That kind of hurts."

Lily grinned. "I'm sure your ego is not damaged. Come inside so I can look at that shoulder."

She unlocked the door and stepped inside. Before she could turn the lights on, Chase slid her arms around her waist. And kissed her.

"That's what I've been thinking about all night. Didn't get much sleep," Chase murmured. "I want you, Lily. So damn much. Kiss me. Please."

Lily didn't even think about protesting. She put her arms around Chase's neck and leaned into the kiss. Chase tasted faintly of coffee and peppermint and heat. Her lips were firm and silky. Lily ran her tongue over Chase's bottom lip and tugged it lightly between her teeth.

Her fingers curled of their own volition into the fabric of Chase's T-shirt, gripping her shoulders. Chase's muscles trembled beneath her palms. She loved feeling all that power melting beneath her touch.

Chase's thigh, lean and hard, edged against hers, and she parted her legs to let Chase closer. Chase's hand drifted up her side and cupped her breast, the sensation so exquisite she might as well have been naked. A rush of heat swamped her, and pressure instantly built between her thighs. She lifted her hips, and Chase's thigh rocked rhythmically into her center. So much need—too much.

Mistake.

The press of heat and muscle made the blood pound in her clit.

She stepped away, and her back touched the door.

Chase pressed her mouth to Lily's ear. "Lily, lock the door."

"No," Lily gasped.

Chase groaned and dropped her forehead against Lily's. "This is killing me."

Lily closed her eyes and took a long, long breath. "Me too."

Chase shuddered, and Lily nearly gave in. She brushed the sweat-damp hair from the nape of Chase's neck and stroked her tense jaw. "This is crazy, you know that, right?"

Chase leaned away, her eyes dark oceans of blue. "I can't seem to stop."

"Mmm, but you do." Lily kissed her, just long enough to satisfy the ache to touch her. "And that makes me want more."

"I'm not gonna be able to think about anything except you all day," Chase said.

"Good." Lily kissed Chase's throat and licked lightly at the curve of her jaw. "I love your body."

"I really need to touch you," Chase whispered.

"What *I* need," Lily said with supreme effort, her voice shaking as she gently disentangled herself from Chase's arms, "is to look at your shoulder."

Chase eased away until a fraction of distance separated them, and clasped Lily's hips. Her eyes glinted as she leaned close, her mouth brushing Lily's. "What else do you need, Lily? Just tell me. Tell me so I can give it to you."

Damn her, but Chase's words made Lily nearly melt. That had never happened before.

"You know what I want," Lily said. "Another day when we don't have to stop."

Chase kissed her, swift and hard. "Then you kiss me first next time, and then I'll know I won't have to stop."

"When I don't want you to stop," Lily murmured, "I'll make very sure you know."

CHAPTER THIRTEEN

Chase had near-miraculous healing powers.

"Your wound looks excellent," Lily said, spraying a liquid bandage over the rapidly closing lacerations before applying a waterproof outer covering. "You'll need to be careful with heavy upper body activity."

"I can probably manage that." Chase grinned. "I'm a woman of many talents."

Lily rolled her eyes. "Really. One minute you're the sexiest woman to draw breath, the next you're insufferable."

Chase caught Lily's hand as she started to turn away, tugged her just a step closer until Lily was nearly standing between her spread thighs, and murmured, "You don't help my restraint by saying things like that."

"I haven't noticed an overabundance of that no matter what the conversation." She smiled when she said it. Chase had unfailingly given her space, while managing to let her know at every opportunity exactly what she wanted. She wanted Lily. Being wanted had never been a major motivator in her relationships—the absence of drama, now that she looked back at her short-term liaisons, had been the important component. Her daily life had always been so filled with demands and stress, she'd wanted the opposite in her personal life. Chase shattered that mold, and to her surprise, she didn't mind a bit.

"You have no idea how hard it is for me not to touch you."

Actually, she did. Keeping a professional distance while tending to Chase's injury wasn't hard, but every other time she was near her, *not* touching her was a conscious act of will. If she didn't know one touch would lead to another kiss, one she was absolutely certain would end them up in bed, she wouldn't have resisted this long. She'd never in her life been so attracted to a woman. Hadn't even realized she could be so primally driven. Her body had become a stranger to her.

She handed Chase her shirt. "I've seen today's schedule. Promise me you'll be careful."

Chase studied her gravely. "I won't take any risks. No matter what you might have heard about me."

Lily touched her fingertips softly to Chase's jaw. "I don't listen to anyone but you. But I will worry, because I care."

Chase turned her head and brushed a kiss against Lily's palm. "So I'll be extra careful, because I do too."

❖

Marty had been looking forward to this since the first day of camp. They weren't the only experienced wilderness enthusiast in camp, but the skill levels varied so much that the first few weeks of camp had been a little basic. Today might be an intro climb, but every climb was a challenge. They were almost the first to arrive at the meet point, but finally everyone assembled. Ford showed up alone, something that seemed to be happening more often lately.

"All right," Chase called, "everyone line up for gear check."

When the check was done and the group set off up the trail, Ford fell into step beside Marty. "This is a skill I can't imagine I'll need very often. Like never."

"Would be helpful if your car went off the road and you had to climb out of a ravine," Marty said helpfully.

Ford rolled her eyes. "Charming."

"Think of it as an excellent upper body workout. That has to be helpful when you're sailing."

"Yes," Ford said. "And I could get that while *actually* sailing, dimwit."

Marty laughed and so did Ford.

When Chase called a halt, Ford muttered, "I thought they said this was a freaking climbing wall. That's a cliff."

Marty kept silent. Pointing out that it *was* a climbing wall, only a natural one, and that if Ford looked closely, she'd see the natural foot and hand holds as well as a few strategically placed pitons, did not seem like a good idea. They were figuring out that Ford tended to have a negative view of most of the events, but when it came time to participate, she tried. And usually excelled, even when some people—frequently Shannon lately—made sarcastic comments about her efforts. Funny, today Shannon seemed to ignore Ford—although Marty caught her watching them every once in a while.

"How many of you have done any kind of climbing?" Chase asked.

"Yo," a guy called.

Susie, one of the youngest and most athletic girls at camp, raised a hand. Marty followed suit.

"Good," Chase said. "You'll go first."

That suited Marty. They liked climbing with no one above them. And climbing walls could get crowded. Even ones like this.

"I'm going to drop guidelines from the ridge up there," Chase said, pointing. "Before you begin your ascent, you'll clip onto one of those lines and get an all clear from Alisha or Philippe. No one steps onto the wall until that happens. Understood?"

"Yes, ma'am," Marty said automatically and heard a few snickers.

"Got it," the guy called, and Susie added, "Certainly."

A few people snickered at that too.

"Right." As Chase checked her lines and adjusted her harness, she said, "Today's objective is to reach the top."

"No shit," someone muttered.

Chase glanced over the group and grinned. "No shit."

That got more laughter.

"It's not a race—in fact, speed is not your friend when you climb. On the other hand, do not freeze. Do not look down. Look to your next hand or foot hold and move on to it. Let your body take control. Don't overthink your moves. That's it. See you at the top."

"That's it?" Ford glanced at Marty. "I don't think I can do that. It's gotta be like three hundred feet or something to the top."

"I think it's more like eighty," Marty murmured. "And you can do it. I bet you've done plenty of climbing around the sailboats."

"Yes," Ford said, "but falling into the water is a lot different than falling down a cliff."

"Good thing you're not going to fall, then."

Chase turned, stepped up to the wall, and without even seeming to pause to look, practically floated up the rock face, one fluid swing and push after another. In no time she hung just below the lip of the crest and, holding on with one hand, swung the other arm up to grasp the ledge. Her other arm followed and, for a second, her legs dangled in the air as she pulled herself up and over.

Ford snorted. "Even if I make it all the way up, I'm not sure I can pull myself over the top like that."

"I'm pretty sure Chase and some of the counselors will be up there. They won't let you fall."

"Theoretically." Ford squinted at them. "You've done this before, haven't you?"

"A few times, yeah."

Ford rolled her eyes. "You're so full of it sometimes."

Marty's chest warmed, not from embarrassment, but because the way Ford said it had held a hint of friendliness. Not sarcasm.

"Could be," Marty said.

When it was their turn to go, Philippe stepped over, checked their harness, and said, "Looks good. Have a good climb."

Marty checked the tension on the guideline just to be sure and assessed the wall. They'd been studying the wall while Chase climbed and had mapped out a course that looked doable. There were plenty of hand and foot holds, but they had to account for their height and their leg reach and how strong their arms were relative to their legs. Philippe tapped them on the shoulder. "Go."

Marty stepped close to the nearly vertical cliff face, judging the incline to be perhaps fifteen degrees, decided on the first handhold, stretched up an arm, gripped, and rose. From there, they forgot about the sounds from below or the voices from above, aware only of the sun on their back, the rough rock beneath their fingertips, and the next crack to wedge a toe into. The slight swing of their shoulders to stretch out and up for a new handhold, the push of thigh and the curl of knee to set a toe and push up, became a rhythmic counterpoint to the rush of their breath and pounding of their heart. They had no idea how long it took before an arm and a hand stretched down.

"Forearm grip," Chase called.

Marty pressed close to the cliff face, braced their thighs to steady themself, and reached. Their hand closed around Chase's forearm. The guideline tightened even more, and in the next instant, they were standing on level ground. The exhilaration of having completed the climb rushed through them then.

"Very nice," Chase said, focused on the next climber. "Water and some nutrition back there a ways."

Marty grabbed a PowerBar and some electrolytes and waited a few feet back from the ledge. Ford came up before too long, and when she got her feet under her, Marty said, "Nice going."

Ford's face was flushed, her eyes gleaming. "That was awesome!"

Marty laughed. "Told you."

Ford rolled her eyes and punched Marty lightly on the shoulder. "Yeah, yeah, I remember. I'm starving now."

Grinning, Marty said, "Come with me."

"Hey, Ford," Shannon called a few minutes later. She'd been one of the last to emerge over the top right after Derek, a guy from cabin one who always seemed to have something sarcastic to say. They stood together now, apart from the others.

Ford nodded to Shannon. "Hey."

"What are you doing over there? Can't find any better company?" Shannon smirked. "Come hang with us."

Marty knew how this was going to end. Ford would suddenly act as if standing next to them was risking something contagious and hurry away. That's how groups worked. No one wanted to be associated with the outsider. That's also why teams *did* work. When everyone had the same goal and trusted each other to look out for one another. Marty steeled themself for the disappointment and reminded themself of what their father always said.

You just need to find your team, Marty.

They just needed to find their team. That would happen. Sometimes, though, it was hard waiting.

"I'm good," Ford said.

Shannon snorted and turned her back. "Yeah, looks like it."

"How do you know her?" Marty asked quietly.

"We were in the same prep school until last year. Then Shannon transferred," Ford said quietly.

"Oh, so you've been friends for a while."

Ford gave her a look. "No, not exactly." She shook her head, making a disgusted noise. "Actually, not at all. But when she showed up here, at least we had something in common."

"I don't know about that," Marty said softly.

Ford glanced over at Shannon and Derek. "Yeah, me neither."

❖

From Lily's vantage point at ground level, the rock wall seemed dauntingly high. And despite Chase's assurance that there were plenty of hand and foot holds, Lily was having a hard time imagining herself climbing it. Chase, on the other hand, scaled it with the speed and agility of a monkey clambering up a tree. Watching her climb was like watching an artist bring an image to life with a few magical strokes of a brush. Clearly she was an artist, and just this small exhibition of her skill underscored how much she had lost, and how very much she must miss it. Lily watched her guide the kids up the wall, calling encouragement and instruction. She was good at teaching, despite her frequent protests.

"You don't have to go up, you know," a low voice said from just behind her shoulder.

Lily smiled and turned to Natalie. "What, and be the only weenie in the whole group?"

Natalie laughed and shaded her eyes with a hand to her forehead. "I see they managed to get all of them up there this year. Usually there is at least one who freezes halfway up."

"Oh, that must be traumatic." Lily had already imagined herself in that position. Maybe weenie wasn't such a bad designation after all.

"Sometimes," Natalie said with a philosophical tone, "but it makes for an excellent lesson on rope rescue."

Lily narrowed her eyes. "That's just mean."

Natalie smiled. "There's really nothing to worry about. Chase wouldn't bring them up the wall if they weren't ready, and if it wasn't perfectly safe. But it can be pretty scary the first time. So…"

"Check my gear, Lieutenant. I'm going up."

"Not trying to impress anyone, are you?" Natalie laughed.

Lily drew herself up in mock affront. "Most certainly not."

"Then enjoy yourself—it's as fun as it looks."

"That's what I'm afraid of," Lily muttered.

Natalie double-checked her harness and secured the top rope to Lily's harness herself. "You're ready. Have you plotted out your course?"

"As a matter fact, I have. The easiest way up." At least she hoped. With a deep breath, she strode to the wall, worked her foot into the first toehold, and reached for the closest depression where she could get a grip. Like so many things she'd had to do in her life that seemed challenging, even at times undoable, she put one foot—and this time, one hand as well—in front of the other and worked her way up. The muscles in her back began to protest by the time she'd made it a third of the way up. She had a second or two to wonder how Chase's back was holding up before she refocused on what she needed to do not to end up back at the bottom. When she'd watched from the ground, she'd imagined it would take forever to gain the crest, but in just a matter of a minute, or so it seemed, an arm came into view and she grasped the tanned, muscular forearm the way she'd seen everyone else do. She tilted her head enough to look up.

Chase smiled down at her. "I've got you."

Lily found a burst of energy and propelled herself up and over onto solid ground. When she got to her feet, Chase was very close and their eyes met. "I know. I knew you'd be there."

"You did great." Chase's eyes gleamed. "Ready for a little bouldering?"

Lily tilted her chin. "Can't wait."

Laughing, Chase turned away to gather the group.

Bouldering, as it turned out, bore some similarities but, instead of a completely vertical ascent, was more like climbing stairs. Very large stairs that sometimes required one to use hands and feet simultaneously. At last, when everyone was suitably exhausted, Chase had pity on them and led them up an easier trail to the summit.

Lily stood on an outcropping of rock and tried to absorb the view. Chase joined her after all the campers reached the summit.

"I understand now why people climb. At least one of the reasons," she said to Chase.

"Why do you think?" Chase asked.

Lily swept a hand toward the mountain range off to their left, and the valley and lake below them. She couldn't even see the camp, shrouded by the forest between them. "All of that. I don't know where to look first." She turned to Chase. "What's your favorite part?"

"Where the lake disappears into the mountains over there," Chase said, quietly pointing. "I've always thought it sort of mystical, how the two join."

"That's very romantic," Lily murmured. "But then, so are you."

Chase smiled a little ruefully. "I can't say anyone else has ever said that before."

"Then they weren't paying attention," Lily said.

"No, but you do."

"I can't help myself." Lily tucked her lower lip between her teeth. Most of the campers were too busy with their second round of trail mix and nutrient drinks to pay attention to them, but conversations like this could only go one place, especially feeling what she felt just looking at Chase. "Will you have much work waiting for you when we get down the mountain?"

"I'll have to answer whatever calls are waiting. So hard to tell. Why?"

"I was thinking we could go for a swim later."

Chase's eyes sparked. "I'll come find you."

Lily smiled. "Good."

"Soon as I can," Chase said.

The hike down was much easier than the climb up, and Lily was secretly glad. She'd thought she was in reasonable shape just from the hours she'd spent on her feet in the ER, but she hadn't done any concentrated exercise in longer than she wanted to admit. The feeling of straining her muscles, of challenging her body, was a welcome reawakening, but she'd rather not do it all at once.

She took a long hot shower to ease some of the stiffness in her shoulders and legs, enjoying a few visual memories of Chase's shirt clinging to her shoulders and back, and the way her climbing pants pulled tight against her thighs. Probably not the best thing to be doing when she really ought to be heading down for the day's windup and the briefing for tomorrow's activities. She stepped out of the bath and was just wrapping a towel around her torso when a sharp knock sounded on the door.

Chase called, "Lily!"

Lily hurried to the door and pulled it open. "Chase? What is it?"

Chase's gaze swept over her. "A 9-1-1 call from a tourist just came in. There's a hiker down on the West Mountain switchback trail. A couple of med students are doing CPR out there. We're the closest."

Lily pulled on shorts and a T-shirt and stepped into her hiking boots. "We'll need a defibrillator and meds."

"I've got a med box. And a portable defibrillator."

Lily raced down the stairs after Chase. A few heads turned as they ran through the great room and out the door, and sprinted to the Jeep. Within thirty seconds of the time Chase had come to her door, Lily was hanging on to the grab bar as the Jeep hurtled down the mountain.

CHAPTER FOURTEEN

W here are we going?" Lily asked as the trail they'd been bouncing along disappeared into a rock-strewn gully and Chase veered off into the adjacent woodlands. The night abruptly darkened as tall pines closed in overhead, obscuring all but a few patches of sky. The headlights skittered off tree trunks and boulders in a dizzying parade of swiftly changing shapes. If Lily hadn't ridden with Chase before, she might have been nervous about their speed over the wild terrain—make that just short of terrified—but she didn't have the luxury of fear. She trusted Chase, and if anything, she wanted her to go faster. She wasn't used to being the one en route to a trauma, when seconds might matter. The medics brought the injured to her by ambulance or helicopter, most already stabilized in the field and often with a preliminary diagnosis. She had time to plan a course of action, to ready herself and her team, so the instant the patient arrived they could institute treatment.

Tonight she was literally in the dark—worse, she was out of her element. She'd run more codes in the ER halls and even the parking lot outside the hospital in the last two years than she would ever likely run again, but even then she'd had all the equipment, all the meds, and all the personnel she'd needed. All they had now was whatever Chase had in the Jeep—and why hadn't she ever thought to ask what that might be before now—and a portable defibrillator she hoped to heaven had a fully charged battery. Her chest tightened. She hadn't been this uncertain since her residency days, at least not until the pandemic descended without warning. But this was not then. This was Chase's world, not hers.

As soon as the realization struck her, Lily's apprehension dissolved. She wasn't the expert here, Chase was. In the ER she was the team leader—tonight, in the wilderness, she was the assistant.

"We can't get up the hiking trail in this," Chase replied, both hands on the wheel and her eyes straight ahead. "Too narrow, and there's a rope bridge at one point—can only traverse that on foot. But we can get close to the reported location off-road."

The route they took gave a whole new meaning to the term *off-road*. As far as Lily could tell, they were simply forging their way through completely virgin forest by some innate compass in Chase's head. All around them, the wilderness lay untouched with absolutely no evidence of anything that resembled a trail.

"How far away are we? If they're doing CPR, we don't have much time."

"We're close," Chase said.

"When we get there," Lily said, "just tell me what to do."

"You assess the patient—I'll break out the gear. Just think of it like you're in the ER, Lily."

As if anything about this was remotely familiar.

Lily decided to stop thinking at all. She'd handled every kind of emergency there was at some point in her career. She'd just have to adapt. Less than a minute later, Chase halted the Jeep on the crest of a rocky ledge and shut off the engine. The canopy of trees thinned, and Lily picked out what must be the trail, just wide enough for two people in some places, wending up the mountainside.

"Come on," Chase said. "We'll have to get up to the trailhead on foot. Watch your step—don't break an ankle."

"I'll be fine. Don't worry about me." Lily jumped out, careful of her footing on the rocky track, and determined never to wear anything except hiking boots again. Possibly even in New York City. Chase yanked open the rear door of the Jeep, reached in, and pulled out a red backpack nearly as tall as Lily and shrugged it on with practiced efficiency. She handed Lily a red tackle box with a white cross on its side. "Meds and the defibrillator. Can you handle it?"

"Yes," Lily said before she'd even gripped the handle. No matter how heavy it might be, she had no choice. "I'm good. Let's go."

Chase checked her red DEC vest with multiple pockets, donned a half helmet with a headlamp that she switched on, and started off. Lily followed Chase and the narrow beam of light as closely as she could, not bothering to search for any sign of the trail but concentrating on putting each foot down on stable ground. Somehow, Chase managed to pick her way with the ease of a mountain goat through clumps of boulders and densely packed trees, until as if by some miracle, the trail widened and the terrain became more level.

"This way, just another quick climb."

"Go, go," Lily said. "I'll be right behind you."

Chase, of course, could sprint up the trail. Lily gave a fair showing, and by the time she reached the small circle of people standing around a young man and woman kneeling over a prone figure in khaki pants, boots, and a green T-shirt, Chase had the backpack open and was pulling out emergency supplies. She set a battery-powered lamp on the ground that added to the eeriness of the scene by illuminating the key figures in harsh white light while the surrounding forest receded into ominous gloom.

Taking a deep breath to steady her mind, Lily knelt next to a dark-haired young man who looked to be in his midtwenties who was doing chest compressions. Sweat streaked his face, leaving thin dusty rivulets down his cheeks. A woman about his age and half his size kept the unresponsive man's airway open with her fingers supporting his flaccid lower jaw. From the sheen of sweat on her face, the two of them had probably been alternating compressions, a back-breaking and exhausting physical undertaking.

"I'm a doctor," Lily said, thumbing open the latches on the med box. At a quick glance, the male patient appeared to be in early middle age—somewhere around forty—and fit looking. She saw no immediate signs of trauma to suggest he had fallen from any great height. All four extremities lay in a natural position with no evidence of blood loss on his person or the surrounding ground. His eyes were closed, his skin tinged a faint blue gray. She pressed her fingers to his neck and felt a faint pulse of blood each time the student compressed his chest. "What's the situation here?"

"We were a hundred yards up the trail," the young woman said, her voice tight but steady, "when we heard a man shout for help. We got here within twenty seconds, probably, and this gentleman was on the ground. He did not appear to be breathing, did not respond to commands, and we could not find a pulse. We immediately began CPR."

"Good. Did anyone with him know anything about his medical status?"

"I-I don't know. We didn't—I didn't ask."

Lily called, "Chase, can you get the leads on?"

"Right here." Chase leaned down, pulled a big pair of bandage scissors off her belt, and slit the man's T-shirt down the middle. As she positioned the EKG leads and defibrillator pads, she said, "He was hiking alone, apparently. The guy who yelled for help just told me he came around the bend and saw this guy on the ground."

Lily grimaced. "He didn't see him fall?"

"No."

"So we don't know how long he's been down." She looked at Chase, whose grim expression matched what she was feeling. "Anything?"

Chase looked at the EKG readout and shook her head. "Flatline."

Lily extracted the defibrillator paddles, slapped the moistened pads over his right chest and lower left side, and said, "Charge to 150."

"Ready," Chase said.

"Clear." Everyone leaned away, and Lily triggered the charge. The body gave a faint tremor. "Rhythm?"

"Nothing," Chase said.

"Charge to 300," Lily said again.

"Go," Chase said.

"Clear." Lily shocked him a second time.

"Flatline," Chase said.

"Intracardiac epi?" Lily glanced over her shoulder at Chase.

"I'll get it." Chase pulled the ampule, attached the five-inch needle, and handed it to her.

Lily felt for the landmarks. The patient was fit, and she easily found the lower edge of the sternum, angled the needle at forty-five degrees toward his left shoulder, and inserted it beneath the breastbone. She felt the faint resistance of the cardiac muscle, and then she was inside the ventricular chamber and pushed the epi directly into the heart.

"Flatline," Chase said. As Lily had worked, Chase had managed to get an intravenous line into an arm vein.

"Push bicarb," Lily said.

"Running," Chase said. "Atropine?"

Lily ignored the pressing sense of impending defeat. They would try everything, per protocol, and then they would try some more. They were this man's only chance. His last chance. "Yes, and let's shock him again."

"Ready."

"Clear," Lily said and discharged the paddles again.

"Nothing."

Lily looked at Chase, who nodded. They ran through everything they had again, using every med to stimulate the heart, reduce the strain on the failing organ, and support blood flow to the brain. The heart failed to respond.

Finally Lily asked. "How long has he been down?"

The male student, his voice quivering, said, "Uh, almost twenty minutes since we got here."

"And an unknown time before that." Lily leaned back. She did not look at Chase. "Stop compressions. Time of death, 7:42 p.m."

Chase stood and addressed the small circle of onlookers who had slowly congregated as they'd come down the trail upon the scene. "I'm going to need everyone to back away now."

Everyone did, and she thumbed her radio. "This is Fielder. We need a recovery team with a stretcher. Alert the local authorities and the ME."

Natalie's voice came back over the radio. "Baxter and Rodrigues are already en route. ETA ten minutes."

"Roger that."

"What now?" Lily murmured to Chase.

"It's now an undetermined death, and we have to investigate it that way. I'll get the interviews with this group started. Someone may have seen him earlier. We'll try to recreate what happened if we can. It would help if you talked to the two med students."

"I'll record it," Lily said, lifting her phone. "Will that work?"

"Perfect. Thanks." Chase paused. "This might take a while. If you want to go down with the retrieval team, you can catch a ri—"

Lily smiled for a fraction of a second. "I'm staying if you're staying."

Lily pulled the two students aside, asked their names, and asked if they consented to her recording their recollection of the event. They did.

"Josh Petrie," the young man said. "I'm a fourth year at Albany Med. I will be, I mean, in September."

"Ada Marinda," the second student said. "Me too."

"Can one of you go over everything you saw and did one more time?"

Josh looked at Ada, who nodded. Their story was still the same—no one was sure how long the man had been lying there before the second hiker came upon him. Both agreed that when they found him, he showed no signs of life.

"You did all that could be done," Lily said when they had finished.

Ada repeated what they'd both already said. "We got here as quickly as we could. We didn't wait more than twenty seconds before starting CPR, and we never let up."

Lily nodded. "I'm certain of it. We won't know what happened until there's a postmortem, but I suspect it was a massive coronary. There was probably no chance of resuscitating him even if you'd been standing beside him when he occluded."

"Will someone call us when the post is done?" Josh asked quietly.

"I will. One of you put your number into my phone. I'll text you." She handed it to Ada to enter the information just as two rangers and a sheriff's deputy arrived with a stretcher. While the deputy talked to Chase, the two rangers covered the deceased with a blanket, carefully transferred him to the stretcher, and strapped him in for the trip down the mountain.

"I've got the interviews here," Chase said to the female ranger, a young blonde about Chase's age who lingered a moment to say something to Chase in a low murmur.

Lily looked away.

"Thanks for the assist," the blonde said, engaging the lift on the portable stretcher. She and her male partner each took a side to guide it on the trek down the trail to where they'd left their vehicle. The deputy followed them a minute later.

"Do you two need a ride?" Lily asked the two students. "We're not too far from here—it would be crowded, but we can get you down the mountain."

"I'd rather walk," Josh said.

Ada nodded. "Me too."

"Thank you for everything that you did," Lily said.

The two of them still looked uncertain and discouraged, but she knew that would pass. She understood their feelings. Losing a patient never got easier.

"They okay?" Chase asked quietly.

"They will be." Lily sighed. "As well as they can be. This is probably their first time losing someone."

"How about you?" Chase asked.

"Not my first time," Lily murmured, "and it still makes me sad and damn angry."

Chase cupped the back of Lily's neck. Her grip was firm and warm, comforting in its certainty. "It's a rough ride back to the camp in the dark. There's a faster route down but it takes us a bit out of the way." She shrugged, her fingers lightly stroking Lily's neck. "Goes pretty close to my place. It makes sense to stay there, if you don't mind plain accommodations."

Lily looked around. All the onlookers had left. They were alone with only Chase's flashlight to push back the dark. That, and the warmth of Chase's palm against her skin.

"I like plain just fine. As long as there's plain coffee involved in the morning."

Laughing, Chase said, "That's a promise."

Lily looped her fingers around Chase's belt at the base of her spine. "Then I accept."

❖

"Hey," Chase murmured softly. "Lily. We're here."

Lily came awake with a start and shifted to face her. "Oh, I can't believe I fell asleep. I'm so sorry."

"You don't need to apologize," Chase said. "If you could sleep on that ride, you needed it."

Lily rubbed her face. "I don't think I've ever done that before. Just checked out."

"Maybe because there was always someone else waiting for you to take care of them."

"It wasn't always like that," Lily said, half to herself. "I wish I could remember that."

"Give yourself some time, Lily. And maybe for tonight, just let it all go."

Lily nodded. "I'll try."

"Good." Chase came around the side of the Jeep and opened Lily's door. "Sorry there's no outside lights here. Too much animal activity. If I had motion sensor lights, they'd be going on and off all night."

She held out her hand. Lily grasped it and stepped down from the Jeep, pausing when she reached the ground. She didn't take her hand away, and Chase held on. Nothing could have felt more natural. The moon was high and bright, and only a few clouds streaked the otherwise clear sky. Lily's face was illuminated in the nearly bright-as-day silvery glow, and Chase's chest tightened with unfamiliar longing that eclipsed even desire. Lily was so beautiful, Chase had a hard time believing the moment was real.

Lily slowly turned and took in her surroundings. Chase tried to imagine it as Lily saw it: a small clearing in the otherwise unbroken forest, her sprawling single-story cabin, the chimney at one end and the small rectangle of garden surrounded by deer fence out behind the other. A porch just big enough for her to sit on with her coffee at dawn, along with an extra chair for visitors she never had.

Chase cleared her throat. "I told you simple—I guess I forgot to say rustic and secluded."

Lily laughed. "I think both of those terms are a slight understatement. Honestly, is there anything anywhere around us at all?"

Chase's gut tightened, this time for a different reason. What had she expected? Of course this place—hell, probably even *her* now that Lily could see what her life looked like—would seem foreign and unappealing to Lily. "Not for a good twenty-five miles to the nearest road. There's plenty of wildlife out there—deer, of course, and bear, the occasional moose. All the small animals, and there's been a few mountain lion sightings, but mostly the cats are bobcats. Sorry, but it's perfectly safe here."

Lily tilted her head and regarded her quizzically. "I wasn't worried about safety. I was just marveling at how amazing it is to be standing in a place like this."

"Oh," Chase said, feeling as wrong-footed as she probably sounded.

"Sometimes in the city," Lily went on as if she hadn't noticed, her voice pensive, as if she was drifting in the memory, "I'd look around me and at all the buildings soaring so high above me, filled with thousands of people, and the streets packed with thousands more, and feel completely alone. My *smallness* was unsettling and disorienting." She turned slightly to Chase, still holding her hand. "This is nothing like that. Out here, I don't feel apart from all the life around me."

Chase carefully clasped Lily's waist and kissed her, as softly as she could manage and far more briefly than she wanted. "I had to do that. You're not only beautiful, Lily, but you see what I love out here, and that makes me ache."

Lily drew in a sharp breath and gently touched Chase's cheek. "You, Chase, are the most beautiful thing that I see."

Chase muttered a half-hearted curse. "I really didn't bring you here to seduce you, but damn, I want to."

Lily's brow rose. "Oh?"

"I brought you here to get some sleep. That was tough, up there on the mountain, more for you, I imagine, than me."

"Why?" Lily said. "Why me more than you?"

"I wanted that guy to live every bit as much as you did, I think," Chase said. "I want all of the ones we find to live."

"But?" Lily prodded.

"But…it's not personal for me."

"And it is for me," Lily said distantly. "Or it's all *become* personal, and maybe that's part of the problem. Somewhere in the past few years, I've lost my professional shields. And that's what's made it so hard for me to do my job."

"Lily," Chase murmured. "Come inside. For tonight at least, forgive yourself."

"Is that what you think I need to do?" Lily asked curiously, her tone still slightly distant, as if her mind was working on some other problem, somewhere else.

"I think you must've done every single thing that could be done, but there was much that couldn't be." She tugged on Lily's hand, and Lily followed her across the clearing, up onto the porch, and inside.

"This summer you're supposed to be getting away from all of that, and when you do, you'll see it more clearly."

Lily drew in an audible breath. "Yes. I didn't consciously think of it that way, but this summer is a chance to find my perspective again."

"So doing something totally different is just what you need."

Lily laughed. "I think so far I'm succeeding in that."

"Hold on for a second." Chase found the propane lantern on the small table next to the door and turned it on.

Lily laughed, and the lightness that had returned to her voice made Chase's heart swell. "No electricity?"

"There's a generator out back for when I need power. The freezer is solar powered. Most everything I actually need in the way of food is canned or dry goods. Plus fresh, in season."

"I don't suppose any of those necessities include a bottle of wine?"

"As a matter fact, they do. I think the only thing I've got is red, though."

"Red would be perfect." Lily glanced past Chase's shoulder to take in the rest of the cabin—a large main room with a stone fireplace at one end taking up most of the wall, a neat stack of cut lumber piled beside it, and a sofa facing it. A low pine table sat in front of that, and off to the left, a galley kitchen with a few cabinets above a sink and two-burner stove, counters to either side, and a plain round wooden table with two chairs in front of a window. On the far side facing the door they'd come through, an open door to a bedroom and another to the bath.

In the flickering light of the propane lantern, she couldn't make out the details, but a number of landscape paintings hung on the walls.

Chase must've followed her gaze. "My mother painted. Those are hers."

"I can't wait to see them in the daylight," Lily said.

"Make yourself comfortable on the sofa. I'll get the wine. I've also got some crackers and a vacuum-packed container of cheese. As I recall, now that I think of it, we didn't have any dinner."

"I'm not actually hungry, but the food is probably a good idea with the wine, if you don't want me seducing *you* after a glass or so."

Chase shot her a look. "I don't think you'd hear me complaining, but I'd rather you not regret it in the morning."

While Chase opened cabinets, Lily settled on the sofa and leaned her head back, willing the tension and the memory of what had happened up on the mountain to fade a little. When Chase sat down beside her and handed her a glass of wine, she sipped it and sighed. "I'm so glad we came here. Thank you."

"You're the only visitor I've ever had, other than Sarah," Chase said. "My hospitality skills might be a little rusty."

Lily took the cracker with the cheese spread on it that Chase offered and took a bite. She didn't think she'd ever tasted anything quite as delicious. "Believe me, all your skills are superb."

Chase's hand rested on the back of the sofa, her fingertips very lightly touching the top of Lily's shoulder.

"I know this place must seem strange to you."

"I can see why you'd think that, but it doesn't. Not knowing you. It seems perfect."

"Knowing me?" Chase asked.

Lily waved a hand to take in the cabin. "Efficient, sturdy, solid, and practical—in a wild way, beautiful."

Chase's expression went from amused to intense in a heartbeat. "If we're going to keep this civilized," Chase said, "you might want to ease up on the compliments." Her words were rough with desire.

Lily smiled over the top of her wineglass. "Civilized. I might have to give some thought to what *un*civilized might look like." She laughed when Chase groaned and finished her wine. "Do you have anything resembling a shower here?"

"I do. At the moment, however, it would be pretty chilly. In the morning with the generator running, I can get you lukewarm."

"Then in the morning, I'd like a shower and that coffee you promised." Lily rose and poured another half-glass of wine. "Right now I need some sleep."

"Take the bedroom, Lily," Chase said. "I'll sleep out here on the sofa."

"You know what?" Lily said. "I'm going to take you up on it, because otherwise there'd be an argument over it, and you'd still end up sleeping out here."

"I'm not sure I like how well you know me," Chase said with a wry smile.

"Really?" Lily said softly. "I'm sorry, then, because I really want to know you a whole lot better before the summer is over."

Chase swallowed, need so tight in her throat the words wouldn't come.

Lily rose and set her wineglass on the table. "See you in the morning."

CHAPTER FIFTEEN

Lily was certain she wouldn't sleep. Her mental review of every step she'd taken up on the mountain—every physical sign she'd assessed, every med she'd administered, every decision she'd made—was only the beginning. She'd search for what she had failed to do, even knowing far too well that sometimes there was nothing she could do. That postmortem would have kept her awake even if the strangeness of her surroundings and the faint sound of Chase's footsteps in the other room weren't enough to drive any remnant of fatigue away. Still, she was glad she'd come here and not gone back to the lodge, where she would be lying in a bed nearly as strange as this one, without the stirring of excitement of being near Chase. Smiling at that thought, surprised as always that a near-constant state of arousal could also be so delicious, she closed her eyes. Even the semblance of rest would be better than none.

When she opened them again, her unerring internal clock told her she'd slept till an hour before dawn. Close to four.

She rolled over to check her phone out of habit: 3:57.

She might be in a world very different than her own, but her body still worked the same. So did she. Somewhere in the hours she'd been asleep, her mind had settled the issue of what had gone on the night before. She'd told the students the truth—they'd all done everything they could.

The cabin was not completely silent. Things that she hoped were acorns or stout twigs clattered on the roof. Those sounds certainly weren't the skittering of little feet. She eyed the window as a distant woof that probably didn't emanate from a Labrador sounded quite clearly. And close. The top of the window was down six inches, letting a breeze in, but hopefully nothing more. The screen might keep mosquitoes out but wouldn't provide much of a barrier to anything else. Her heart raced for a second and then settled. She'd had almost a month to get used to the night sounds in the mountains, and to appreciate that the wildlife had no more interest in running into her than she did with them. This land, which a few weeks ago she'd considered completely foreign, had become familiar in so many ways, and she was no longer a stranger in a strange land.

Lily turned on her side and peered through the open bedroom door into the main room of the cabin to where Chase slept twenty feet away. Moonlight sent shadows dancing around the sofa. She'd been close enough to Chase to kiss her—more than once—and for far longer than was wise, but this moment struck her as more intimate than when they'd touched. They were alone—not just far away from the lodge and Sarah and four dozen restlessly simmering teens, but secluded in the untouched wilderness where the outside world with all its misery and guilt could not encroach.

Right here, right now, Lily was completely free. And Chase, with the excitement she roused and the ecstasy she promised, slept only steps away. Waiting for Lily to take those steps.

Lily sat up and strained to catch some sound from the other room. She smiled to herself. Chase didn't snore. Or maybe the silence meant something else. Maybe Chase was as awake as she was. Maybe Chase was thinking of moonlight walks and midnight swims and kisses that promised endless pleasure. Lily shifted restlessly. Imagining Chase lying in the semidarkness, thinking of her, perhaps listening for her as she listened for Chase, perhaps aching as she ached, birthed a heavy longing deep within her.

Her heart skipped a beat. Her throat tightened even as she went liquid inside. If she walked out into the other room right now, Chase would welcome her. Oh, Chase's kiss the evening before had been delicate and careful. Not chaste. Never that, not when Chase touched her. But restrained. Chase had held back, had ended the kiss, even as her eyes had smoldered. Knowing that Chase was excited by her, that Chase *wanted* her, aroused her more than any of the sex she'd had in the past. She'd never been wanted the way Chase wanted her.

Never *wanted* a woman to desire her the way Chase desired her. With undisguised ferocity. Seeing that fierce craving in Chase's eyes and feeling the way Chase's body trembled when they touched ignited something within her. A hunger, a yearning, beyond anything she'd ever known. Imagining Chase's kiss, aching to make Chase shudder beneath her hands, caused a pulse to beat heavy and thick between Lily's thighs. Insistent, persistent, urgent. Clamoring for her to touch. To be touched.

To be filled.

Lily swung her legs out of bed, reached automatically for her shorts, and then stopped. She'd gone to bed in panties and a T-shirt. The breeze coming through the window was faintly cool, but the cabin itself still held the heat of the day. Barefoot, and only in what she'd worn to sleep in, she made her way into the other room by moonlight and over to the sofa without running into anything. Chase lay on her side in a light ribbed tank with a pale sheet draped over her hips and legs. Her face in repose lost none of its strength, despite the softness that cloaked the bold planes of her jaw. A shimmering band of bare skin lay exposed along her lower abdomen, and Lily's stomach clenched. She closed her hands against the seething need to reach out and stroke the sensual perfection of her.

Kneeling, she whispered, "Chase?"

"Couldn't sleep?" Chase murmured, her gaze meeting Lily's.

The instantaneous connection, raw and primal, slammed through Lily with the force of an avalanche cascading over everything in its path. She shivered, drawn into a place beyond thought, adrift in sensation.

"I did sleep." Lily struggled, and failed, to control the need in her voice. "Then I woke up and started thinking about you."

"Oh?"

Chase watched Lily, a half smile and her satisfied silence only making her all the more desirable.

"Yes," Lily said, pushing the covers down with one hand to expose Chase's bare thighs. Chase, like her, had gone to sleep in just the tank and a pair of bikini briefs. She left her hand on Chase's thigh. "I started thinking about kisses, and the way your body feels when I touch you, and the way mine feels when you touch me."

"Are you going to tell me about it?" Chase asked hoarsely.

"No." The taut need in Chase's voice drove Lily forward, instinct her only guide. She rose above Chase and pressed both hands to her shoulders until Chase turned fully onto her back.

Lily put a knee on the sofa and slid the other across Chase's hips, straddling her. "I thought I'd show you instead."

Chase groaned, grasped her waist, and pulled her down into a bruising kiss. Chase's mouth was hot and hard and demanding, and Lily fell into it. She stretched out along the length of Chase's body, sliding her thigh between Chase's. She braced herself on her elbows on either side of Chase's shoulders, her breasts against Chase's, their bodies touching everywhere.

Chase lifted the back of Lily's T-shirt and stroked her back, down to her hips, and beneath her panties. Her palm, hot and firm, clasped her rear possessively.

Desire curled between Lily's thighs, and she pressed against Chase's leg.

Chase tugged at Lily's tee. "Can we take this off?"

"Yes," Lily gasped, leaning back to pull the shirt over her head. Then she pushed at Chase's underwear. "These too."

Chase bridged her back and pushed them down as Lily rose to her knees and pulled hers off, lifting one leg and then the other to strip them down her calves and drop them on the floor. Then they were naked together, and everywhere they touched was fire. Lily played her fingers over the taut muscles and smooth skin of Chase's middle until she reached her breasts. Caressing her, molding her breast in one hand, she kissed Chase's jaw and the side of her neck, found her mouth again. Chase's hands roamed over her as if she couldn't touch her enough, sliding down her back, clasping her hips and drawing Lily hard against her, forcing Lily to rock against her thigh until every stroke was blissful agony.

Lily threw her head back and swallowed a cry as the pressure turned to a rush of electrifying pleasure. "Chase…"

"Don't stop, Lily," Chase said, an order and a plea. "Don't stop."

Lily reached out, blind with the surge of release, and Chase's hand gripped her. Her hips rolled of their own accord, hard sharp thrusts until she came with a jolt, her body bucking with each titanic contraction. Cries ripped from her throat as her neck arched and her eyes lost focus.

Chase sat up, her arms around Lily's waist and her mouth to Lily's throat, holding her as she shuddered.

"You're so fucking beautiful," Chase gasped. "More beautiful than anything I've ever seen."

Lily draped her arms around Chase's shoulders and rested her forehead against Chase's, panting for breath. "God, I don't know where that came from."

Chase chuckled. "I think you do. At least I hope so."

Lily laughed shakily. "All right. Yes. You're fantastic."

"I haven't even gotten started." Chase lowered her head and brushed a kiss across Lily's nipple.

Lily tightened inside again but managed to keep the quaver from her voice. "Well, you'll have to be patient."

Chase snorted. "Not likely."

The predawn sky had begun to lighten, and Lily read the stubborn set of Chase's features. She smiled. Chase liked to be in charge. Not that she would mind that, but right now she had something else she wanted. Very much. Lily finally gathered her strength and pushed Chase back down against the sofa, holding her there with a palm against her chest. "Be still."

Chase could have easily ignored her command, but she obediently relented. Her body beneath Lily quivered with the effort, and Lily instantly wanted to come again. She bit her lip and took a deep breath. "I'm not done with you."

"Please." Chase gritted her teeth. "Lily. Come on."

"Not yet," Lily said sweetly and, before Chase could protest or stop her, slid to her knees by the side of the sofa and pushed Chase's knee up. "Now," Lily murmured as she leaned down to kiss her between her thighs, "I'm going to have you."

"Ah, fuck, Lily." Chase's fingers came into her hair, gently, and simply held her head, not pressing her to go anywhere or do anything. The tender sense of claiming nearly burst Lily's heart.

"You can have whatever you want, Lily," Chase whispered.

Lily kissed her again, brushing her lips feather light across her clit until Chase shuddered.

"There," Lily murmured. "That's what I want."

"Please," Chase said. "Take anything you want."

And Lily did.

❖

When Lily woke again, she was tangled around Chase on the sofa. They'd somehow managed to fall asleep on the narrow cushions, legs entwined and arms around each other. Her head was tucked beneath Chase's chin, and she could feel Chase's heart beat under her cheek.

"Chase?"

"Mmm?" Chase brushed a kiss into her hair.

"I think I'm supposed to be at the clinic this morning."

"Uh-huh."

"I better call Sarah. Can you radio her?"

"I checked in last night with both Natalie and Sarah before I went to sleep."

Lily raised her head and propped it on her bent elbow. "I didn't hear you."

"You went right to sleep."

"No, I didn't. I was lying awake for a long time thinking about... things."

"You must snore when you think, then," Chase said.

Lily punched her in the arm. "I do not snore. I've had it from very good sources that I do not snore."

"Uh-huh." Chase grinned at her. "All the same, Sarah knows you'll be late this morning, and if there's anything urgent, she'll let us know right away."

"Oh God," Lily said. "Sarah knows I'm here with you."

Chase pushed herself up until her back was supported against the arm of the sofa and Lily was cradled against her chest. "That's a problem for you?"

"No, not in theory. I just prefer my private life to be private."

"Sorry, but technically we were both on duty last night, and I needed to check in."

"Of course, and I understand. It's fine."

"It doesn't sound fine. Are you having second thoughts?"

"About that," Lily said, "I don't do things that I'm going to regret the next day. This was not an accident or the result of some lack of control. I intended to sleep with you last night."

"Is there some reason you didn't tell me beforehand?"

"I intended it when I came out here with you. I didn't intend it earlier."

"Okay." Chase kissed her. "So we're good."

As long as what you said still goes—no obligations or expectations. Lily didn't insult Chase with the words—she trusted Chase to be honest with herself as well as Lily. And she needed to do the same. No obligations, no expectations, no regrets.

"We're good. Last night was amazing."

Chase deftly rolled Lily over and settled on top of her. Her weight was unexpected and unexpectedly arousing. Lily opened her legs for Chase to settle between them.

"It's still really early," Chase said.

"Then let's not hurry."

Chapter Sixteen

H ow's the coffee?" Chase asked.
        Lily looked over her shoulder, appreciating the view for the thirtieth time that morning. Chase wore the ribbed white tank she'd slept in and a pair of midthigh khaki shorts, which Lily knew had nothing underneath. With her tousled hair, her long muscled limbs, and the ever-present rakish grin, Chase looked better than any fantasy Lily'd ever had. Then again, she hadn't even been able to imagine anything close to this. She kept that to herself. Chase didn't need to know she was exploring uncharted territory, especially since she was looking forward to leaving that reality behind for as long as this fantasy lasted. She was going to grab on to this wild adventure with both hands.

Lily lifted her coffee cup in salute. "This is amazing. Funny, somehow instead of a French press I imagined you with one of those old-fashioned tin percolators with the glass thingy on top where the coffee shot up when it came to a boil. This is much better."

Chase laughed. "I'm a forest ranger, not a cowboy. And it's still the twenty-first century, even out here."

"Well, this is my definition of decadence." Lily gestured to her bare legs propped up on the coffee table. She hadn't bothered to do more than pull on her T-shirt and the panties she'd retrieved from the floor where she'd tossed them away in abandon a few hours before. If she cataloged her firsts since she met Chase, she'd have a very long list. Kissing a woman she barely knew—the younger sister of her best friend at that—and waking said woman up at four a.m. for sex being at the top.

"Be prepared to add to your list," Chase said as if reading her mind—something else she was very good at, along with the already noted kissing and exceptional sex. "The water's ready for the shower."

"Wonderful. I'm more than ready for it." Lily swallowed the last sip of her coffee, set her mug on the coffee table, and headed for the bathroom.

"Oh, it's not in there."

Lily frowned, having assumed the shower was behind the curtain she'd noticed when visiting the bathroom the night before. "Sorry?"

Chase pointed a thumb toward the back door leading outside from the kitchen. "It's this way."

"Outside."

"All except for the winter months. Then I'll divert the water inside, but the maintenance is easier this way." Chase grinned. "And the view is better."

"Of course," Lily murmured.

Chase grabbed a stack of clothes from the counter. "I pulled out a shirt and shorts that I'm pretty sure will fit you. Might be a little loose."

"Thanks," Lily said. "I doubt it will take long before the news of where I spent the night makes the rounds at the lodge, but I'd prefer not to show up waving the flag of yesterday's shirt."

"The kids have archery this morning. The counselors will have them set up and ready to head out just about the time we're getting back. You might be able to sneak in without shame."

Lily laughed. "I'm not going to worry about it. At least I'll be clean. Lead on."

Chase took her hand, a motion that was becoming more frequent and more familiar and more right every time she did it. Lily laced her fingers through Chase's and stepped out into a glorious summer morning. Despite the fact that it felt like she'd been awake and busy for hours, it was barely seven and the air hadn't acquired the early July heat that would likely be stultifying by midafternoon. The sky, its usual crystalline blue, hosted a scattering of pure white fluffy clouds. Bird songs chorused, the trees rustled, and even the breeze seemed to carry the melody.

She halted abruptly on the deck that ran along the back of the cabin and stared. What could only be the shower at the far end consisted of a five-by-five platform with a big metal reservoir above it with a chain dangling down to head height.

"That's it?" Lily said. "That's all of it?"

Chase looked from the platform back to Lily. "There's not much reason to enclose it out here."

Laughing, Lily shook her head. "No, I don't suppose you have to worry about the neighbors."

Chase pulled off her tank and pushed down her shorts with the same unconscious abandon that she stripped to go swimming. Lily took a moment to take her in against the backdrop of forest green and cerulean blue. Of course she looked perfectly a part of the wild surroundings and of course completely arousing. Lily nearly shuddered with the instant rush of desire.

Chase quirked a brow. "You'll be more comfortable if you don't have your clothes on when you shower."

"As if I'm not going to be uncomfortable in every other way," Lily muttered to herself as she pulled off her clothes.

Chase stepped up onto the platform and held out her hand. "Water supply is limited, so best we share."

"How much time do we have…with the water?" Lily asked.

"Three or four minutes, if we're efficient."

"Don't turn it on yet, then." Lily climbed onto the platform, wrapped her arms around Chase's neck, and pressed against her. Thrusting a hand into Chase's hair, she kissed her. The hunger she'd been holding back flooded through her. She tugged on Chase's lip with her teeth and swept her tongue over the spot and into her mouth, tasting a hint of coffee, fresh mountain air, and the tangy heat that was all Chase. Everywhere their skin touched, her body came alive.

Chase hissed as everything inside her tightened, the coiled spring of need that accompanied her every waking moment around Lily ratcheted another turn. She swept her hands down Lily's back and cupped her hips, returning the kiss that satisfied one need while stoking another. She could kiss her forever and never be finished. She would always want more. She tasted and teased her and drank her fill—and still ached for more.

Lily swayed against her and moaned softly, and Chase slipped one hand up to clasp her breast. When she rubbed her thumb over Lily's nipple, Lily pushed her parted thighs against Chase's leg.

"I can't believe how hot you make me," Lily gasped. "I need you to make me come right now."

"Anything." Chase tightened her grip around Lily's waist and slid her hand down Lily's stomach and between her thighs. Lily was ready for her, hot and open, and took Chase inside with a tilt of her hips and a whispered plea.

"Don't tease."

"Hold on, baby." Chase stroked her, cupping her as she moved deeper each time, until Lily pressed hard into her palm, her body quaking. With a strangled cry Lily buried her face in Chase's neck and sagged in her arms. Chase closed her eyes and struggled to memorize every single second.

"There's a lot more to this mountain air than I ever knew," Lily finally muttered against Chase's throat.

"It's a closely guarded secret." Chase was pretty sure she didn't need the mountain air, or any air at all, to sustain her as long as she could drown in Lily's kisses. When Lily tilted her face to her, Chase kissed her again and muttered a protest when Lily pulled away. Struggling to contain the need that clawed at her deep inside for just one more moment, she said, "Ready for the shower?"

"I don't want to waste water," Lily said, "and I believe," she added, pressing her palm low on Chase's belly, "we might need to wait a bit longer."

Lily found Chase's clit and stroked. Chase dropped her head back against the wall and shivered. She hadn't even realized she was right at the edge. All she'd known was Lily. "Shouldn't take long."

"Don't hurry," Lily whispered and kissed her throat.

"Too close." Chase came, an explosion that trailed off into languorous aftershocks. When she finally opened her eyes, feeling dazed, Lily was watching her with an intensity she couldn't read. "What?"

Lily kissed her. "You're glorious."

"If you say so." Before she changed her mind, Chase reached up behind her head and pulled the chain. Lily gave a shout as the water cascaded down over them. Chase took the bar of soap from the wooden ledge next to the water reservoir and glided it over Lily's chest and breasts and down her belly. Lily returned the favor, and they quickly scrubbed and rinsed their hair, managing to finish before the water ran out.

Dripping, Lily pushed the hair back out of her eyes and shook herself like a dog. She laughed. "That was wonderful."

"Which part?" Chase pulled a towel from a peg and handed it to Lily.

Lily toweled her hair, then wrapped it around her torso. "I think the shower was my favorite part."

Chase shook her head. "I'll have to work on my technique, then."

As Chase opened the kitchen door, Lily said, "Believe me, there's nothing wrong—"

The radio crackled to life. "This is District Five Supervisor Natalie Evans. Reported rockslide east face of Big Bear. Hikers trapped above the slide. Emergency services en route. All officers report time to vicinity."

Chase grabbed the radio. "Fielder. Copy that. Twenty minutes out." She turned to Lily. "I'm going to have to go."

"What is it?"

"Could be just a trail washout—but we've got people to secure first," Chase said, already hurrying toward the bedroom.

Lily's stomach lurched. How many other dangers would Chase face as part of her routine work that had never even occurred to her? "How will I…"

Chase held up a finger and spoke into the radio again. "Fielder, calling Thunder Ridge Lodge. Come in please."

"This is Thunder Ridge," Sarah's voice came back. "Over."

"I've got a callout. Can you come get Lily at the cabin?"

"Be there in thirty."

"Copy that. Thanks."

"You'll be careful," Lily said.

Chase kissed her. "Always."

Chase dressed with the same kind of speed Lily was used to when answering an emergency call at the hospital. In less than a minute she was out the door, and gone. Lily dressed in the borrowed clothes Chase had left for her, checked the cabin, and tidied up the coffee cups. The door hadn't been locked when they'd arrived, and she left it that way.

As she sat on the front steps and waited for Sarah, the kernel of worry that always settled in her stomach when Chase was out on a call returned.

❖

Sooner than Lily expected, the mechanical rumbling of an engine drawing near cut through the soft background noise of the forest. Sarah, driving the Kermit-green Jeep, emerged from the trailhead into the small clearing in front of the cabin, and Lily rose, dusted off the back of her borrowed shorts, and climbed into the passenger seat.

"Sorry to drag you all the way out here," Lily said.

Sarah three-pointed a turn and headed back down the trail before speaking. "It's fine. These things happen."

These things happen. Well, yes, they probably did, to most people, possibly, but not to her. Her night with Chase—her entire affair, and she really ought to call it that although the word made her cringe for some reason—was definitely not on the spectrum of her usual behavior. She was far too busy and far too…grounded—yes, that was a good word for it—to have a torrid one-night-stand with a hot younger woman. But she had and was contemplating doing it again as soon as possible the next morning. She'd spent the time waiting for Sarah drifting in the still-fresh sensations of sex with Chase. Viewing herself in retrospect, as she'd never imagined herself to be. Aggressive, demanding, and—to use another word she'd never dreamed of applying to herself—wanton. She smiled to herself. Surprisingly, it fit, and she didn't mind. Chase made it easy to accept what she wanted, to give and take pleasure of every kind freely. A rare gift she'd never expected and hoped she had returned with all the joy and wonder she'd experienced.

"This is a little awkward," Sarah said.

Lily really, really hoped all of that had not shown on her face. "I know. You first."

Sarah half smiled, still watching the road. "Ordinarily, I'd tease you about your activities of last night and try to get you to tell me how it was. That feels a little weird now."

Lily laughed. "You know I wouldn't tell you anything interesting anyhow. At least not much."

"You always were pretty stingy with details."

"That's because there weren't any good bits to really share," Lily said, intending to divert the conversation away from her sex life but realizing instantly that her previous encounters really *hadn't* been particularly interesting ones. She'd had what she considered good sex, satisfying for both parties, she hoped, but nothing that had expressed or spoke to what had been burning deep inside her for probably all her life. The need to connect with another person as deeply, more intimately, physically—and as a consequence, emotionally—as she had the night before with Chase. The realization was stunning and terrifying.

Her silence must've registered something of her quandary because Sarah said cautiously, speaking slowly, as if feeling her way across a quagmire that she might sink into up to her neck if she wasn't careful, "And I'm taking it that last night was different?"

Lily wanted to answer in the same careful way, choosing what she hoped was the diplomatic path with Chase's sister. "Chase is a very special woman."

Sarah erupted into laughter. "That is such BS. Of course I know that." She shot a look over to Lily, no judgment in her expression. "She's hooked you, hasn't she."

"I…" Lily searched for an answer. "I don't know. I'm not sure I would know what that felt like. And truthfully, I don't *feel* caught. If anything, I feel like Chase is giving me all the room to run she possibly can."

"Hmm." Sarah nodded. "How much do you know about fishing?"

"Sorry?" Lily said, totally at a loss. Fishing? How did they go from sex to fishing, and really, yuck.

"When you want to hook a fish and be sure you don't lose it, you give it enough line to run until it tires itself out." Sarah snapped her fingers. "Then you set the hook."

"I could have spent the rest of my life without knowing that." Lily was about to add that analogy was ridiculous, until she considered it. The theory, in a way, made perfect sense. Chase had been letting her run for weeks. Still, she was a person and not a fish. Thankfully. "I'm not running, and I'm not caught. So that destroys your theory."

"If you say so," Sarah said in a voice that said she didn't agree at all.

Lily huffed.

"I'm not going to say anything else," Sarah said, "because I'm turning over a new leaf."

"Really?"

"Uh-huh. No meddling."

"That sounds painful."

Sarah laughed again and turned up the trail to the lodge. "Surprisingly, it feels really good." She slowed to a stop in the parking area, turned off the engine, and released her seat belt to face Lily. "Seriously. I love you both, and I'd hate to see either one of you get hurt. But you're both way past your majority, and you don't need a supervisor. So if you're happy and she's happy, then I am too."

"Thank you."

"So, was it great?"

Lily felt the color climb into her face as she stepped out of the Jeep. After a second, she leaned down, met Sarah's eyes, and said, "Incredible."

Sarah gave a little hoot and came around the Jeep to join her.

"And as penance for missing sign-out last night *and* the morning briefing," Sarah said, "I'm assigning you a group for archery this morning."

"Archery?" Lily actually heard herself squeak. "I know the definition, but not much more than that. I certainly know nothing educational about it."

Sarah looped an arm around her waist as they walked. "All you have to do is make sure they don't shoot each other with arrows."

"I can do that," Lily said.

At least, she sincerely hoped she could.

❖

Marty nocked the arrow with a single fletching pointing away from the bow, sighted to the target, drew back until the bowstring was maximally taut, and released. Their arrow hit the edge of the center orange spot at the junction of the next ring out. They'd misjudged the wind and needed to correct for that. They stepped back so the next camper could move up to the shooting line to take their shot.

"You know," Ford muttered, "that right there? One of the reasons I hate you."

Marty chuckled. They were getting used to Ford's peculiar form of friendly banter. "I thought it was because I was just weird."

"Oh no," Ford said, "weirdness is not necessarily a negative. But being good at everything? That rises to the seriously not-to-be-tolerated level."

"I'm not good at everything," Marty said. "I can't cook anything that doesn't come in a foil packet, I'm really crappy at math, and I don't know how to talk to strangers." They paused. "Or anyone, really."

"You've been talking to me," Ford pointed out as the line shuffled forward, those who'd taken their shot moving to the back to rotate through again.

"Only because you started it."

"No, I didn't!" Ford said indignantly.

Marty shook their head. "You pretty much did. That night you came outside—when you were looking for Shannon."

Ford grimaced. "You mean covering her ass with Alisha?"

Marty looked away. They'd noticed Ford and Shannon weren't tight any longer, and Shannon had even laid off taunting them. "She's your friend. I get it."

"No she isn't." Ford snorted. "She just likes to have someone around who tells her everything she thinks is great. I didn't measure up."

"Because you disagreed?" Marty said.

Ford shrugged. "Because I didn't say yes to everything." She shrugged again. "You know what? It's fine. As to your list of things you're not good at, I don't see that any of those are lethal failings. Although, if you loosened up a little, you'd probably be better at the social thing."

"Loosen up?"

"Yeah. You're pretty funny and you have opinions about stuff, but nobody knows that. Put it out there more."

Marty looked away.

"What, which part of that freaked you out?"

Marty sighed. "The more visible you are, the bigger a target you make."

Ford snorted. "Okay, that's one of those things your dad taught you, right?"

Marty stared. "What're you talking about?"

"Some of the things you say make you sound like a recruiting poster." She tilted her head. "You know, you'd look pretty good on one."

"Cut it out," Marty hissed. "And what do you mean about my dad?"

"Look, he sounds like a terrific guy and a great dad, but he's a soldier, Marty. You're not. Maybe all his rules don't really apply to you."

"Maybe you've never been a target."

"Maybe you're making assumptions. You think having a father like mine doesn't draw attention from crazies?"

Marty frowned. Their dad was a hero, and not just because they loved him. But he also taught them to consider all sides of a situation before settling on a course of action. And that meant gathering intel. "What do you mean?"

"Hey, I know he's not popular with a lot of people. Fuck, I don't agree with most of what he says. And sometimes..." Ford looked around as if to check that no one was paying them any attention. "I get weirdos showing up on my social media, making gross comments mostly, but sometimes they make threats. Happens to my father in real life sometimes. Doesn't mean anything," she added quickly. "Mostly. But it's...it can be scary, and then I'm stuck with security following me everywhere."

"Oh man, that really sucks. I'm sorry."

"It's okay. I just mean, most of us get attention we don't want sometimes. I'm sorry that you do."

"I'm sorry you do too."

"You're still weird, though."

Marty laughed. "Yeah, I know. You're up."

Ford made a creditable attempt at following the steps Alisha had shown them, and she hit the target, but way outside the rings. She shook her head. "Why do I need to do this?"

"You never know when you might be stranded in the forest and have to eat squirrels," Marty said.

Ford gave them an incredibly disgusted look. "That is gross."

Marty smiled, walked to the line, nocked their arrow, made a mental correction for the wind, pulled across their chest while sighting the target, and gently released. Bull's-eye.

Better.

They walked to the back of the line, and one of the girls they recognized from cabin seven came over to them.

"You're a really good shot," the girl said. "I'm Suwallia, by the way. Do you compete?"

"Um, no." Marty hesitated, then held out their hand. "I'm Marty."

Suwallia, her dark eyes filled with humor, shook their hand. "Yeah, I know. We go to the same high school."

"We do?" Marty caught Ford, who stood behind Suwallia, rolling her eyes, and blushed. What? What had they done wrong already?

"I'm in the year behind yours."

"Oh. Okay." Marty took a breath. "That's great."

Suwallia glanced at Ford hesitantly, then back to Marty. "Listen, we have archery team tryouts right after the school year starts. You should come try out. You'd make it for sure."

"I...I'm not really much into sports."

Suwallia arched a brow. "This isn't like that. We shoot as a team, sure. But you're competing individually too. I'm team captain. You should come. Really."

"Yeah, okay. Yeah. Thanks."

"Good. I hope the rest of your summer is fun." Suwallia waved and went back to her line.

Ford chuckled. "Ha. She's cute."

Marty stared. "What?"

Ford leaned closer and lowered her voice. "Ace doesn't mean no romance, does it?"

"I guess sometimes it does, but I...I don't know about me. For sure."

"So there you go. Be sure you make it to the team tryouts." Ford laughed again, and Marty shot a glance over to the adjacent line as everyone jostled forward. Suwallia turned, saw them, and smiled.

Maybe you just haven't found your team yet, Marty.

Their dad was a soldier, and maybe all his rules didn't apply to them all the time, but he still got an awful lot right. Archery. Yeah. They could do that.

CHAPTER SEVENTEEN

Chase still hadn't returned when Lily got up the next morning. By now she'd come to recognize that long callouts happened frequently, but that didn't make the waiting any easier. Having no idea where Chase was and only the vaguest picture of what she might be doing didn't help either. She wasn't prone to catastrophic thinking—at least she never used to be—but then anxiety was a foreign emotion too until the pandemic, when uncertainty and apprehension became the order of the day. She'd started to reprogram while she'd been at camp, finding the steadiness that had always come naturally to her. Still, on the third morning with no sign of Chase's Jeep and no word from her—at least no word to her—Lily was done with waiting.

"Have you seen Sarah?" she asked Alisha, who was curled up in her usual spot on the sofa in the great room with her morning coffee.

"Mmm," Alisha said. "She walked through a few minutes ago with coffee. Went out the front, so I don't think she's in her office."

"Thanks," Lily said and hurried to get coffee before starting her search. Besides, she had a pretty good idea where she'd find her.

"Muffins are ready," Clara called when Lily walked into the kitchen. "Lemon poppyseed."

"Can I take two?" Lily detoured to the big stainless steel counter and the cooling racks of muffins.

Clara laughed. "Honey, you can take as many as you want."

Lily wrapped two in a paper towel along with a couple of napkins and walked down the trail to the lake. Despite her never-go-anywhere-without-them boots, she watched the path for any early morning sunbathers. The evenings rarely cooled off more than a few degrees below the sizzling daytime temps, and the wildlife seemed most active in the very early hours.

People too, it seemed.

Sarah sat on the far end of the little dock, facing the lake with her legs dangling over the water. She didn't turn as Lily approached, though she must have felt her as the dock swayed and creaked with every step.

"Hi," Lily said as she carefully juggled her coffee and muffins to sit down beside Sarah. "Muffin?"

"Lemon poppyseed?"

"Uh-huh."

Sarah held out her hand. "Thanks."

"So," Lily said, sipping her own steaming cup of coffee, "I was wondering—"

"She's still up at Bear Mountain," Sarah said. "Natalie just radioed an update, or I would have told you sooner."

"Did they get the hikers out okay?"

"Yes—a trio of very lucky tourists who were a few hundred feet farther up the trail when the slide started. They had water with them, luckily, but not much in the way of food."

Lily sighed. "They obviously never spent a summer at a DEC camp."

Sarah laughed. "Really—most wilderness adventurers could benefit from it. Of course, we'd need a lot more camps and a lot more counselors and a hell of a lot more money." She eyed Lily. "And of course, medics."

"I could be persuaded to volunteer again," Lily said without a second's hesitation. She'd never actually considered it until then, but as soon as she'd said it, she knew it was true. Her role had turned out to involve so much more than just tending to the routine illnesses, injuries, and occasional emotional issues that were commonplace in every ER and primary care practice. She'd led discussion groups on topics from career paths to family planning, and learned more from the teens than she could have at any seminar on adolescent medicine. And she'd learned things about herself she'd never guessed at—like her bizarre desire to excel at outdoor activities. With the exception of fishing. That ranked high on her activities-to-be-avoided list. Her excitement at the idea of returning quickly turned to disappointment. "I don't know how I'd swing the time off, though."

"You'll have almost a year to work that out," Sarah said mildly. "Tonight's big outing marks our halfway point. In another five weeks the kids will have to start thinking about going back to school—and a couple will be heading off to college."

"Do you think Chase will make it?" Lily asked, feeling just a little selfish that she didn't want to spend the Fourth of July celebration without her.

Sarah shrugged. "Hard to know. Natalie said they were still clearing the rockfall, and then they'd have to repair the trail washout. If the ground is dry enough for them to maneuver the Bobcats and backhoes in there."

At Lily's blank look, Sarah laughed. "Bobcats are like mini bulldozers. Very agile in close quarters. Great for moving rocks and dirt around."

Lily thought of Chase's newly healed shoulder, and the older back injury that had changed Chase's life. "That's hard labor."

"Pretty much everything they do is," Sarah said.

"She's amazing," Lily said almost to herself, thinking about what it must've taken for Chase to physically recover to the point she could do this work—despite never being totally pain free.

"Amazing," Sarah murmured. "Amazingly stubborn, more like it."

"That stubbornness is what made her incredible recovery possible," Lily said gently.

"She told you, didn't she," Sarah said. "About the fall."

"Yes," Lily said simply. "And I've seen the damage. I treated her, remember."

"And seen her naked," Sarah pointed out.

Lily stiffened but kept her tone mild. "Afterward, yes."

Sarah grimaced. "Sorry. That was an asinine comment."

"You're worried about her. I understand. So am I."

"I'm not sure you really understand."

"Then explain it to me," Lily said. They weren't talking about Chase now, although she wasn't certain Sarah realized that. "What are you afraid of?"

"Did she tell you she was climbing a route that had never been free-climbed before? Did she tell you that more than one older, more experienced climber cautioned her against it?"

"No," Lily said.

"Did she tell you that when they called me they told me she wasn't likely to walk again, if she lived?"

Sarah's anger was so palpable, Lily prayed never to experience the fear that must have bred it. She drew a long breath. "I can't even imagine how terrifying that must've been for you."

"No," Sarah said on a long sigh, "and what made it even worse was that I always expected it. Something like that, at least. The call in the middle of the night that there'd been a car accident, or they'd found her somewhere at the bottom of some fucking ravine."

Lily silently waited.

"And you know what's really the hardest thing of all," Sarah said, her gaze fixed out over the glassy surface of the lake. "I hate, *hate*, that she can't do what she loves to do so much any longer. That she can't climb anymore, not like she did. It's like clipping the wings on a bird. As much as I'm glad that she doesn't free-climb, I hate that she can't."

"Of course you do," Lily said. "You hate that she lost something that she loves, and it hurts her."

Sarah turned toward her suddenly. "I've forgotten how good you are at reading what people don't say."

"Occupational skill," Lily said softly.

Sarah shook her head. "It might make you better at what you do, but it's just who you are. But you didn't read all of that. Not what might be the most important part. Chase told you. She never talks about what happened with anyone. I can't tell which one of you has gotten hooked."

Lily groaned. "Please—can we not do the fish thing again? Have you actually looked at those mouths with all those little pointy teeth?"

She shuddered.

Sarah laughed, though her laughter held an undercurrent of sorrow. "Something monumental must have happened for Chase to tell you that story."

"Maybe it isn't that at all," Lily said gently. "Maybe Chase's healed much more than you think."

"You mean much more than I'm willing to see?"

"Sometimes, we have to let go of our pain—and our guilt—in order to realize that someone else has too."

Sarah quirked a brow. "Physician heal thyself?"

Lily chuckled wryly. "Touché."

Sarah gave Lily a quick hug. "Thank you, Doctor. I'll work on it."

"Will you let me know when you hear anything more?"

"Of course." Sarah rose and held out a hand to Lily. "Come on. I'm willing to bet your clinic is empty this morning."

Lily laughed. "Naturally. No mysterious ailments are in order on the Fourth of July when we have a trip to town and a cruise scheduled."

Sarah nodded. "If I know my sister, she'll find a way to make it. Never one to miss a party."

Lily hoped so. She wanted a few more minutes with Chase when there suddenly seemed to be so little time left.

❖

Chase rewound the winch attached to the front of her Jeep, backed into a turnaround by the side of the trail, and stepped out, carefully stretching the screaming muscles in her lower back and legs. After three days in the cab in ninety-degree weather, sleeping on an air mattress in a bunk in the equipment trailer, and showering for a minute every twenty-four hours, she was tired, sore, and generally grungy. And couldn't be happier. The hikers were taking it easy in some hotel somewhere, all medically cleared, the trail was secured and ready to reopen, and she was going to a party.

"I think that's the last of it," Tom Perry called to her.

"Yep. Nat wants to wait twenty-four hours until things dry out. Should be good to go by then."

"Looks that way," Tom said, pausing beside her as two volunteer assistant rangers, both muddy and bedraggled, trooped past them toward their vehicle. He shook his head. "Gonna be a long summer."

Chase laughed. "I sure hope so."

He gave her a look. They all loved summer, despite the increase in their workload, but something in the way she'd said it must've caught his attention. She shook her head. She wasn't about to tell him that she hoped the summer went on forever if it meant that Lily didn't leave. She didn't want to think too much about that herself.

Lily was here, and if she could read the signals—which she could—Lily wanted her just as much as she wanted Lily. No point in thinking about anything else—especially when there wasn't a damn thing she could do about the future. She'd learned that lesson the hard way—along with the even harder lesson that good things always came to an end. She'd enjoy this while she could and try her best to see that Lily did too.

With a wave, she pulled onto the access road for the trek down the mountain and radioed Nat. "Fielder, leaving Bear Mountain trail, over."

"Copy that," Nat came back. "I'm headed over to Lake George."

"Hold the boat," Chase said.

"Better hurry."

Chase laughed and kicked up the speed on the Jeep. "I'll make it."

She had the best reason in the world to be on that ship—a woman she couldn't get out of her mind.

❖

When Chase pulled in at the lodge, she didn't see a soul, and the lot was empty except for Lily's BMW. With a curse, she hopped out of the Jeep, took the stairs up to her quarters two at a time, took another one-minute shower, pulled on a clean short-sleeved uniform shirt and pants, grabbed her utility belt, and raced back down to the Jeep. After locking her service weapon in the lockbox bolted behind the seat, she took the downhill tract faster than she should have—counting on skill and luck not to blow a tire or break an axle—and broke a few speed limits getting into the village. As she rounded the turn onto the beach road where the big tour ships took on passengers, she let out a sigh of relief. The *William Henry* was still in port, although it looked like everyone was boarded and the crew was getting ready to pull up the gangplank. She quickly slotted her department Jeep into a spot that said *Official Vehicles Only* reserved for village police—hopefully they'd extend her the professional courtesy of not ticketing her—and jogged across the boulevard through throngs of tourists and down the dock to the ship.

"Hold up," she called when she was twenty feet away. One of the crew had just begun unwinding the chain that moored the end of the wide gangplank to the dock. "Coming aboard!"

The sailor—a young brunette Chase knew from the social scene around town—looked up, saw her coming, and smiled. "Cutting it close there, Chase."

Chase grinned as she jumped onto the gangplank. "Thanks, Arden. I wouldn't want to miss this."

Arden gave her another smile as she worked the opposite chains loose. "Look me up later?"

"Appreciate it, but I've got the campers." She shrugged apologetically.

Arden gave her a look and a knowing nod. "Uh-huh. Some other time then."

"Thanks again," Chase said and hustled up the gangplank with Arden, who'd finished releasing the moorings, close behind.

The crew waiting shipside pulled in the gangplank, and the *William Henry* slowly eased away from the dock with its characteristic three-blast salute from the ship's booming horn. As Chase made her way forward, the captain's voice came over the intercom.

"Welcome to the *William Henry*," her voice rang out through the loudspeakers. "Our cruising time tonight is three hours and thirty minutes. We will be traversing beautiful Lake George on a route through the picturesque Islands of the Narrows. Weather report says clear skies and sunny all the way. En route, our guides will be informing you of the natural and historic wonders along the shore as we range first up the eastern shore and return along the western shore at sunset. Dinner will be served compliments of our crew in one hour. Enjoy the ride."

The first level was packed with campers and the majority of their families. Natalie and most of the district rangers not out on call were also present to celebrate one of the favorite evenings of the summer season. Chase wended her way through the crowd, slowing only long enough to return quick greetings, until she spied Sarah on the second level not far from the stairwell.

"Hi," Chase said as she edged into a place by the rail. "Everything okay? Sorry I'm late."

"I thought you'd missed it altogether," Sarah said, giving her a quick appraising glance.

Chase knew the look. Sarah surreptitiously, or so she thought, checking her over. Ever since her fall, Sarah looked for injuries after she'd been out on a call. Before that, she'd been looking for signs of forbidden teen activity. Maybe one day she'd stop trying to protect Chase from herself. Maybe. Chase spread her arms as far as she could in the crowd. "All in one piece."

Sarah smiled. "Always glad to hear that."

"Have you seen—"

"She's up on the top level, toward the bow," Sarah finished. "She wanted a spot with a view."

"Thanks. I'll just go see how's she's doing."

"Chase," Sarah said.

Chase turned back with a questioning look.

"You know what you're doing, right?"

"Relax, Sarah." Chase gave her sister's arm a squeeze. "We've got it under control."

"All right then," Sarah said quietly. "Enjoy the ride."

If Chase didn't know better, she'd think that was a double entendre, but that wasn't her sister's way. Although she fully intended to ride the whirlwind with Lily, for however long that might be.

She found Lily where Sarah had said, facing forward at the bow, one hand on the rail, the other holding a drink. She'd freed her blond hair from its usual clasp at the back of her neck, and shimmering strands floated around her neck and shoulders in the spray wafting up from the water below. She'd chosen a sleeveless, pale green top and white shorts with low-heeled sandals for the evening. Simple, elegant, totally Lily. Chase stopped at the small bar tucked under the captain's observation deck.

"Any chance you've got wine?" she asked the middle-aged bartender whose tailored white shirt and rolled-up sleeves showcased his buff build.

"You're not wearing a red wristband," he said with a grin, "but you look like you're over twenty-one."

Chase laughed. "Definitely in the rearview. How's it going, Jimmy?"

"Well, I'd rather be fishing, but this is a close second." He laughed. "How are the trout running up at Colter's Creek?"

"Plenty of legal size. Not too many out-of-towners that far up the creek either. You headed up that way?"

"I'll take a week up at the camp middle of July."

"Good. Let me know if everything looks okay up that way. I'll swing by when I can."

"No problem. There you go." Jimmy handed her a plastic cup with white wine and a couple ice cubes.

The crowd on the top deck had gotten heavier in the short time she'd been waiting for her drink as sightseers migrated up from the lower levels for the air and the view. Chase angled her way through the jostling, boisterous clumps of teens and families until she made it close to Lily's right shoulder. She rested her fingertips very lightly on the lower curve of Lily's spine and said, "I told you it was pretty out here."

Lily slowly turned and looked up. Her eyes widened with welcome, a warm, sensuous gaze that kindled a fire in Chase's belly. "I don't know how you managed it, but you continually surprise me. Hello."

Chase vibrated with the need to kiss her. The entire time she'd been scaling rock piles and muddy escarpments to reach the marooned hikers and later moving a ton of debris off the trail, she'd been ambushed by images of their night together. Images that churned her up and turned her muscles to jelly. She had to satisfy herself with running her fingertip down Lily's bare arm, out of view. "I told you tonight was special. Did you think I would miss spending it with you?"

"I think you have an extraordinarily demanding job, this is a very busy time of year, and I would understand if you missed it." Lily laughed lightly. "After three days with no word from you, I had reconciled myself to seeing the sights solo."

Chase pressed a hand to her chest. "Oh, you wound me. How little faith."

Lily laughed again, the sound a delighted one. "I doubt very much I've dealt a lethal blow."

"Then let me say that I would be very disappointed to miss you tonight."

Lily sipped her drink and met Chase's eyes again. This time her gaze held an invitation that did nothing for Chase's composure. It was going to be a long night.

"I didn't say I wouldn't be disappointed that you couldn't be here," Lily said.

"Then all my wounds are healed."

Lily shook her head. "Far too easy."

"Where you're concerned." That earned Chase an eye roll, and she added, "I would have gotten word to you if I could have. I hoped Nat would."

Lily squeezed her hand. "I know. And Sarah kept me up to date as much as she could." She paused. "I was worried. I know there's no need to be—I think it's mostly I don't know what you're doing. I only know it's potentially hazardous."

"You don't need to worry," Chase said softly. "I had a very good reason to get back here on time and in one piece."

"I'm very glad for both." Lily gestured at the campers, parents, and staff crowded along the rails and sitting in the central seating area. "This really is fun."

Chase nodded. "How are things going?"

"Well, I think. Quite a number of families showed up, and the campers seem happy to see them, which in and of itself is a miracle considering that teenagers usually aren't keen to spend a night out with their parents."

"I think when the kid's been away half the summer at camp, they're secretly glad, although they probably don't say so."

Lily tilted her head toward the far rail where Marty stood with Ford. "Their families didn't come, but I saw Julia with another woman who I think is also Ford's security."

Chase grimaced. "I guess someone thought Ford would be a flight risk if she left camp. I don't get that feeling, do you?"

Lily shook her head. "I don't. She seems to have settled in, especially since she and Marty have become friends. The two of them have been doing a lot of the activities together, and Shannon and Ford don't seem quite as tight any longer."

"I don't think I saw Shannon on my way through," Chase said, "but I wasn't looking for her either."

"She was on the first deck with Derek. I think the two of them have a thing going."

"I'm sure they're not the only ones." Chase laughed. "We've got a bunch of older kids at camp. That always happens. Usually nothing too heavy."

Lily shook her head. "I guess it does. Obviously, I missed an important developmental milestone by not going to camp when I was younger."

"I really would've liked it if you had," Chase said. "I definitely would've made a move."

Lily stared and then burst out laughing. "Oh, and you're so certain I would've just instantly melted?"

Chase looked around and then leaned closer. She still wanted to kiss her, but there was no way she could do that. Instead, she murmured in her ear, "I can be very persuasive."

"I've noticed." Lily leaned on the rail as the ship steamed through the islands that dotted the lake like green emeralds. "This really is very beautiful. I'm so glad I did this."

"Did what?" Chase asked.

"Decided to come here for the summer. It's an amazing experience on so many levels."

Chase's stomach tightened. *For the summer.* She knew that, she'd always known that. She forced a smile. "I'm glad. You seem like you've found your direction again."

"Maybe that's it," Lily mused, finishing her drink. "In a lot of ways, it feels like I've found more of myself than I've ever actually appreciated." She held out her empty cup to Chase. "Do you think you could get me a refill so I don't miss the excitement up here?"

"At your service," Chase said and took the cup. "What are you drinking?"

"That was seltzer, but I'm ready to switch to white wine."

"Do you have your little red wristband?"

Lily held up her left wrist with the referenced band. "I do, not that I need it."

"Oh, I don't know. You're beautiful enough to raise the question."

Lily regarded her solemnly for a second. "You know, you're far more devastating when you're serious."

"I'll remember that, then. Don't go away." Chase leaned in again. "There will be fireworks later."

Lily murmured, "I wouldn't miss it."

CHAPTER EIGHTEEN

L ily dreamed of fireworks, brilliant bursts of color against a velvet sky, the rising sounds of surprise and pleasure from the people gathered six deep along the rails on the top deck of the *William Henry*, their faces upturned in simple joy. Chase stood behind her, arms wrapped around her waist, her breath warm against Lily's cheek as she laughed. For those brief moments as rockets soared and flamed, as the magic wheeled overhead, everyone—young and old—believed in happy endings. Even her.

Lily woke with the warm memory of Chase's hand lightly caressing her hip as they watched the spectacle, the *William Henry* rocking gently at anchor. Right now, the sky outside her room was tinged with gray, but at any moment dawn would break and color return to the world. The warmth of Chase's hand on her hip was very much *not* a dream. For a little while longer, her touch was very real.

How had she missed the last month passing by since that holiday celebration on the lake? Or had she just been content to fill every day with camp activities, nature excursions, and even a weekend of wilderness survival training for the campers and staff alike? So busy she hadn't had to think about the end.

Endings. The inevitable finale to every adventure, even life itself. For the lucky, the unhappy endings would be few and the ultimate one met with grace and peace. Lily hoped she could manage the one fast approaching with just a fraction of that.

She *had* loved every minute of the summer, discovering skills and interests she'd never even considered before, never tiring of the beauty wherever she looked, and taking unexpected pleasure in seeing some of the teens thrive with the physical challenges, and others—like Marty and Ford—discover something new in the course of becoming friends. She'd rediscovered something also, her fundamental joy in caring for others—even though the worst of her medical emergencies recently had been a fractured wrist she'd needed to splint until the teen could be seen at a local urgent care center, a host of mysterious rashes that still evaded a diagnosis but that thankfully responded to topical steroids, and the never-routine, ever-present challenges of managing nearly fifty teenagers through small illnesses and injuries.

And then there was Chase.

Sometimes Chase would be on-site to lead an excursion or supervise a technical exercise, but just as often she was out on a call, sometimes for several days at a time. Even though Lily's days and nights were full, something was missing when Chase was absent. The expectation of that surge of pleasure when she first saw her, the banter that often turned to seduction, the quiet conversations that touched somewhere even deeper, and the moments when they joined—heart and body. When Lily awakened to the steady rumble of the Jeep cresting the road at dawn, she'd rise, her pulse racing, to wait for Chase at the lake. Chase would appear at the end of the dock, her blazing smile vanquishing the memory of missing her with the intensity of her presence. They'd swim, they'd kiss, they'd make love slowly before the day began and duty called them apart.

Other times, when Chase returned at midnight, she'd come silently up the stairs to Lily's room and through the door Lily'd left unlocked to lie down beside Lily and fold her in her arms. Sometimes, like the night before, Lily's need for her would rise hard and fast, and she'd pull Chase into the whirlwind of her passion. That need grew stronger as the summer grew shorter. Feeling the ache fill her again, Lily pressed into Chase's arms, seeking relief in her touch.

Chase kissed the curve of her shoulder and tightened her arm around Lily's waist, snugging Lily more tightly into the curve of her body. "Morning."

Lily curled her thigh over the curve of Chase's hip, bringing her center closer to Chase's body as her heart beat faster. "Good morning."

"I think it is." Chuckling softly, Chase stroked Lily's back, around the curve of her hip, and slowly trailed up her thigh until she cupped Lily between her legs. "I missed you, Lily."

Lily drew in a sharp breath.

"I should have let you sleep last night," Lily whispered, the ache spiraling beneath Chase's hand clouding her awareness of anything but the urgency of release.

"I always sleep well next to you." Chase kissed her again, her strokes languid and knowing. "And I need *you* more than a extra hour."

"You'll need to get out of here soon before the lodge fills up." Lily gasped. "Soon."

"I don't like to rush the important things," Chase whispered against her throat.

"Mmm, keep doing that *right there* and it shouldn't take very long."

Chase kept stroking exactly where Lily liked it, and almost instantly Lily's stomach clenched, her thighs tightened, and she gasped into the curve of Chase's neck as the orgasm swept over her.

"See? Plenty of time," Chase murmured, starting to draw away.

"No. Don't go just yet." Lily rolled onto her back and pulled Chase with her.

"Can't now." Chase groaned softly and straddled the length of Lily's thigh. "Whatever you want."

"*This* is exactly what I want."

Lily clasped Chase's hips and gently urged her to ride, and Chase did. A half dozen hard strokes, and she threw her head back on a sharp groan and came. The sight never failed to leave Lily breathless with wonder. God, she *loved* her.

How had that happened? How could she have let that happen? And how—given everything Chase had made her feel and everything Chase had opened up around and inside her—could she ever have thought it wouldn't happen?

Chase settled down upon her, careful with her weight but breathing hard. "You know you destroy me, right?"

And this might destroy me. Lily stroked the damp hair at Chase's neck and kissed her. "That's my total intention."

"You succeeded." Chase rolled over with a long sigh. Her hand found Lily's and their fingers entwined. "I really better get out of here."

"I know." Lily didn't want four dozen teens speculating on her sex life—to say nothing of her colleagues. They probably all speculated, but they didn't need to see the rumpled, satisfied proof. "Go jump in the shower."

"Yeah?" Chase sounded hopeful.

"Alone."

Chase sighed but didn't move and, after another moment, asked quietly, "When are you leaving?"

Lily bit her lip for an instant until she was sure her voice would be steady and light. "A week from today. I wanted to wait till all the campers left over the weekend. I imagine Sarah will need help getting the inventory and paperwork squared away too."

Chase's grip on hers tightened briefly. "Will you start back to work right away?"

"I don't know, probably." *Talking* about not being here was almost easier than thinking about it. Thinking about it only brought up a sense of longing, as if her mind got stuck on the one inescapable reality—her life would be one without Chase in it. "I've talked to my boss, and of course he can't wait for me to get back." Lily chuckled wryly. "So I assume sometime next week."

Chase leaned on her elbow and kissed her. "Well, you've got a week left."

Chase's tone was curiously flat, and Lily tried to read her face, but Chase turned away too quickly. The rigid set of her shoulders as she reached for her pants didn't invite a touch, and Lily kept silent.

Chase stood in just her pants, her T-shirt balled in her fist, and a totally neutral expression on her face. "Give me five minutes in the shower."

When she emerged, dressed and hair still damp, less than five minutes later, Lily asked, "I'll see you for breakfast?"

"Yep," Chase said as she headed toward the door. "I've just got to check in and make sure the weather works for today's trip."

"I'll wait," Lily called after her, and then Chase was gone.

Lily sighed. That went as well as it probably could have, even though putting words to the reality left her feeling mildly ill. She'd always known what would happen when this time came, but *knowing* hadn't prepared her for the sinking sensation she carried around with her all day long. She'd never before had trouble dealing with hard truths—all her training had been focused on accepting the randomness, vagaries, and sometimes outright unfairness of life so she could continue to do her job with compassion and hope. She'd struggled with that in the face of so much failure the last few years, but she'd survived it and recovered her professional balance this summer.

She'd expected to miss Chase when she returned to the city the way she'd missed Sarah—a friend she loved, a friend she missed, and a friend she always rejoiced to see again. How foolish she had been. Chase was not her friend—Chase was her lover. Time had no meaning where the heart was concerned, and she'd lost hers.

❖

At four thirty in the morning, Chase was used to the lodge being nearly deserted. Clara was usually up, though, and the coffee was usually hot and ready. Chase wasn't bothered by what Clara might think about her having spent the night upstairs and not in her quarters across the way. Clara had known her since she was fifteen and was used to seeing her come in at all hours, a fond smile her usual welcome.

This morning, Sarah greeted her at the coffeepot.

"Morning," Chase said briefly and reached for a cup. All she wanted was to snag some caffeine and go. She'd been serious when she'd told Lily she had things to do, but mostly she'd needed to shake off the hit she'd known all summer was coming. In a week Lily would be gone. They'd played by the rules—grabbed every moment they could and made the most of it—and each second was more than she'd ever imagined. Oh sure, the sex was fabulous, as anyone looking at Lily for a heartbeat could have predicted. But the rest—the easy silences, the even easier revelations, and Lily's endless understanding—filled a hunger she'd never recognized and knew now she'd never be able to sate with anyone else. She'd never wanted to feel what she felt for Lily, and she should have been more on her guard. Hadn't she seen it before and sworn that would never be her—the one left behind to grieve? She'd watched her mother grieve her father's absence until the day she died, and Chase mourned them both still, as she knew Sarah did.

She had never been looking for love.

"Hi," Sarah said. "I didn't hear you come in."

Chase gave her a look. "I didn't. I was upstairs."

"Ah." Sarah smiled softly.

Chase gritted her teeth. Could she just walk out with a wave? Like that had ever been possible with Sarah.

"It's hard to believe camp season's almost over," Sarah said with studied nonchalance.

"The season isn't," Chase said just as nonchalantly. "Once the campers leave, you'll still have tourists coming up for the guided hikes and the fall foliage shuttles and the Halloween—"

"Stop!" Sarah laughed. "You're giving me a headache. I haven't even gotten the kids out of here yet."

"Everyone will be gone this time next week," Chase said flatly.

Sarah let out a breath. "You know, Chase, Lily mentioned how much she liked being the camp medic this season, and that she might want to come back again."

Chase gave her a long look. "Lily has a job and a life in New York City, Sarah."

"People change," Sarah said.

"Do they? I'm not so sure." Chase shook her head. "Besides, what we had has been what Lily needed. You can see she's ready to go."

"What about you?" Sarah asked. "Has it been what you needed?"

Chase grabbed her cup and said firmly, "It's been exactly what I *wanted*. And I'm fine that it's only been this summer. So don't worry."

Sarah merely nodded, and Chase finally escaped. She'd meant what she'd said. Lily had been who she'd wanted, and that would have to be enough.

❖

Marty stirred when Ford crept out of the cabin before anyone else was awake. Marty debated following for a few minutes, but since everyone would be rising soon for breakfast anyhow, they didn't figure Ford would mind the company, and they could bring Ford the pack she'd left by her bunk. They dressed quickly, grabbed the day pack that they'd readied the night before with everything necessary for the day's activity, and carefully crossed the room to the bunk Ford shared with Shannon. They probably didn't have to worry about waking Shannon, who'd come in just before Alisha made her last rounds at midnight.

Marty usually woke up when Shannon snuck in, and that was most nights now. At the beginning of the summer, Ford used to go out with her, but not any longer. Not since right around the *William Henry* night, as Marty thought of it. That had been a special night—not just cool to see the lake and the fireworks. Which *had* been cool. That was the night they'd known for sure they and Ford were friends.

"So," Ford had said as they leaned on the rail as the *William Henry* steamed up the lake, watching the waves spread out in frothy crests, laughing as the spray drenched them both, "I saw you talking to Suwallia earlier. You going to do the archery thing?"

"Yes," Marty said, "I thought I would."

"That's all good then." Ford paused. "So, um—who was the guy who was there?"

"You mean Keno?" Marty asked. "He's Suwallia's cousin. He came with the rest of her family for the tour."

"Huh. Maybe you can introduce me later."

Marty stared. "Like tonight?"

"Well, yeah," Ford said as if they were clueless.

"Sure. Now?"

Ford gave her another *hello* look. "No, not now. We're talking."

"Okay. Right. Later."

Ford watched the water another minute. "I decided what I'm going to do next year."

Marty struggled to keep up with the conversation. "You mean college?"

"Not college." Ford turned to meet their gaze. "I'm going to join the Coast Guard."

Marty stared. "Wow. That's…that's so awesome."

Ford grinned. "Yeah. Hey, it's sailing, right?"

"So, um, did you tell anyone else?" *Like your parents?*

"Not yet." Ford looped an arm through Marty's. "Come on. Let's go find Suwallia."

The memory still made Marty smile as they ambled down the trail to the lake. Like they'd figured, Ford was swimming off the end of the dock. Marty plopped down on the end and called out, "You know you're not supposed to swim alone."

"You know all those rules and regulations clogging up your head are going to break something," Ford called back and swam with strong firm strokes over to the dock. She flung the hair out of her eyes and smiled up at Marty. "Give me a hand?"

Marty leaned over and stretched down, then hauled Ford up onto the dock. "I brought your pack down."

"Thanks—I'd have had to go to breakfast in my suit." Ford grabbed a towel and T-shirt out of the pack to dry off. "Why are you awake?"

"I wanted to get down to the lodge early to check the weather radar online," Marty said. "If there's a lot of cloud cover we can't go today."

"Oh right," Ford said with mock sarcasm. "We're hiking up a mountain, then we're climbing up a big-ass tower, all so we can look at birds. Have you ever glanced around this place? There's a bird in every bush."

Marty grinned. "Uh-huh. But they're not ospreys, and they don't have fledglings. And if we're lucky, there might be a peregrine falcon. They're endangered but that's a raptor sanctuary up there."

"Right. I'm rapt."

Marty groaned. "That's really bad."

Ford laughed. "I know. Come on, I'm starving."

Ford swung her pack onto her shoulder and, as they walked down the end of the dock, asked, "Have you heard from your dad?"

"Yeah. End of the month at the earliest." Marty shrugged. "That's okay. He'll be stateside for months this time. I can wait."

"So how are you getting home?"

"Oh, I'll be fine."

"Marty," Ford said with exaggerated patience.

"Bus?"

"Um, no." Ford snorted. "You know, if he's not going to be back until September, you could come stay with me the rest of the summer. I could teach you to sail."

Marty stumbled to a halt. The invitation was so outside their realm of possibility they didn't know what to say. "Seriously?"

Ford rolled her eyes. "No, Marty. I'm used to saying things I don't mean. You probably noticed that."

"True. And, um, I'd really like that."

"Great."

"What about your parents? Will they care?"

"No, and even if they did, I wouldn't. No matter what they want, I get to choose my own friends. Only I have to warn you, there may be some security lurking around."

"Oh, that's okay. I'm used to that sort."

"And I'm planning to tell my parents about the Coast Guard when I get home. You'll be my backup."

Marty got that feeling again, like on the *William Henry*, of knowing that this moment *mattered.* "Totally done deal."

❖

Chase didn't come to breakfast, and Lily had no chance to speak with her once they started loading the vans for the trip to the raptor observatory. The campers lined up for the three vans by cabin number while Lily and the counselors checked them off their lists as they entered. Once they were ready to go, Lily climbed aboard the van Chase was driving and settled into the front seat opposite her. The campers' chatter made conversation on the thirty-minute ride impossible, and she might have been imagining it, but Chase seemed…distant. Usually whenever they were anywhere within sight of each other, she could feel Chase's gaze upon her. A brief smile, a wink, a raised brow—all carried a special message that spelled interest. And desire. The absence of those subtle connections left her vaguely uneasy, as if she'd lost something but couldn't see clearly what it was.

"We'll take a ten-minute break at the information center for everyone to fill their water bottles and use the accommodations," Chase announced as she turned into the lot. "Make sure you do—there's no public water available within the borders of the sanctuary. Do not carry any food in your packs. Do not collect any souvenirs—not even stones. This is protected land, so stay on the trails at all times—do not overtake the group ahead of you and stay behind your guide."

The instant the van stopped, the teens tumbled into the aisles in a chaotic shuffle to gather packs and belongings.

Chase stepped over to Lily. "You all set?"

Lily nodded. "I'm looking forward to it."

"Good. It's a special place." Chase smiled, a smile that carried a hint of sadness Lily was certain she was not imagining.

The six groups started off at three- or four-minute intervals with Chase and Lily's group going last. As they walked, Chase elaborated on the nature of the bird sanctuary that encompassed an area of cliffs and undeveloped mountain ranges bordering 12th Lake and the raptor tower—a platform atop a hundred-foot steel base. The crags and crevices were favorite spots for raptor nests, and from the tower, they'd be able to observe the flights and feeding without disturbing the nesting grounds or the young families.

Lily'd already studied the bird guide, so she hoped she'd be able to identify some of the hawks, eagles, falcons, and other winged predators, but in her experience, birds in flight all tended to look the same. But then, Chase was always able to tell them apart, and when their group had climbed the steel stairs to the massive platform at the top, Chase called everyone to the railing.

"Watch the rock face off to your left," she directed. "There's a big osprey nest at eleven o'clock, below that clump of spruce."

"Over there?" someone called.

"No, those are pines," another voice answered.

A few teens groaned.

Someone said, "Now we have to be botanists?"

More laughter while several kids pointed out the direction to look.

Lily smiled. She'd miss this—their energy, their insecurities and bravado, their curiosity and their optimism. She watched Chase move from group to group, answering questions, guiding their observations, explaining the life cycles of the great winged hunters.

She'd miss so many things, but none as much as Chase. She turned away, her throat tight. Blinking away the sudden moisture in her eyes, she scanned the cliff tops and, beyond those, the massive mountain ranges. Strange to see fog so late in the day with the sun so high. She blinked again, but the gray haze remained.

"Chase," she murmured, and Chase instantly appeared at her side. "Lily?"

"Why is it so foggy—" Lily sensed Chase stiffen and glanced at her, instinctive alarm prompting an adrenaline rush that heightened every sense.

Chase's jaw tightened. "That's not fog. It's smoke."

CHAPTER NINETEEN

Is it close?" Lily asked calmly, although her eyes took on that dark, deep hue that usually indicated she was worried.

"Over here," Chase said, motioning for Lily to follow her to the far side of the platform away from the cluster of campers and counselors. Lily was no stranger to a crisis, and from the rate at which the smoke cover was spreading, a crisis was a distinct possibility. "From where I put the fire, there's no danger to populated areas right now, but I can't say yet what we're facing. Let me call it in—chances are good I'm going to have to go."

Lily's mouth set and she nodded. "I understand. Is there anything I should do here?"

"If I have to leave, Alisha will be in charge until you're all back at the lodge. No reason for the regular schedule to be interrupted." Chase pulled her radio off her belt. No reason to mention the fire was closer to the lodge than where they were right then. "This is Fielder, I'm at the raptor tower in Little Neck. Smoke sighted about seventy-five miles north-northwest, vicinity of Eagle Peak."

"This is Evans," Natalie came back. "Roger that, dispatching aerial surveillance. Will advise."

"Copy that. Fielder out." Chase cupped Lily's elbow and drew her an inch or two closer. "Lily, if I need to go, there's no telling when I'll be back."

"I can wait," Lily said quickly.

"No, that's not what I mean." Chase shook her head. Lily had spoken quickly, no doubt meaning what she said, but she didn't know what they might be facing. Chase forced a smile she didn't feel. "You've got responsibilities elsewhere, and I could be gone a week or two. I want you to know that I get how important your work is, not just to you, but to the patients you take care of. I think you're an amazing woman. I think what you've done for thousands of people, who don't even know it, is incredible." Her throat tightened and she swallowed. She was out of time, and she needed to say this. "And for me, Lily. Thank you for this summer."

Lily drew in a slow deep breath and held Chase's gaze. "I don't want it to end like this, but if it does, you need to know I—"

Chase's radio blared. "This is District Supervisor Natalie Evans. This is an all call. We have an unprescribed burn cresting Eagle Ridge. Ground teams from Bolton Fire, Lake George Fire, and Ticonderoga Fire Rangers responding. All district five officers report to the station for briefing and deployment. I repeat, all call."

"That's me," Chase said. "I've got to go, Lily."

"You be careful," Lily said, gripping Chase's shirt with one hand. "Do not take any chances."

Chase knew this might be the last time they were together, and she didn't care who was watching. She pulled Lily close and kissed her. Lily leaned into her, returning her kiss with a fierceness that flamed Chase's senses. Cradling Lily's cheek in her palm, Chase drew in the scent of her, absorbing the sweet and tangy taste that ran like life over her tongue. When she drew back, her body quivered. "You too, Lily. Be careful down there."

Chase turned and took the steps down the middle tower without looking back.

❖

Lily quickly crossed to the far side of the platform and watched Chase's figure disappear down the trail and kept watching for long seconds after she'd disappeared. What had just happened? She understood emergencies, of course—the stat page that terminated conversations midsentence or the phone call that interrupted an intimate moment one too many times, putting an end to any chance of another evening with that person. Events that demanded whatever personal pleasure or problem of the moment be set aside to allow the gears to shift, the mind to focus, and the job to come first.

But this was different—this was not a casual moment she could shut off and forget. Chase was gone. Their summer had just ended. Everything they had shared was neatly tied up and dispensed with. They had just said good-bye, while her lips still tingled from the heat of Chase's kiss and her blood raced with wanting her.

Lily gripped the railing to steady herself, reeling to take in the abrupt departure—as final and traumatic as an amputation—while struggling to keep the well of sadness that brimmed within her from spilling out.

"Something happening?" Alisha asked at her shoulder.

"Forest fire."

"I saw the smoke. Looks like it might be sizable."

Lily turned when she was certain she had control again. "Chase said we should keep to today's schedule. I'm without a compass here. How worried do I need to be?"

"Don't need to worry yet." Alisha checked to see that the other counselors had the campers engaged before continuing. "Fires aren't uncommon during high summer when there hasn't been much rain and the forests are dry. Added to the danger of natural causes like a lightning strike, we've got the most hikers dispersed throughout the area as we'll have all year, increasing the chance of a careless campfire or tossed cigarette."

"How difficult are they to get under control?"

Alisha grimaced. "The fire protocols are very effective—establish the natural local barriers—a stream or rock face where the fire won't jump, shore up the defenses by cutting clear any underbrush or flammable foliage, starve it out from the air with retardants spread over the burn. Usually once the fire lines are secured to prevent it jumping into adjacent areas and after dampening the burn from the air or with ground water—if there's any nearby—the fire will burn itself out." She frowned. "If the weather cooperates."

"Cooperates how?" Lily railed inwardly at her ignorance. She hated there were so many things she didn't understand about this life, about *Chase's* life. About the things that could endanger Chase's life. For Lily, understanding was comfort, the lessening of worry and anxiety.

Although that worry would never completely go away whenever Chase was out of sight. Except that had already happened, hadn't it? She might've said good-bye to Chase for the last time already. When would that reality ever not shock her?

Her hands trembled and she carefully slipped them into the pockets of her shorts. She focused through the frustration and pain. "Wind, you mean. That's what drives the flames, gives it air to breathe, to grow." Her hands clenched tighter. She wouldn't voice what could happen—the wildfire that roared down mountainsides, changing direction unexpectedly, jumping fire lines, trapping firefighters. She would not give those images any more power to terrify her.

"The best thing we can do," Alisha said, her expression kind and gentle, "is just keep on with our regular routine. Sarah will be in constant contact with the DEC and keep us informed. The kids only have four days left, and they're busy ones. If they have questions, we'll answer them as needed."

Lily nodded. She would do her job just as Chase was doing hers. And she would trust in Chase to be every bit as good at hers as she knew her to be. She *did* trust her, or else she never would've given Chase her heart. Even if she hadn't realized that's what she had done until now.

❖

Lily watched the smoke while circulating through the groups of teens, none of whom except Marty, who stared in the direction of the fire, seemed concerned by the distant black smudges hanging above the treetops.

"It's quite a ways away," Lily said as she leaned on the rail next to them.

"No rain in the forecast," Marty said. "I checked it this morning."

"I understand they drop fire retardant from the air." *Thank you, Alisha, for the brief lesson in fighting wildfires.*

Marty nodded, their gaze still distant. "It's a little bit like war, I guess. You're trained to fight, right? So when you have to, you do." They looked at Lily. "So Chase and the rest of them—they'll be okay."

Lily hugged them quickly. "Yes, they will." She didn't say *and so will your dad*, but the tension eased from Marty's shoulders, so Lily knew they'd heard. "Come on—I think it's time to head down to the vans."

The moment they returned to the lodge, Lily sought out Sarah. "Do you have any word yet on the situation out there?"

Sarah shook her head, her eyes full of undisguised concern. "Nothing yet. Nat will get in touch when she has time, but until the teams are deployed and the aerial surveillance provides detailed information on the location, they won't know the scope of the burn." She sighed. "If we hear before tomorrow, I'll be surprised."

Lily let out a sigh. "That long. Waiting has never been my strong suit."

"All the responders are veterans of this kind of thing," Sarah said. "Wildfires are always unpredictable, but everyone out there knows that. The teams are very well trained, and there's always the chance they'll have it under control in a couple of days if not sooner."

"Right. And we carry on."

"We do. The next two days are kind of highlights of the summer season, and the campers usually love it."

"I imagine for them playing accident victims and medics beats climbing rock faces or learning water rescue techniques."

"For some of them," Sarah said with a smile.

"Ha," Lily said, "I'm willing to bet most of them volunteer to be accident victims."

"There's something about the bandages and the fake blood," Sarah said, forcing a laugh. "And I won't take that bet."

"Care to wager on who volunteers to be medics?"

"Oh, that's an easy one. Marty for sure, probably Ford. And of course, Merrick from cabin three, who we all know plans on being a flight surgeon."

Lily laughed, the camper in question having made his military career plans clear to everyone on a daily basis. His excitement, however, was contagious, and no one seemed to mind. "I haven't done a field training like this in a decade. Under other circumstances, I'd be looking forward to it too."

Sarah squeezed her arm. "I know it's useless to say don't worry, but try not to. This isn't Chase's first rodeo, you know."

"You're right, of course." Lily forcibly shook off the anxiety she could do nothing to assuage. "You'll let me know as soon as you hear anything?"

"Of course."

"Thanks. I'm off for a quick shower before dinner, then."

She needed the shower after a day hiking, but even more, she needed a few moments to compose herself. She thought she'd have a week to prepare for leaving, and now it appeared she had no time at all. The thought of returning to the city without seeing Chase again was intolerable. She sank down on the side of her bed and tried to take stock of what she was feeling.

She couldn't. This sense of being lost somehow and not even knowing how or why or where the right path lay was completely foreign to her. She'd never been indecisive in her life. She'd known from childhood that she would follow her parents into medicine. She knew from her first day in medical school that she was destined for the emergency room. She knew where she would practice, in the largest metropolitan area in the nation and one of the largest in the world, where anything could happen and *had* happened. She'd known that a serious relationship—when and if—would happen how and when she was ready. And now here she was in the last place on earth she would ever expect to be, about to return to the life she'd made, and all she could feel was sadness and uncertainty.

❖

Chase pulled on her Nomex pants and flipped the suspenders up over the shoulders of her yellow shirt. She checked the contents of her backpack for the air filters, the heat tent, the extra water, the salt tabs, the MREs, and her goggles before shouldering the pack and tucking her hard hat under her arm. Tom Perry jogged over to her.

"Knew this was coming," Perry said. "No rain for three weeks."

"Maybe we'll get lucky and the forecast will be wrong," Chase muttered. No rain was forecast for another week at least.

Tom harrumphed. "Wouldn't count on that. Without bad luck, I wouldn't have—"

"Any luck at all," Chase finished with a wry laugh.

When they walked into the conference room for the briefing, Nat was already there with the fire chiefs from three neighboring towns and the fire ranger captain from Ticonderoga. Nat nodded to Chase and Perry and indicated the aerial map of the fire location projected on a wall screen. "Preliminary reports have the burn encompassing sixty woodland acres, projected to double that hourly. Satellite images"—another image came up—"show a large grassland area in the potential fire zone, depending on wind shift and fire movement."

Chase grimaced. Wildland fires traveled faster in grassland than in heavily wooded zones, making it all the harder to contain them. Especially if the wind picked up to drive the fire uphill.

The Bolton fire chief, a heavyset man in his sixties with a gray crewcut and summer tan, grunted. "When do we think about evacuations?"

Nat shook her head. "There's a lot of forest between the burn and any populated areas, but we will be sending teams out to clear any hikers or campers who might be in the red zone once we set up our perimeters."

She turned back to the satellite images. "We've got a water barrier here"—she traced a line with her laser pointer—"and a rocky escarpment along this eastern peak. We'll put our lines there." She circled a spot just off the barely visible thin line of an access road that ended below the location of the fire. "Incident command post here. Questions?"

No one had any—the approach to fire containment was standard, although anything but routine. The terrain, the wind, the dryness of the soil, the moisture level in the air, and the ability of firefighters to reach the areas where they needed to work were all unique factors, which would have to be addressed on the ground as the situation evolved.

"I'll see you out there," Nat said, and the teams dispersed to head for their assigned locations.

As Chase jogged toward the helicopter, she let her mind drift for the last free moments she'd have before the job ahead demanded all her attention. Her last glimpse of Lily's face—a little pale and worried—mirrored the emotions swirling through her now. Good-byes were hard, even when necessary, even when expected. She knew that. She and her father hadn't had a chance to say good-bye, but she and her mother had.

This felt a little bit like that, like a little piece of her had died. The pain in her chest was real, and she hadn't realized that could happen. But her heart felt bruised. She settled into the jump seat next to Tom and pulled on her headgear. She had to let that go for now. After all, she'd have a lifetime to miss Lily and knew that she would.

CHAPTER TWENTY

Lily spent a restless night, her dreams punctuated not by fireworks, but by flames. She woke up with a choking sensation a few minutes before her alarm was due to go off. Smelling smoke, she shot upright, her chest tight, her heart pounding.

Think, assess. Don't panic.

Lily took a deep breath, blinked the night's clouds from her eyes, and scanned the room. Nothing. Nothing but the remnant of a dream.

Rising, needing to be sure, she pushed the window open wide and leaned out, both hands braced on the sill. Thunder Ridge, an unbroken collage of green beneath a steel-gray sky not yet giving way to the dawn, rose unmolested above her. Somewhere beyond that pristine ridge, fire devoured the forest. Somewhere out there, Chase and dozens of others stood in the fire's path and denied it passage. How close was the fire? How long before Chase and the others battled it into submission?

She'd resisted the urge all evening to find Sarah and pester her for an update. Sarah would come to her with any news as soon as she could, and reminding her—reminding them both—of their helplessness was simply cruel. Folding her arms across her chest, Lily suppressed a shiver that had nothing to do with the damp morning mountain air, an anomaly that would disappear by noon when the day lay heavy as a cloying blanket beneath the blistering sun. That discomfort barely registered now, not when somewhere out there—*where* she wasn't exactly sure, considering her natural compass was sorely lacking despite a summer tramping through the surrounding forests—Chase was undoubtedly hard at work. She would be hot and dusty and tired beyond anything Lily could imagine, facing one of nature's most violent displays of temper. Had she slept? Had she eaten? Was she whole and uninjured?

"Damn it," Lily muttered. She'd had moments—hours verging on days that hazed into weeks—of frustration and rankling impotence over the last few years, but unlike now, she'd had weapons of her own with which to fight back. Now she was sidelined, helpless, and the stakes were personal. She was tucked away here, safe and secure, and whatever Chase faced out there, there was absolutely nothing Lily could do to help her.

Lily lifted her chin and turned her back from the window to gather her clothes. She had a full schedule ahead, and a camp full of kids who would still benefit from what she could help teach them. Chase was doing her job, and she'd do hers.

She carried her coffee and a slice of toast that she had no real appetite for over to the clinic, unlocked the door, and then sat on the porch. For the last two weeks, her early morning clinic hours had been pretty quiet. The campers had all acclimated to the various challenges of living in the mountains, had become accomplished, almost despite themselves, at wildland lore and procedures, and rarely fell prey to the common injuries that seemed to beset so many day-trippers who flooded the trails and lakes all summer. She'd already updated all her pertinent records and entered them into the statewide medical system for reference. Should one of the campers have medical difficulties in the future related to anything that had happened at camp, her treatment would be documented.

At a little before seven, Marty and Ford walked down the trail from the cabins, saw her, and waved.

"Morning," they called in unison.

"Headed to breakfast or a swim?" Lily called.

"Food first!" Ford called back.

"We want to be ready for the simulations," Marty said, their grin quicker and easier the last few weeks. "Do you happen to know our assignments yet?"

Ford gave them a playful push. "Will you relax. You know you're going to get to be one of the medics."

"Maybe I want to get airlifted into a helicopter," Marty said archly.

Lily laughed. "I'm not sure that's going to be a volunteer position."

"It will be if Marty has a say." Ford snorted. "Come on. I want a Coke."

Marty groaned. "When are you going to start drinking coffee like a grown-up?"

"When I've lost my sense of taste or the stuff stops tasting like stewed tennis shoes."

"You just haven't had good coffee. The coffee here..."

Amused, Lily watched the two teens amble off, arguing about the caffeine benefits of Coke versus coffee, weighed against the taste or lack thereof, and thought how glad she was to have watched them both, especially Marty, grow strong, confident, and happy over the summer. At her first meeting with Marty after she'd received the anonymous note about the bullying, she'd been struck by Marty's resilience and maturity but had sensed their loneliness too. Over the course of the summer, they'd changed. Marty laughed more easily and had connected with quite a few of the other campers. Ford's friendship no doubt had a lot to do with Marty's happiness, but Marty's natural wit and subtle magnetism drew others to them too.

For a while, Lily had thought Ford might have been the one to leave the note reporting the bullying, but Ford's friendship with Shannon at the beginning of the summer had made that seem unlikely. When Lily had learned from Suwallia's family on the Fourth of July cruise that Suwallia and Marty went to the same school, she'd suspected Suwallia had been the author of the note. Now, Marty and Suwallia were friends as well.

She'd miss that, when she started back in the ER—the chance to know people on a deeper level, to watch the people she cared about change and triumph. The absence of long-term patient relationships was the trade-off, she supposed, for no office hours and no late-night calls when she was off-call. Just another thing she'd learned about herself that summer, and something else she'd miss.

Her coffee cup was empty and the toast a distant memory, and with a long, physically demanding schedule ahead, she opted for a real breakfast. Hungry or not. She passed on the invitations to dine with Alisha and Philippe and several of the other counselors. Her mind was too distracted, her thoughts elsewhere, to make her reasonable company. At eight thirty, she joined the rest of the staff outside to await the arrival of the team from the regional medical center who would be staging their field training sessions with the help of the campers. Supervising the ER residents, PA students, and campers as they'd resuscitate the pseudo accident victims and ready them for transport would keep her busy for the next two days. Lily welcomed the work, but no matter how busy she was, nothing would dispel her worries over Chase and what she was going through.

❖

Chase flagged down the driver of one of the equipment carriers headed down to the base camp. The big trucks hauled ATVs, power saws, and hoists, even backhoes, and followed the line crews as they pushed to stay ahead of the fire front. "Got room for a passenger?"

The driver, a young guy with a two-day beard, shadows of fatigue riding his cheekbones, and a weary grin, motioned her around to the passenger side. "Climb in."

"Thanks," Chase said. "Fielder, DEC out of Bolton."

"Michael James—Fire Rescue from Fort Ann. How's it going out there?"

"We're holding," Chase said as she leaned her head back. "But we're not winning yet."

"Reports say the wind's coming up overnight."

"Yeah." Chase sighed. She hadn't had a shower in thirty-six hours, and not much more to eat than a few rushed cups of coffee, a couple of prepackaged peanut butter and jelly sandwiches, countless bags of Cheetos, some kind of meat on a bagel, and a power drink. She had charge of one of the twenty-man hand crews cutting timber, clearing underbrush, and digging the fire lines behind the hotshots working up close who constructed firebreaks, doused hot spots, and directed the flyover retardant drops to help suffocate the fire. The front was less than a mile away from the incident command post, on the other side of an unpopulated valley with a narrow stream running through it. They were clearing both sides of the stream and deploying as much of the water as they could pump to stop the advance of the fire. Chase's crew, being closest to the hotshots, also had to maintain the evac routes in case the wind picked up and the front moved faster. A really hot wildland fire could move ten miles an hour or more, and they'd all need to get out in a hurry. Her hunger vanished as she considered what might happen if the teams could not reach secure trails and strategically located vehicles.

"Thanks," she said when she jumped out of the truck. She needed to be back on the line in an hour. She stopped at the mess tent and grabbed a plate of fried potatoes and something with gravy on it from one of the assistant rangers maintaining the supply lines. Carrying the food, she located Nat in the command center.

"I was just about to radio you," Nat said.

"Something happened?" Chase said, pausing with a forkful of food on the way to her mouth.

"Jumped the line at Eagle Peak," Nat said.

Chase's stomach clenched. "Anybody hurt?"

"No, they saw it coming and evacuated, but the front has moved upslope, and we need to get around it."

Chase glanced at the geographic images up on the wall, but she didn't need to. She knew Eagle Peak. She'd climbed all over there as a kid. That's where she'd taken her last fall. "I wouldn't have thought it could get past that rock face."

"The wind kicked up enough to send a few fireballs upslope."

"If it keeps moving in that direction, it could crest Thunder Ridge." Chase's stomach churned.

"It's a good fifty miles from the lodge, but I'll let Sarah know to be on notice." Nat pursed her lips and pointed to a new red line just below the crest of Eagle Peak. "We'll need your crew and Charlie and Delta to reform up here."

"Tell Sarah to evacuate," Chase said.

Nat's brows rose. "That's pretty premature."

"The kids will all be going home at the end of the week. Why risk it?"

"You've got a point. I'll talk to her about it."

"Thanks." Chase hesitated. "Give Sarah a message for me, will you?"

"Of course."

"Tell her to make sure Lily goes home."

"That's it? Will she know what that means?"

"She'll know."

"If we weren't in the middle of this," Nat said quietly, "I'd ask what's going on. But there's no time for it now."

"No," Chase said. "No time at all."

There'd never really been enough time. She just hadn't wanted to see that.

"I'm headed back to spike camp," Chase said. "We'll need to hike all night to get up on that ridge before the fire does."

"Radio your location if you stop early. I don't want a crew getting cut off out there," Nat called as Chase carried her half-finished plate back outside.

"Copy that."

Fifteen minutes later, she was showered, had donned her spare Nomexes and a clean shirt, had replenished her water and food, and was back in another truck, headed up the mountain. She had a fire to fight and a crew to safeguard. With Lily out of danger soon, she didn't need to worry about what Eagle Peak had in store for her this time.

❖

"Did you talk to Chase?" Lily said after Sarah related the details of the call from Nat.

"No, and I don't expect to. Cell service is nonexistent up there. Everyone's family knows no news is good news—sometimes it's a week or more between contacts. We're lucky Nat is a friend or we might not hear anything at all until Chase shows up back home."

Lily gritted her teeth. "So how bad is this news—about the spread, I mean? Is it more dangerous for them?"

"No more than usual," Sarah said. "Sometimes it takes weeks to contain the fire, and that's if it's small. With a hundred thousand acres burning like they have on the West Coast at times, it could be months."

"So we just wait," Lily said, her voice tight with frustration.

Sarah nodded. "They'll be there at least another week, at the soonest, I would think. Even if they contain it within a day or two, there will be small hot spots to put out, brush that needs to be cleared, new trails cut for access. They don't just need to put out the fire. They need to secure and restore the area too."

"Well, can't they send someone else in to do that? So they can relieve the crews that have been working for weeks?"

"Did they send in reinforcements when you were working two or three weeks straight in the ER?"

"Not when it was all hands on deck," Lily said quietly, "like it is for them now."

Sarah squeezed her shoulders. "Nat didn't sound particularly worried. So you should try not to too."

"What about the kids?" Lily asked. "What do we tell them?"

"We're putting out calls to all their families to pick them up earlier if they can, starting tomorrow. We'll be done with the field trauma exercises then, and they won't miss much after that."

"Not all the parents will be able to change plans," Lily said. "Some of the kids will probably still be here until the end of the weekend. I'll stay until then at least."

Lily turned to leave, another night of restless sleep all she could look forward to.

"Lil," Sarah called after her.

Lily turned back. "Yes?"

"You should get out of here too. We can manage here without you."

Lily bit back a sharp reply. Sarah wasn't the cause of the anxiety squeezing her heart into a painful weight in her chest. "I'm staying until the kids are gone, and until—"

"She's not going to be back right away."

"I'm sure I can arrange another week or so off before I need to get back," Lily said quickly.

"Why, Lily?" Sarah asked flatly. "So you can say good-bye again?"

Lily's temper did flare then. "What does it matter, Sarah? It's our business."

"I know, you're absolutely right. It's probably better you stay until Chase gets back anyhow—that might head off any rash decisions."

Lily frowned. "I'm sorry, what?"

"By the way, you probably realize this, but rangers have to live where they work."

"Yes, I know that."

"There are a lot of postings in the New York City area." Sarah snorted. "In fact, they're always looking for people down there because, well, it's not exactly the kind of posting most rangers are looking for."

Lily narrowed her eyes. "Why are we talking about this?"

"Chase has a history of making pretty impetuous decisions, and if she thought there was some kind of possibility, long-term, I mean…" Sarah shrugged. "I can see her transferring."

"Chase would *hate* that." Lily couldn't even imagine Chase living and working in a metropolitan area. The mountains were as much a part of Chase as she was of the mountains. This wasn't just Chase's life, this was her life's blood. "Don't even mention it to her," Lily said. "It's not possible."

"Oh," Sarah said quickly, a note of apology in her voice. "Sorry. I misunderstood. I thought you loved her."

"Of course, I…" Lily caught her breath. "That was low, Sarah."

"I know," Sarah said with a hint of a sigh. "But I couldn't think of any other way to tell you that it would be better if you weren't here when she came back."

Lily turned away. The message had been devastatingly clear. "Good night, Sarah."

CHAPTER TWENTY-ONE

Despite knowing she was about to be disappointed, Chase's heart beat faster as she crested the track to Thunder Ridge Lodge. She'd never learned not to hope, not when her mother'd been ill, not when she'd been lying in the hospital with everyone telling her she'd never walk normally again, let alone climb, and not when she'd said good-bye to Lily. She slowed approaching the main building, heaviness replacing the buzz of anticipation in her depths that she hadn't been able to crush. The lot was empty except for Sarah's green Jeep. Of course the place was deserted late on a Sunday night. The campers had been gone for two weeks, the fourteen days she'd spent at a remote spike camp on Eagle Peak, too far from a trail for anything except a flyover airdrop of supplies every few days. They'd been lucky and kept the fire contained to minimal forest loss. The area would reforest and, given time, repopulate with the animals that had fled the conflagration. The burn had remained safely away from developed regions, and too far from cell service for calls home or even texts. Most of the crew— her included—were too busy mopping up, suppressing the few hot spots that flared up, and securing the trails to think about much except food and sleep. She'd thought about Lily, though, in the scant minutes of awareness after crawling into her shelter for a few hours of stuporous sleep. She wondered when Lily had left, if she'd left, and what she was doing now.

Chase parked, got out, and walked a short distance up the trail to look at the closed cabins and Lily's now vacant clinic. Closed and shuttered until next summer. That answered the all-important question. Lily had left.

"She left the night the last of the campers went home," Sarah said from behind her. "Two weeks ago, now."

Chase took a breath and schooled her features, turning to face her sister. "Good. I guess you haven't heard from her?"

"She texted me to let me know she'd gotten back to the city safe and sound. I haven't heard anything since then."

Chase pressed her lips together and nodded. "I imagine she's pretty busy."

"I imagine," Sarah said pensively. Hurrying on, as if not sure of what she intended to say, she added, "You know, I'm not so sure telling her to go home was such a good idea."

"That was always the plan," Chase said. "We both understood that."

"Yes, well." Sarah sighed. "I might have suggested she go home— for your sake."

Chase narrowed her gaze. "For my sake."

"Uh-huh."

"And how exactly did you do that?"

"I might have suggested that it wouldn't take much encouragement for you to hare off asking for a transfer—which you *know* you would get—to some municipal posting downstate." Sarah bit her lip. "I'm sorry. I just can't stop meddling when I'm worried about you!"

"Did she scream and run off at that scenario?" Chase hesitated. "I might not tell you everything I'm planning, but I did vow a long time ago not to lie to you. I can't say I haven't considered the idea."

"She screamed—at least, what amounts for a scream for Lily. She raised her voice and proclaimed you were to do no such thing."

Chase smiled.

"What?" Sarah said. "What don't I get about this?"

"Lily knows me." Chase shrugged. "I'd try it—you're right—if she asked. If I thought she wanted me there. Hell, who knows. Maybe I'd even like it."

Sarah snorted.

"Okay. No. But I'd trade what I have here for her."

"Lily would never forgive you," Sarah said.

"I know. She'd never be happy." Chase shook her head. "I wouldn't do that to her."

"This is a mess," Sarah said. "How are you really?"

"You don't have to worry," Chase said.

"That's not an answer, but I love you. And I trust you." Sarah pulled an envelope from her back pocket and held it out. "Lily left this for you."

Chase stared at it. This she hadn't expected. She'd expected Lily to leave, even when she'd hoped she hadn't. Now Lily'd surprised her again—just like she'd been doing all summer. She reached for it. "Thanks."

"Chase," Sarah said, "I'm sorry."

Chase smiled. "Don't be. I wouldn't have traded this summer with her for anything."

"That's quite a statement."

"Lily is quite a woman."

Chase turned and headed back for her Jeep. She sat behind the wheel with the envelope in her hand for a few minutes before she finally opened it and read the single line. Her hand shook as she read it again and then a third time.

There's always another summer.

Chase leaned back and closed her eyes. Sarah'd said Lily had talked about returning for another season. *Next year.* Summer flings were supposed to end, and they sure as hell weren't supposed to turn into love. One thing she'd never be able to do was pretend another summer with Lily would ever be enough. She couldn't do it.

Summoning the will that had gotten her through every other trial set in front of her, she radioed Nat. "Fielder, reporting back."

"You're off rotation for a week unless we get an emergency," Nat said.

"Not necessary," Chase said. "I'm good."

"Not optional."

"Copy. Fielder out." Chase clicked off the radio and headed for home, debating whether to stop to buy groceries. She passed the convenience store without pulling in. Whatever was in the freezer would do along with the bottle of wine or two she'd stocked for the times Lily visited.

Lily. Everything came back to Lily.

Chase turned up the track to her cabin, more a glorified deer trail than anything else, and rolled all the windows down. Usually traveling these last five miles gave her the chance to throw off the hassles and stress of the job, to let the fatigue slide away like an unneeded cloak, and to purge her mind of worries and regrets. She loved leaving everything behind as the pines closed in on either side, as the Jeep bounced from hot sunlit glades into dense cool shade and out again and, with the windows down, as the fresh clean air flowed through the Jeep, carrying the sounds of the wild.

Today, the sunlight seemed duller, the shadows grayer, and the forest bereft of song.

She slowed entering the clearing in front of the cabin, a quick flash of hope quickly smothered by uncertainty and the fear of being wrong. An unfamiliar Jeep stood in front of her cabin. She parked behind it, got out of her vehicle, and walked toward the cabin. No one waited on the porch. Chase stopped below the stairs and watched the door.

A moment later it opened, and Lily stepped out. She looked exactly as she did in all Chase's memories—effortlessly beautiful in casual navy-blue shorts, a scoop-necked white top with a row of small multicolored stripes along the edge of the sleeves and waist, and low hiking shoes. What grabbed Chase's attention and held her captive, though, was the intensity in the depth of Lily's green eyes. A fierce focus Chase could feel from feet away.

"It wasn't locked," Lily said, her voice as soft as her gaze was potent, "So I took that as an invitation to enter."

"You have a standing invitation whenever you want it, Lily." Chase tempered the urge to bolt across the space between them and pull Lily into her arms. Lily had the lead here. "How long have you been here?"

"Just since this morning. I was about to raid your freezer."

Lily shrugged and grinned, a motion Chase found about as sexy as anything she'd ever seen. Her stomach actually rolled with the need to touch her. She swallowed hard. "Nice vehicle."

Lily smiled. "Sarah always told me I needed a Jeep. She was right."

"Can't argue there." Chase laughed. "But raspberry, Lil? Really?"

"Nothing says you can't have a pretty Jeep."

"Where'd you leave the Beemer?"

"My parents are safeguarding it."

Lily's smile widened as she came down the steps and stopped only inches from Chase. The familiar aroma of coconut and vanilla and an undercurrent of dark spices hit Chase hard. The ache in her midsection dropped lower, and her hips tensed. "What are you planning to do with that 4-by-4 in the city?"

"I didn't buy it for the city," Lily said.

Chase carefully framed Lily's face, running her thumbs along the edge of Lily's jaw. Lily made a sound a lot like a purr, and her lids flickered. Lily's skin was so soft, her gaze so deep and inviting, Chase trembled. "What are you doing here?"

"Did you get my message?"

"I did."

"Well, that's why I'm here."

"I don't...I don't understand." Chase's throat tightened, want so fierce her body refused to move. "You said next summer...I thought you meant you'd be back then."

"Mmm. That too." Lily threaded her arms around Chase's neck and kissed her.

The kiss was everything Chase remembered and more, warm and sweet, like the air she breathed, and as wondrous as every dream she'd stopped dreaming. She didn't want the kiss to end, for the moment to pass, for whatever came next to shatter the perfection. She didn't move, her fingertips lightly grazing Lily's cheeks. "Help me out, Lily. I'm out on the edge here without a guideline, and I'd rather not fall."

"You won't. I'll never let you fall." Lily leaned back, her gaze on Chase's. "There will always be another summer, and I want to be here for all of them. But I don't want to leave when summer ends, not as long as you want me."

"Lily," Chase said, "I will never not want you."

"That's good," Lily said, "because I love you. And I want you for as long as I live."

"Ah, Lily." Chase closed her eyes and rested her forehead against Lily's. "I love you, baby. So damn much. But—"

"I quit my job, Chase."

"What?" Chase stiffened. "Lily, no. You—"

Lily laughed. "Don't worry. I didn't turn in my doctor card, and I'm not having a midlife crisis. More a midlife awakening."

"But—"

"I know we have to talk," Lily said, pressing into Chase again, her breasts tauntingly soft against Chase's chest, "but I really need you. Can we please talk later and make love first?"

Chase's inertia imploded on a surge of desire. She scooped Lily up and crushed her to her body. No matter what it took, no matter what she had to do, she wasn't letting her go. Nothing mattered as much as a life with Lily in it. "Anything you want, Lily, anything. But absolutely that."

She crossed the porch, pushed the cabin door open with her foot, and carried Lily through.

❖

Lily tightened her grip on Chase's shoulders and pressed her face to her neck, drawing in her scent, that unique mixture of earthy mountain fragrance and crystalline air. She'd thought of that scent— missed it—every time she'd stepped out into the city these past weeks. Her senses felt blunted, as if she couldn't quite experience everything as clearly as she had all summer. The sun was certainly just as hot, but not nearly as bright, filtered through the ever-present haze that hung over the metropolitan area. She'd never really noticed it before, but then she'd rarely actually looked up. Her world had been concrete, steel, and stone, not earth and sky and green growth. She'd lost the exhilarating sensation of being surrounded by vibrant life everywhere she looked, and the loss only intensified the ache that was constantly with her—the hollow void inside her chest that was missing Chase.

"You didn't get hurt out there, did you?" Lily murmured, trying and failing to touch all of Chase as she carried her through the bedroom door to the bed.

"Nope. Bumps and bruises." Chase leaned over and gently laid her on top of the covers and then eased down beside her. "Nothing serious. And right now, I've never felt better in my life."

Chase's tone was low and heavy, and she kissed Lily with slow, probing restraint. Her fierce control fired Lily's need, and Lily tugged Chase closer until Chase lay full-length upon her. "You should keep kissing me like that, and maybe I can make you feel even better."

Chase groaned, a sound that shot through Lily like heat lightning, bright and sharp and tinged with wild sky. She gripped Chase's shirt and tugged it from her pants, needing skin. Needing the feel of Chase's firm muscles, the sweeping planes of her back, the power that she longed to set loose.

Chase's kisses came faster, harder and more insistent, and Lily sensed her tremble on the edge of control. She pulled away and struggled to form words through the longing that tightened her throat. "I want to be naked with you. I *have* to be naked with you. I need you."

"Lily," Chase gasped, her mouth on Lily's neck, her lips tracing the pulse down Lily's throat. "I love you, Lily."

"Oh," Lily sighed, a lightness of wonder filling her, "I love you too. God, I love you."

Chase sat up, her knees on either side of Lily's hips, and tugged at her shirt. Buttons flew and Lily laughed. "You're ruining your shirt."

"I don't care. Take your clothes off, Lily."

Lily half sat and pulled off her top and everything underneath. She opened Chase's ruined shirt and kissed her breast. "I don't ever want you to move." She traced Chase's nipple with her lips. "You are gorgeous."

Chase threaded her fingers through Lily's hair and hissed out a breath. "Lily, let me get you naked. I want you. I've wanted you for weeks. Please."

Lily leaned back on her arms, bare to the waist. "Be careful—I'm so aroused I feel like one of those rockets on the Fourth of July—I'm afraid I'll go off the second you touch me."

"Then we'll just start over." Chase climbed off the bed, kicked off her boots and shoved her pants down, and, an instant later, unbuttoned Lily's shorts. Her fingers were deft, the backs of her hands warm against Lily's belly as she slid the shorts down her thighs along with her panties. The air in the cabin was hot and still, the last bit of sunlight drifting lazily through the windows, etching Chase in golden tones.

"You're beautiful," Lily whispered.

"I'm yours, Lily. However you want me."

"Always, always."

Chase knelt on the bed between Lily's legs and played her fingertips lazily up and down the insides of Lily's thighs. Lily quivered, each stroke coming closer and closer to where she needed Chase most.

"Tease me later," Lily said, knowing she sounded desperate and not caring. She wanted Chase to know how very much she needed her. "Take me now. Go slow later."

Chase laughed, a wild, primitive, possessive sound that drove Lily even higher. She wanted so badly to come, and she wanted so badly to stay right at that pinnacle of urgent need and incredible desire and consuming, magnificent pleasure that flowed from Chase's every touch. She wanted to lose herself in loving Chase.

"I love you," Chase murmured, covering Lily's sex with her palm.

Lily's hips tensed. "I can't wait. Please."

And then Chase was inside her, deep and knowing and filling her, stroke after stroke. Lily cried out.

Oh, now.

Her eyes closed against her will. Colors more glorious than sunrise played across her inner landscape, and the roar of the wind and the rush of the waterfalls flashed through her consciousness. And she came, gloriously long and gloriously hard until her muscles went limp on a sob. Chase was above her then, her mouth taking Lily's again, hard and deep. Chase straddled her thigh, her hips thrusting wildly.

"*God*, Lily." Chase groaned and came, quivering in Lily's arms.

When Chase lay stunned and loose-limbed upon her, Lily stroked her hair. "I love you. I love it when you make me come. But I love making you come more."

Chase shuddered and kissed the corner of her jaw. "Win-win."

Lily laughed and filled her hands and her heart with all that was Chase, stroking her, wrapping herself around her, reveling in being with her again.

After a few minutes, Chase rolled onto her back next to Lily and reached for her hand. "I don't know what to say now. You're here, and I'm not sure what's next."

"Say what you need to say," Lily whispered, lacing her fingers through Chase's. Whatever it was, whatever Chase needed, whatever troubled her, they'd find a way.

"I'm crazy in love with you, Lily," Chase said quietly. "And it will make me crazy if you leave again, so I'm scared, right down to my boots."

"Well, that part's easy." Lily leaned over and kissed her. "I'm not leaving again."

Chase's brows furrowed and worry swam in her eyes. "But, Lily, I can't ask—"

"You never asked. And I know you never would." Lily held Chase's gaze, making sure Chase could see the truth in hers. "I'm here because this is where I want to be. I told you I wanted to be with you for the rest of my life, and this is where we belong."

Chase took a long breath. What she needed to say was the hardest thing she'd ever said. "This is where *I* belong, Lily. But you—"

"No," Lily said, pressing her finger briefly to Chase's lips. "This is where you belong, and this is where I *want* to be. Because of you, yes, but for me too. Can you listen? Can you hear me?"

Chase trusted her, believed in her. And knew that Lily would always speak her truth. "I'm listening, baby."

"On the drive back to New York, I realized something." Lily laughed a little unsteadily and shook her head. "God, it took me a long time. I told you about my parents, right, about meeting in a war zone?"

Chase nodded.

"At the time," Lily said, "they were both doing what they'd always known they would do. And then, after they'd met and fallen in love, they wanted something else. They came back here, and they made a different life."

"I'm with you."

Lily settled her cheek against Chase's shoulder and wrapped an arm around her waist. Chase rested her chin against the top of Lily's head. She'd never been so content, so thoroughly *happy* in her life, just lying with Lily in her arms.

"I'm my parents' daughter. I wanted to be an ER doc, and I am. I wanted to work in the most challenging, demanding, wildly unpredictable place I possibly could, like they had done—short of going to war—and I did that. Then I *went* to war, and now my war is over."

"Lily," Chase whispered. "You'd be giving up everything you've worked for."

"I want more than a job, Chase. I've discovered something else that I want in my life, what my parents found. Not just you," she said quickly, "although I want you more than I have the words for, but I want you *and* the life I could have here with you. A life with love in it. I didn't know how much I needed that. I can be a doctor in an ER up here, and I can still make a difference in people's lives. I learned that this summer."

Chase kissed her. "I always knew the summer would never be enough. I fell in love with you the first time we kissed."

Lily sat up. "We were never meant to be for only this summer, Chase. Our love is for every summer, and all the times in between. You are who I want, and this is the life I want. Will you have me?"

Chase framed Lily's face for another kiss. A kiss that said forever. "Always, Lily. I'm yours for all the summers of our lives."

EPILOGUE

Chase rolled over, emerging from a restless sleep, and checked her watch. Almost two a.m. She lay awake in the early June morning, almost exactly a year from the day she'd first met Lily. She'd been waiting for Lily then too, but she hadn't known it. Hadn't known her life could be full and bright and filled with expectation, all because she'd opened herself to love and be loved. Love changed her life—changed her, and every day brought possibilities. Along with the joy came a little kernel of anxiety that took up residence in the pit of her stomach whenever she waited for the rumble of the Jeep coming up the track, bringing Lily home. Lily's shift was over at midnight, and she should be home anytime.

Most of the time Chase was the one coming home in the middle of the night, but Lily had been trading shifts pretty regularly to accumulate time for her leave, and night shifts were the ones everyone wanted to switch. For the next two months, Lily wouldn't be traveling back and forth forty-five minutes to the ER.

Chase sat up at the sound of the cabin door opening, and a moment later Lily came into the bedroom.

"Have you been awake long?" Lily asked, leaning down to kiss Chase. Somehow, even in the middle of the night after a twelve-hour shift, she managed to smell like a fresh morning breeze.

"Just a couple minutes," Chase said, watching Lily's figure in the moonlight as she moved around the bed, taking off her scrubs. She'd cut her hair to just above her shoulders—easier in the ER, she said—and her generically shapeless scrubs hid the swelling in her midsection

Chase swore she could see, even though Lily said it was too soon. "Your T-shirt's on the chair over there."

Lily chuckled softly. "You straightened up, didn't you?"

"Wasn't much to do."

"Were you awake worrying?"

"Nope, just woke up."

"Uh-huh," Lily murmured. "How did things go up at Big Bear with the hiker who fell?"

"She'll make it. Broken femur. She was lucky to get away with just that. She fell fifty feet, and we needed the helicopter to get to her."

"Rough insertion?"

"Not really. The helicopter drop was a little tricky. It was windy."

Lily made a slight huffing sound. "You know, I'm a lot better at this than I was a year ago."

"Better at what?"

"Being the wife of a forest ranger. I know what you do now. And *helicopter* and *windy* do not equal easy or simple."

Chase pushed back the sheet, and Lily settled in beside her. "Tricky's part of the job."

Lily kissed the angle of her jaw. "I know that. Just remember, I speak ranger now too, so I'll know if you're obfuscating."

"Obfuscating?"

"As in sugarcoating the rough stuff."

"I'll remember that." Laughing, Chase ran a hand over the curve of Lily's belly. "How are *you* doing?"

"I'm happy to report that I have progressed from water and crackers for breakfast to oatmeal. I'm fine."

"You know, I was thinking, maybe we ought to get a place in town."

"And why is that?"

"So you don't have to drive the Jeep up and down the track."

Lily laughed. "Love, women ride horseback until they're practically ready to deliver. The Jeep is a lot more comfortable than that, and the track is not exactly a rock face."

"Yeah, but still…"

"It's way too soon for you to start being worried. In fact, there's nothing to worry about at all. Childbirth is a thing that women do pretty naturally." Lily kissed the corner of Chase's mouth and settled her hand in the center of Chase's abdomen. Lily's skin was warm and soft, and the slight pressure sent distracting sparks southward.

"Yes," Chase muttered, trying to ignore the growing arousal, "but you're *my* woman."

"I am. And right now I'm a woman with needs." Lily pulled off the T-shirt she'd just put on and slid on top of Chase. In the moonlight, her eyes glinted with humor and something else Chase recognized. Something that brought more heat to her belly and a fist of need to the center of her chest. "Aren't you tired?"

"Not even a little bit," Lily murmured. "The other nice thing about being pregnant and not feeling queasy is I'm horny."

"Is that something new?"

Lily ran her nails down the center of Chase's belly. "No, but when it hits, it's pretty urgent."

Chase skimmed the muscles in Lily's flanks and cupped her hips, pulling Lily tightly against her. Lily was hot and wet, and Chase hissed in a breath. The pulse beat faster between her thighs. "You're beautiful, and I want you so damn much."

"Show me?" Lily murmured and leaned down to kiss her again.

Chase did, with all the tenderness and fervor and love that burned through her, hour after hour and day after day. When Lily lay in her arms again, her hand straying down between Chase's thighs, Chase sucked in a slow breath. "You should go to sleep."

"I will," Lily said. "Starting tomorrow, life gets easy."

Chase, her concentration torn between the light stroke of Lily's fingertips brushing over her and the lull of Lily's voice in the darkness, managed to mutter, "How's that?"

"Camp starts. I've got ten weeks to spend up here in the mountains, and I heard from Sarah that Marty's coming back. They're going to be a camp counselor this year."

"That's nice," Chase said, the words strained with a little hint of desperation.

Lily laughed. "What's nice, my love?"

"Lily," Chase groaned. "Come on. You know."

"You're right, I do know. I know you love me. And I know what you need. And by the way, I love you." Laughing, Lily kissed Chase again and took her to that place that felt like summer, every time.

About the Author

Radclyffe has written over sixty romance and romantic intrigue novels as well as a paranormal romance series, The Midnight Hunters, as L.L. Raand.

She is a three-time Lambda Literary Award winner in romance and erotica and received the Dr. James Duggins Outstanding Mid-Career Novelist Award from the Lambda Literary Foundation. A member of the Saints and Sinners Literary Hall of Fame, she is also an RWA/FF&P Prism Award winner for *Secrets in the Stone*, an RWA FTHRW Lories and RWA HODRW winner for *Firestorm*, an RWA Bean Pot winner for *Crossroads*, an RWA Laurel Wreath winner for *Blood Hunt*, and a Book Buyers Best award winner for *Price of Honor* and *Secret Hearts*. She is also a featured author in the 2015 documentary film *Love Between the Covers*, from Blueberry Hill Productions. In 2019 she was recognized as a "Trailblazer of Romance" by the Romance Writers of America.

In 2004 she founded Bold Strokes Books, one of the world's largest independent LGBTQ publishing companies, and is the current president and publisher.

Find her at facebook.com/Radclyffe.BSB, follow her on Twitter @RadclyffeBSB, and visit her website at Radfic.com.

Books Available From Bold Strokes Books

A Haven for the Wanderer by Jenny Frame. When Griffin Harris comes to Rosebrook village, the love she finds with Bronte de Lacey creates a safe haven and she finally finds her place in the world. But will she run again when their love is tested? (978-1-63679-291-0)

A Spark in the Air by Dena Blake. Internet executive Crystal Tucker is sure Wi-Fi could really help small-town residents, even if it means putting an internet café out of business, but her instant attraction to the owner's daughter, Janie Elliott, makes moving ahead with her plans complicated. (978-1-63679-293-4)

Between Takes by CJ Birch. Simone Lavoie is convinced her new job as an intimacy coordinator will give her a fresh perspective. Instead, problems on set and her growing attraction to actress Evelyn Harper only add to her worries. (978-1-63679-309-2)

Camp Lost and Found by Georgia Beers. Nobody knows better than Cassidy and Frankie that life doesn't always give you what you want. But sometimes, if you're lucky, life gives you exactly what you need. (978-1-63679-263-7)

Fire, Water, and Rock by Alaina Erdell. As Jess and Clare reveal more about themselves, and their hot summer fling tips over into true love, they must confront their pasts before they can contemplate a future together. (978-1-63679-274-3)

Lines of Love by Brey Willows. When even the Muse of Love doesn't believe in forever, we're all in trouble. (978-1-63555-458-8)

Only This Summer by Radclyffe. A fling with Lily promises to be exactly what Chase is looking for—short-term, hot as a forest fire, and one Chase can extinguish whenever she wants. After all, it's only one summer. (978-1-63679-390-0)

Picture-Perfect Christmas by Charlotte Greene. Two former rivals compete to capture the essence of their small mountain town at Christmas, all the while fighting old and new feelings. (978-1-63679-311-5)

Playing Love's Refrain by Lesley Davis. Drew Dawes had shied away from the world of music until Wren Banderas gave her a reason to play their love's refrain. (978-1-63679-286-6)

Profile by Jackie D. The scales of justice are weighted against FBI agents Cassidy Wolf and Alex Derby. Loyalty and love may be the only advantage they have. (978-1-63679-282-8)

Almost Perfect by Tagan Shepard. A shared love of queer TV brings Olivia and Riley together, but can they keep their real-life love as picture perfect as their on-screen counterparts? (978-1-63679-322-1)

The Amaranthine Law by Gun Brooke. Tristan Kelly is being hunted for who she is and her incomprehensible past, and despite her overwhelming feelings for Olivia Bryce, she has to reject her to keep her safe. (978-1-63679-235-4)

Craving Cassie by Skye Rowan. Siobhan Carney and Cassie Townsend share an instant attraction, but are they brave enough to give up everything they have ever known to be together? (978-1-63679-062-6)

Drifting by Lyn Hemphill. When Tess jumps into the ocean after Jet, she thinks she's saving her life. Of course, she can't possibly know Jet is actually a mermaid desperate to fix her mistake before she causes her clan's demise. (978-1-63679-242-2)

Enigma by Suzie Clarke. Polly has taken an oath to protect and serve her country, but when the spy she's tasked with hunting becomes the love of her life, will she be the one to betray her country? (978-1-63555-999-6)

Finding Fault by Annie McDonald. Can environmental activist Dr. Evie O'Halloran and government investigator Merritt Shepherd set aside their conflicting ideas about saving the planet and risk their hearts enough to save their love? (978-1-63679-257-6)

The Forever Factor by Melissa Brayden. When Bethany and Reid confront their past, they give new meaning to letting go, forgiveness, and a future worth fighting for. (978-1-63679-357-3)

The Frenemy Zone by Yolanda Wallace. Ollie Smith-Nakamura thinks relocating from San Francisco to her dad's rural hometown is the worst idea in the world, but after she meets her new classmate Ariel Hall, she might have a change of heart. (978-1-63679-249-1)

Hot Keys by R.E. Ward. In 1920s New York City, Betty May Dewitt and her best friend, Jack Norval, are determined to make their Tin Pan Alley dreams come true and discover they will have to fight—not only for their hearts and dreams, but for their lives. (978-1-63679-259-0)

Securing Ava by Anne Shade. Private investigator Paige Richards takes a case to locate and bring back runaway heiress Ava Prescott. But ignoring her attraction may prove impossible when their hearts and lives are at stake. (978-1-63679-297-2)

A Cutting Deceit by Cathy Dunnell. Undercover cop Athena takes a job at Valeria's hair salon to gather evidence to prove her husband's connections to organized crime. What starts as a tentative friendship quickly turns into a dangerous affair. (978-1-63679-208-8)

As Seen on TV! by CF Frizzell. Despite their objections, TV hosts Ronnie Sharp, a laid-back chef, and paranormal investigator Peyton Stanford have to work together. The public is watching. But joining forces is risky, contemptuous, unnerving, provocative—and ridiculously perfect. (978-1-63679-272-9)

Blood Memory by Sandra Barret. Can vampire Jade Murphy protect her friend from a human stalker and keep her dates with the gorgeous Beth Jenssen without revealing her secrets? (978-1-63679-307-8)

Foolproof by Leigh Hays. For Martine Roberts and Elliot Tillman, friends with benefits isn't a foolproof way to hide from the truth at the heart of an affair. (978-1-63679-184-5)

Glass and Stone by Renee Roman. Jordan must accept that she can't control everything that happens in life, and that includes her wayward heart. (978-1-63679-162-3)

Hard Pressed by Aurora Rey. When rivals Mira Lavigne and Dylan Miller are tapped to co-chair Finger Lakes Cider Week, competition gives way to compromise. But will their sexual chemistry lead to love? (978-1-63679-210-1)

The Laws of Magic by M. Ullrich. Nothing is ever what it seems, especially not in the small town of Bender, Massachusetts, where a witch lives to save lives and avoid love. (978-1-63679-222-4)

The Lonely Hearts Rescue by Morgan Lee Miller, Nell Stark & Missouri Vaun. In this novella collection, a hurricane hits the Gulf Coast, and the animals at the Lonely Hearts Rescue Shelter need love—and so do the humans who adopt them. (978-1-63679-231-6)

The Mage and the Monster by Barbara Ann Wright. Two powerful mages, one committed to magic and one controlled by it, strive to free each other and be together while the countries they serve descend into war. (978-1-63679-190-6)

Truly Wanted by J.J. Hale. Sam must decide if she's willing to risk losing her found family to find her happily ever after. (978-1-63679-333-7)